THE JOURNEY OF BET

STEVEN HAMMOND

ROCKHOPPER BOOKS

THE JOURNEY OF BET
Copyright © 2018 Steven Hammond
All rights reserved.
ISBN-10: 0-9986234-3-1
ISBN-13: 978-0-9986234-3-6 (RockhopperBooks)
1st Edition

Edited by Ella Medler
Cover art by Gabriel Barbabianca
Interior layout by Tanya Adams
Find out more at:
STEVENHAMMONDBOOKS.COM

Dedicated to

To all those who make dreams reality.

ACKNOWLEDGMENTS

Thank you to everyone who supports me along this journey. Joy, for her belief; Cathy, for her enthusiasm of my stories and reading early, unrefined drafts; Michelle and Rodney, for their friendship, encouragement, and eagerness to help; Ella, for making me a better writer; Tanya, for all of her work at all hours of the day; Gabriel, for creating the art that gives life to the words; and everybody at the Book Barn, for the constant support. And Buster Dog, for being a good boy.

OTHER BOOKS
BY STEVEN HAMMOND

THE STAFFS OF OMIA SERIES

The Talents Of Bet

THE RISE OF THE PENGUINS SAGA

Rise Of The Penguins

The Warlord, The Warrior, The War

Crosscurrents

Whispers Of Shadows

The Royal Creed

Order Of Kings

Preeminence (Coming Soon)

THE JOURNEY OF BET

One

Firelight danced across a gleaming white marble floor, creating a flickering ballet of amber and black, punctuated by bursts of orange and dashes of vermillion. Exquisite, hand-woven runners cut a path through the spectacle of light from the hearth to a large and lavish bed in which King Dalverious slept alone, lost in faded dreams of conquest and glory. Shadows wavered against polished granite walls, casting odd forms against tapestries depicting past victories in the war against the Whist and the conquest of past generations.

The black, shapeless form of the Reacher crept along the walls, rustling the tapestries, moving slowly to the edge of the king's bed. It hovered for a moment, swept over the silk quilting, a living shadow hidden by the night. The king's eyes fluttered, nearly opening, but remained closed, keeping him in his dreams.

The shadow swirled around the bed, twisting into a shape resembling a man, and stood at the bedside. A wisp of a hand shot forward, seizing the king by his night shirt, and lifted him in the air, then threw him to the marble floor. "Awake, you fool. We have work to do!"

Dalverious howled in fear, and dove for his sword hanging in the scabbard on the bed post. Hilt in hand, he stood, facing his attacker, ready for battle. Wide, dark eyes stared at the shadow, hands clenched, arms trembling yet ready to strike.

"Calm yourself," the Reacher hissed. "Had I wanted to kill you, I would have done so long before now."

The chamber doors burst open. Two of the king's guards rushed in, alerted by the shout, rifles at the ready. The shadow swirled around the men before they could react. A tendril of black touched each of them on the forehead simultaneously. Their bodies went rigid, surrendering control to the Reacher's whim. Bringing their long rifles up slowly, they trained them on the king. The guards stood, eyes wide, horror-stricken faces grimacing at what they were about to do.

"What are you doing?" Dalverious shouted, bringing his sword up as if it offered protection. He looked at the Reacher, the nostrils on his sharp nose flared in a mixture of fear and impotent rage. "Enough!"

The shadow spat a sickly laugh, raised a smoky arm, and the men turned away from the king, training their weapons on each other. "Your guards are weak-willed. They will prove useless in the Whist. I should kill them and spare them of their ineptness."

"They are competent enough against flesh and blood. Stop this," Dalverious demanded, his voice betraying his fear and doubt.

The Reacher snaked toward the king, white eyes burning with unworldly malevolence. Several moments passed in tense silence. "If you insist." The guards lowered their guns.

Dalverious took a breath and walked to the guards. He studied their unblinking eyes gripped by fear. "Release them, please."

Black threads quivered from the Reacher's shapeless arm and danced before the men. "Leave and forget," he said in a hissing voice. The guards shouldered the weapons and left the room without speaking, closing the door behind them.

"Can you only come at night or do you simply delight in disturbing my slumber?" King Dalverious said, sounding bolder than he felt. He tossed the sword on the bed, watching it sink into the soft mattress. He sighed and pulled a long blue velvet robe from the post hook.

"Mind your tongue or I'll take it for my own."

Dalverious stared at the undulating mass of black. Turning his back on the Reacher, he cinched his robe briskly and walked to the fire. "What is this work that needs doing that couldn't wait until morning?"

"It is time to complete the Staff of the Din."

The king's thin blond brows rose. He turned to the Reacher, trying his best to look impassive, but an oily smirk tugged at the corner of his mouth. "You have the final piece?"

The Reacher extended his shapeless hand, showing him the shard. "It is mine."

"The girl is dead then?" Dalverious said, touching a patch of hair on his chin.

"No," the Reacher said, withdrawing his hand. His voice betrayed a hint of doubt. "She has proven herself resilient. But no matter. When the staff is complete, the Whist will be mine."

"You mean ours." Dalverious took a cautious step closer.

"Yes, yes. You may have her land, the game, and her cities; I only desire their lives."

Dalverious sniffed a laugh. "There will be plenty to take if you can truly reconstruct the Staff," he said, walking to a teak wood bureau. He threw off his robe, revealing a sinewy frame made hard by the passage of time and war.

"If you harbor such doubt, perhaps the King of Valdivia would be a more suitable ally."

"Valdivia lacks the resources of Persk."

"If greed is a resource, I stand corrected," the Reacher said, gliding toward the fire.

The king watched the Reacher hover before the flame while dressing in black pants and tunic. The firelight shone through the translucent darkness of the Reacher, and he wondered if the shadowed being could feel the warmth, or anything at all. He tied back his long blond and gray hair, pulled on tall, fine-leather square-toed boots, strapped his sword, and grabbed a long black overcoat. "I'll summon the workers," he said, clearing his throat.

The Reacher stood motionless, as if transfixed by the flame. "Have you gathered the girl's caretakers?"

"We have," he said, adjusting his coat and taking gloves from the pocket. "They're being held in the dungeon."

"We will go to them before we begin. I have questions."

"I assure you they have been interrogated several times. Nothing of any real use was revealed."

The Reacher drifted from the fire, and stood inches away from the king. "You are incapable of finding the answers I seek."

Two

King Dalverious walked alone through a stone corridor deep below the citadel. Booted footsteps bounced echoes off the concrete walls. Firelight flickered from brass sconces, casting the gray hall in straw-yellow light. Flames wavered as he passed, creating the illusion of the king being followed. He looked back to make certain the guards hadn't disobeyed their orders. They had not.

He casually strode by empty cells that had once held Users during the war as they awaited their perfunctory trial only to be executed. Now those of the Whist were few and far between, and common criminals were held in highly visible prisons as a deterrent. On occasion the dungeon still housed those who the king thought would be of interest to the Reacher, who would persuade them to his cause. If they held no value, the phantom would wipe their memories and send them away, or simply have them killed.

He rounded a slow curve and spotted the Reacher melt away from the wall like a living oil stain, black and viscous. The king knew the Reacher could go anywhere he wished without his assistance. The thought of his freedom of movement filled him with helpless anger, but their alliance was a necessary means to an end.

For five years after his defeat by the actions of Fealist-Marsh, Dalverious had sent teams of huntsmen and inquisitors to find a way back into the Whist. But it was as if that world no longer existed. All that remained was a scarred battlefield. The very landscape had changed. The familiar forest, mountains, rivers and seas had vanished, leaving behind unfamiliar terrain. At first he thought of it as a boon; new lands to fall under his kingdom. Though trees grew and waters flowed, crops refused to yield and the settlers sent to form the new land claimed the place cursed. Eventually only the heartiest of hunters remained, gathering the pelts and meat of the abundant wildlife. On the fifth year, the anniversary of the end of the war, the Reacher came, and with him he brought the promise of absolute victory.

Dalverious grabbed the key ring from a rusted iron hook, a remnant from the days of his forefathers, before concrete forms, before popular law, before the altruistic Users threatened to tear down his right to rule his kingdom as he saw fit. He brought the keys to the scraped and tarnished padlock and glanced at the wavering shadow of the Reacher, seemingly antsy to enter the cell and inflict whatever horrors it had in store on the occupants. The king wondered why he even needed to be present when the specter could enter the lockup on a whim. He guessed the Reacher wanted the captives, the less fortunate citizens of the realm, to see that they had been betrayed, that their king was in league with what he had sworn to destroy.

The thoughts vanished from his mind and he turned the key. The lock popped open with a whispered clunk. He slid the steel door open, steel casters grinding on steel tracks, echoing its screech through the murky hall, revealing a second door. Fumbling with the keys, he unlocked the second, and once more looked back at the Reacher, who hung as still as a windless flag. Pulling the door open, he motioned for his ally to enter.

"Watch," the Reacher breathed as he swept past the king.

The low glow of a sconce hung high in the ceiling bathed the room in rusty light. The smell of excrement and unwashed bodies, punctuated by the scent of fear, stung the king's nostrils when he stepped across the threshold.

Sitting on a low, time-worn wooden bench, shackled by heavy chains to uneven stone walls, Putrice Malweather lifted her round head searching sightlessly behind blindfolded eyes. "I count the minutes 'til morning. It's not breakfast yet." Neither answered her words.

A feeble scraping of chain against stone scratched from a darkened corner of the cell. The old man, Harrelle, sat with age-worn knees drawn to his naked chest, bare feet tucked close to his body, eyes peering over pant-less legs. He sucked a hiss when the king stepped into the light.

"Who's there?" Putrice demanded from her wall. "Tell me, won't you? Or are you afraid to show your face to an old woman?"

"Remove her band that she may see," the Reacher whispered in the king's ear, slinking back into the shadows.

Dalverious shivered at the cold touch caressing his lobe. He pulled a small blade from his belt and walked to the woman. His hand hovered over her head as he searched for a way to carry out his task without touching the filth of her unwashed hair. He cut the blinder and shuffled back.

Putrice blinked ugly little sunken eyes until they found purchase on the king. She coughed and stammered, finding her breath. "My lordship. Forgive me. Please. I am a loyal servant to the crown. The guards…your guards feed me only twice a day. My mind is weakened by starvation. I suffered long. Have you come to release me? Pardon my impudence. I'm hungry. I count the moments 'til breakfast. It is my only comfort in the hell you have me in. Why do you keep me? I've answered your questions. Let me out. Let me out, you bastard son of a pig! Oh! Forgive me my words. Hunger gnaws at me. Look at me; a woman of wealth cast in a pit not worthy of hogs. Release me, you motherless dung hauler. I demand it!"

Dalverious placed his hand on the hilt of his sword. "Mind your words or I'll take your head." He pulled the blade half way, taking a step toward the woman.

Putrice tucked what chin she had into her neck.

"No. Don't kill her. She is merely scared and angry. Rightfully so," the Reacher said, slinking into the light.

"Demons!" Putrice screamed at seeing the Reacher. "Mercy on me, foul thing."

"What know you of foul?" the Reacher hissed.

The woman shut her mouth, shook her head, wobbling rolls of flesh beneath her swollen face.

The Reacher went to her, hovering just before her eyes. "I have questions. You will answer me truthfully or I will take them from your mind. Do you understand?"

Putrice nodded. "Yes, demon."

"Good. The girl. Tell me about the girl."

"I answered all of them questions to the guards," Putrice croaked, squeezing her eyes shut.

"Tell me." A wisp of blackness caressed the woman's face.

She opened her watering eyes. "The girl. Yeah, I can tell you about her. Worst purchase I ever made, not including that waste of a man."

Harrelle lifted his head slightly, the flickering firelight accentuating his disgust of the woman in his eyes.

"Bought her 'bout a year back—auction at the orphanage in Hammerton. Didn't want a girl. Girls're always trouble. But she was the sturdiest of the lot. Put her to work on the farm. Last one I had died of the choke-pox. She was insolent from the get. But she did her work 'spite the sass. Beat her enough you'd a thought she'd learn, but the sass stayed in her 'til she runned off."

"Why did she *runned off*?"

"She was always dotin' on the animals. She took a fever and started talkin' in her deliriums. Found out she was one 'em. *A User.* She talked to the critters. She slept a few days, and while she's out, I took the wagon to town and got a message to the courts. Told 'em to send the inquisitors. I hoped for a reward to get my expense back. But I knew it was the right thing to do. She come to while I waited for them. She came out her room as strong as I'd ever seen her. You'd 'spect a thin girl to be weak after a fever. But she wasn't. She ate a little, no meat, mind ya. She refused it. Always did. Ain't natural. She saw I cooked one of her critter friends and turned violent."

"Violent?" the Reacher asked, sounding almost lustful.

"Violent. Girl tore off for her room, came out with bags packed. She pushed me down. Me, an old lady. Felt like I got kicked by a mule. She swore a bit and made for outside. Girl tore the knob clean off the door. Ain't seen her since."

The Reacher edged closer. Putrice didn't flinch, caught under the spell of the darkness. "Where did the girl go? Surely you looked for her."

The woman shook her head. "It was rainin' out. Sent that worthless stalk of a man to find her. He came back nearly a half hour later sayin' he lost her trail in the mud. Said she was likely headed toward Hammerton. If you ask me, I say he helped her. He did it to spite me."

"What makes you think he helped her?"

"Came back without his gear. Lyin' that he lost it in the creek followin' her track. He came back with her sass, too. Called me things I won't say in front of royalty."

The Reacher's smoky tendrils danced around Putrice's head. The woman swayed beneath the touch, lolling sideways, back and forth, until he released his grip. "She has told me all she knows. All but one thing."

"I told you all. I swear it!" Putrice howled, sweat breaking on her brow.

"Why did she run?" the Reacher said, his voice dark and heavy with threat.

Putrice shook her flabby head. "It was Harrelle. He done it. He musta warned her they were coming."

"I'll get to Harrelle soon enough. Now tell me."

The woman's eyes pooled up, she shook and quivered. "I done it. I teased her. Laughed 'bout eatin' her friends. Didn't know she was strong like that. Cost me my reward," she sobbed pathetically, remorseful over her lost reward.

"You are lucky to be alive," the Reacher said, sounding sadistically parental. "Users, as you call them, can be dangerous…deadly."

The woman's beady eyes narrowed at the old man. "It was Harrelle. He helped her. Maybe sent her to Raisin Town. He knew she was one all along."

"Swallow a tooth, woman!" Harrelle yelled from the corner.

The Reacher seemed to tremble in the dank light, quivering in twisted delight at what was to come. A flowing arm reached forward enveloping the woman's head. "You have done well tonight, and you will get your reward. But first you will fulfill your purpose."

Putrice's eyes beamed with hope and greed.

"Of course. All *Users* are not what you think of us. Some are much, much worse." He whispered something indecipherable in her ear and slid back admiring her confused expression. Without warning, the blackness sprang forward, twisting and encircling the woman. The inky form entered her eyes, nostrils and mouth. Putrice's body shook in jiggling spasms, but she made no sound, no screams of pain or protest. The woman writhed violently, pulling the chains from their hold.

King Dalverious stepped to the door, drawing his sword. He watched the woman gyrate and contort, twisting like a wrung cloth, until her body hung in the air, arms where her chest should have been and legs where her absent shoulders once were. He heard a muffled gasp escape Harrelle in the otherwise silent display. Putrice Malweather's body spiraled once more, swelled, then flattened, finally exploding into a spray of gray dust, speckling the stained floor. The king reached for the handle, not taking his eyes from the apparition emerging from the cloud.

"Steel your nerve, King of the Realm," the Reacher croaked. White eyes observed nearly formed five-fingered hands, no longer smoky tendrils. The fingers stretched and balled into fists, repeating the movement again and again. He stared at them almost longingly, until they returned to their previous state. "Now I will talk to the man."

The king's eyes met Harrelle's, and the old man's eyes stabbed hatred at the king.

Three

Bet stood on the edge of a charred boardwalk watching the sky, mesmerized by the bright orange Andolan airships hanging vibrantly against the brilliant blue, cloudless canopy as they began their slow descent on the outskirts of Illguard. She leaned against a strap-worn hitching blackened by the fiery attack days before. Wanting a better look, she stepped onto the dirt road, craning her neck, and blundered into a child carrying a long wood plank from the Supply Hut.

"So sorry. Let me get that for you," Bet said to the girl of no more than nine wearing a tattered yellow dress and a too big, brown workman's coat. She decided she should probably use her Talents to help with town repairs rather than stand gawking at the Andolan airships.

The girl clutched the wood, saying nothing. She gave Bet a crooked smile and vanished, wood and all.

Bet jerked in alarm. She spun on her heels, unsure of what had just happened, wondering if she had imagined the girl or was having some ill effects from her encounter with the Reacher. She shuffled to the middle of the road, twisting her head, searching for the apparition. Her eyes were drawn to a man's loud voice singing praises toward someone. She spotted the girl halfway down the lane, standing in front of a burly man who took the long plank off the child's shoulder. The girl turned her head toward Bet, gave her an impetuous smile, bright white teeth radiant against her dark brown skin, and scampered up the boardwalk.

Bet laughed to herself, instantly liking the kid. "Now that's a Talent I'd like to have."

"And what Talent is that?" a familiar voice said from behind.

Bet swung around to find Errel Handover standing with hands on hips, wearing crisp black slacks and an equally smooth blue and white, bibbed button-down shirt, looking as clean and unfatigued as he had the first night she'd met him. She waved her hand toward the young girl. "That kid just teleported, or something like that, halfway across town."

Errel sniffed a laugh. "Misty? She likes to show off for newcomers. Her games will wear thin after a while." His eyes showed he meant no disparage to the child.

"I don't know if any of this will ever wear thin. There's so much. So much I never knew existed."

Errel nodded with a half-smile. "Come along. Old Babbers is awake, and she's asking for you."

Bet's eyes lit with joy. It had been three days since they returned from their battle in the Waste, and Old Babbers had been unconscious since they arrived. Her heart pounded with excitement at having her friend back from the edge of death. She started to walk but stopped. "What about your friends?" She motioned toward the swollen air ships.

Errel followed her hand, spotting a three-horned Terranod grope at a guy line tossed from the gondola below the aircraft. He seemed to hesitate. "They'll keep." He motioned for Bet to follow him.

Bet fought the urge to run. Instead, she kept pace with Errel's long strides. The tall, blue-skinned Andolan smiled down at her as they made hurried steps through the maze of workers rebuilding the damaged town. "Is she awake-awake? Or just, you know, kinda awake?" She considered reaching out to get a sense of the woman, but in the days since confronting the Reacher, she committed herself to using her Talents only when necessary. However, she did allow her senses to remain vigilant for any threat, to the point of it becoming second nature.

"Awake-awake," Errel said, matching the girl's giddy tone.

They hopped up on the boardwalk in front of Gus Wumple's Barber Shop, which had become a makeshift infirmary in the aftermath of the attack. Bet swung the door open with far too much enthusiasm, banging it against the interior wall. The shop had received surprisingly little damage, with the exception of the broken advertising window, which was now boarded up. She winced when she saw Gus.

"Quiet down. There's people recoverin' here," the old man of unknown years barked from beside a wash basin. Long, white and yellow hair dangled in front of his dark brown eyes. He pushed it aside to see who had caused the ruckus.

"Sorry." She smiled when he spoke, always amused by his appearance. It seemed the man had cut the hair of everyone in town who had hair at the expense of his own. Bet wondered how he performed his tasks from beneath the mop. She waved apologetically.

He made an indecipherable grunt and returned to his work at the sink.

Bet took special care in opening a door at the back of the shop, tip-toeing through the ward, hoping not to disturb healers from their work. She paused a moment, watching a robust chartreuse-skinned K'vin rub a tacky balm over the body of a badly burned man while chanting incoherent utterances in a baritone melody. Bet fought back a pang of guilt for having brought such catastrophe on the peaceful hamlet.

Errel placed his hand lightly on Bet's shoulder. "This is the Reacher's doing, not yours. Keep that with you, not your guilt."

Bet nodded, blowing a sigh through her nose. She gave Errel a fake smile and looked at the stairwell leading to Old Babbers' room. Her false smile turned genuine and she bolted upstairs, padding quietly on moccasin-covered feet.

Four

Bet laid her hand softly against the brass push plate on the time-stained wooden door. She hesitated and yanked off her wide-brimmed, black canvas hat, the one Old Babbers had given her. Taking a deep breath, she stepped in, carrying a cautious, but anxious smile. She glanced at Pooch-kin, cradled in Bathezine's bulging arms, who sat with legs sprawled in a chair much too small for his bulk. Her eyes fell on Old Babbers, involved in a conversation with Mandi-lyn. The motion caught the woman's attention, and she looked at Bet with a tired, but warm smile.

Taking hesitant steps, Bet crept closer to her friend.

Old Babbers chirped a laugh. "Get over here, girl. I ain't all that broken no more." She lifted her arms, inviting a hug.

Bet shook her head with a smile and raced to Babbers. She fell across the cot, giving her friend a warm embrace, while being careful not to squeeze too hard. She held the woman, whom she now considered her sister, until Babbers patted her back in submission.

Babbers tussled Bet's red hair, wincing slightly at the motion. "One rib still ain't quite healed," she said at Bet's worried expression, glancing at Mandi-lyn.

"I can only do so much," the Flursh said, scratching underneath her tricorn hat. "If the nurses catch me, I'll spend the rest of my days as a healer, perpetually sequestered, healing diaper rashes and broken toes."

"I'm sure they'll put you to greater use," Bet laughed.

"No, no, they won't. Children, especially human children, find my appearance comforting. I would be stuck in pediatrics until the end of my days."

"Well, you do look like a big hamster," Bet said through a smirk.

Mandi-lyn chittered something indignantly, straightened her hat, and shuffled to the corner of the small room, turning her attention to a bag of nuts.

Old Babbers scooted higher in the bed as Errel propped a pillow behind her back. "How ya holdin' up? Bathezine filled me in on what happened after I got walloped." She made a motion at the Ursian, who only grunted his confirmation between snores.

Bet shrugged. "Okay, I guess. I feel a certain sense of, I don't know, freedom. If that's the right word. Kinda like a dog let off a leash. But I know that leash will come back. Sooner than I hope, I suppose." She pulled her eyes away, suddenly finding the view outside a small window very interesting. Truth was she wasn't *okay*. Her sense of freedom was stippled with anxiety, a kind of nervousness over the unknown.

Doubt over what she had done stained her every thought. *What if the Reacher completes the Staff of the Din before I reach the next Ancient One? What if I don't find Fealist-Marsh? What if all of my friends die because I gave the stone up to protect them?* These and a hundred other doubts filled her mind constantly.

To make matters worse, she hadn't been in contact with Fealist-Marsh since that day in the Waste. She had slept and dreamed, but her dreams were simple dreams—images of scattered memories mixed with nonsensical scenarios and faces of people she didn't know, or used to know. None seemed to hold any real importance, like they had when she held the facet. It was as if she had been cut off from the greater world she had come to know since entering the Whist.

She stood and pulled the flimsy sun-bleached blue drape aside, and stared through the glass at the wooded hillside. Her throat tightened. The leash was returning.

"I told ya before, and I'll tell ya again. Ya did good, girl. That Reacher fella would've dogged us to the end of our days if'n ya hadn't given up that rock." Bathezine's meaty paw of a hand gripped Bet's arm just below the elbow. "Might've even killed ya."

Bet turned away from the window, her expression both appreciative and doubtful. She shook her head. "I've been thinking about that, and that's one of the things that bother me. I don't think he *could have* killed me. Knock me down, sure. But outright kill me? No. That's why he sent his minions. They had to do the killing for him. If he could've, he would've the moment he knew I had what he wanted. He could control the weak-minded, or Foul, but he couldn't physically harm me."

"Well, a mind-controlled Mastive could do plenty a harm," Bathezine said, raising his snout at Old Babbers.

"Lucky punch," the woman said, snorting a laugh, then grimacing at her unhealed rib.

"It was only lucky because it didn't kill you." Bet gave her a worried smile.

Old Babbers waved Bet's words away. "Ah, it'll take more than a snot-drippin' Mastive to send me to my end."

Bathezine shifted in his chair, carefully adjusting the sleeping Chook-chook. "Point is, if'n ya hadn't a done it, more woulda came. The stars know there ain't no shortage of weak-minded fools round here, and Foul too. Even if we'd managed to escape with our hides from that particular mess, there'd a been more. And if the next batch was a swarm of them wasps that nearly killed ya? Then we'd a been in a heap."

"And *what if*, by my giving the stone up, that gives him the power to kill without needing a host or an army of hill folk, or a criminal?" Bet sat back on the edge of the cot, smiling weakly at Babbers.

"We've been through this. He ain't got no need of ya now." Bathezine settled back in the chair, gently stroking Pooch-kin's ears.

Bet looked at the two. A warm flush crossed her face. Bathezine, for all of his gruffness and ill-mannered behavior, had taken a shine to the little Chook-chook. Pooch-kin had, at first, been reluctant to return the affection, but had given in when Bet suggested that maybe the Ursian needed someone to protect, and maybe he was giving the big bear-man a sense of security and was keeping Bathezine safe from the demons in his mind after all of the violence. She knew Bathezine's path of redemption, back to the Fair, had been interrupted by her arrival in the Whist, if not outright lost. But she also knew he still clung to that hope, the same way Bet had clung to Pooch-kin to keep her sanity in the madness she'd fallen into. Pooch-kin said mammals were much too clingy.

"Bathezine is correct," Mandi-lyn said through a mouthful of egg-nuts. She scooted forward, nudging Errel to make room for her to pass. "The Reacher will be too preoccupied to give you—us—any real problems. For the time being, that is. We need to focus on what we *do* know, not the *what ifs*. What we do know is that we need to reach the Caves of Moth, sooner before later. Now scatter, the lot of you. I need to work on healing her rib."

The swing door swooshed open, and the K'vin healer pattered through much more gingerly than her corpulent frame seemed capable of. "Did you say *you* were working on healing the patient?" she said to the Flursh, with a raised, suspicious brow.

Mandi-lyn shook her head a little too vehemently. "No, no. You misheard. I said she's healing and needs her rest. I'm a Charge, a historian, not a healer. None of that in my bloodline. None."

The K'vin seemed to consider Mandi-lyn's words, then shrugged it off. "Let me have a touch. Make room." The K'vin looked at Bathezine, then went to the opposite side of the bed, squeezing the Flursh aside.

Bet watched the healer's soft touch against Old Babbers' brown skin, caressing the wounded ribcage beneath while chanting in a more alto voice than the baritone melody she had heard earlier. Bet guessed there were different tonal ranges of chants, depending on the injury.

The K'vin smiled a toothless grin at Babbers. "Bone healing takes a little longer than simple cuts, but you are healing remarkably fast. You'll be out of here in no time. Now that you're awake, you should eat."

Old Babbers smiled up at her. "Yes. Thank you. I'm famished." She rolled her eyes at Bet when the K'vin turned away.

"Amateurs," Mandi-lyn said when the K'vin had gone. "Now where was I? Oh yes. Scat. All of you." She extended a stubby pink hairless finger toward Old Babbers.

"No!" Old Babbers protested. "Don't you put me to sleep again. I swear I'll shave you bald and—"

Mandi-lyn touched Babbers between the eyes and the woman instantly fell asleep. "Get out," she barked at the others.

Bathezine handed Bet the Chook-chook and stood. Bet was happy to receive her old friend.

"I can walk, you know," Pooch-kin said, sounding irritated but not overly so.

"When we get outside. Don't want Gus Wumple yelling at me for something else." Bet looked back at Babbers once again and let Errel lead the way.

"Let's go check on Tiny, then get somethin' ta eat," Bathezine said grumpily, then pushed his way past Errel.

"Back to his old self, I see," Errel muttered.

Bet only shrugged and followed after him.

Five

The boardwalk creaked beneath the weight of Bathezine's heavy steps, audible even over the sounds of hammering, sawing, and shouts of workers going about their repairs of shops and homes across the small town.

Bet skipped to catch up with the Ursian's purposeful strides while watching the busy citizens working with no complaint, almost happily, seeming to hold no grudge over the tragedy that had befallen their quiet hamlet. She spied Misty, the teleporting young girl she had met earlier, standing on the porch roof, pulling charred shingles away with a crowbar, carrying a cheerful expression. Chores at Malweather farm had always been so dreadful for Bet. She couldn't imagine doing such work under Biscuit Head's scornful glare without feeling animosity and dread. Maybe it was because here there was no threat of punishment if the task wasn't performed exactly as told, like at Malweather...or the orphanage, for that matter. Misty didn't seem to mind the work. Bet envied the girl's carefree attitude. Curiosity about the child welled up in her and she caught up with Errel to find out more.

"Who are Misty's parents? She seems like a good kid," Bet asked, coming alongside the tall Andolan.

Errel gave Bet a sideways glance. "Misty came here from the Din about, oh...four years ago now. Her parents were barren of Talents, so they sent her to the Whist alone to protect her from the inquisitors."

Bet's heart sank a little at hearing she had been given up by her parents. Misty was an orphan old enough to know she was being sent away. Bet lowered her head, unable to find words for the pity she felt for the child.

Errel glanced at Bet's face, reading her concern. "Misty has adjusted well. She knows her parents did the right thing for her. Her Talents were well expressed for one so young, and that would've caused trouble for them all, perhaps even gotten her executed along with her parents."

A flash of anger rose in Bet's chest. Her own experience notwithstanding, she wondered how people could be so cruel to someone so young. King Dalverious had always been portrayed as the beneficent leader who governed his realm with good will for all. *What a crock of lies*, she thought. He had tried to eradicate the Whist, even going as far as to write them out of history. The king was just as bad as the Reacher, if not worse.

"How'd she end up here? I'm guessing she wasn't dropped off in the mountains by a three-headed crow, like I was."

"No," Errel laughed. "She arrived in Azural like everybody else. Well, almost everybody. Mokep the Black assigned her to Illguard where we were short of youth. The Spiller family became her guardians."

"Good people, then?"

"You can't foster a child if you've turned Foul. So, yes. Good people."

Bet was about to ask more when they arrived at the end of the boardwalk and spotted an enormous silver airship floating weightlessly high above, dwarfing the bright orange ones she had seen earlier. The midday sun sprayed beams of reflected white light, dazzling her eyes and all who took the time to watch the spectacle. "Amazing," she said beneath an awestruck gasp. "I've never seen such a thing."

"They don't have airships in the Din?" Errel said, looking at the shimmering light show.

"I'm sure they do; I've just never seen them." Bet stopped in the middle of an alley between the center of town and Old Babbers' Supply Hut, unable to pull her eyes away from the display. She heard Bathezine snort.

"Well, the Andolans have arrived. Days after they were needed, of course," the Ursian grumbled.

Bet stole a glance at Bathezine. "They're here now. It looks like they've brought supplies to help rebuild the town."

Bathezine snorted again, nodding at Errel. "You've seen your boys. Immunuh go check on Tiny. You comin', girl? Or ya gonna stand here and gawk at their show of wealth and…*benevolence*?" he asked, not trying to mask his disdain.

Bet's shoulders slumped as she watched Bathezine march toward the woods behind town. "I'll come," she said in a quiet, disappointed voice and started to follow. She craned her head back at Errel. "Are you coming? Or do you have to meet somebody?"

Errel hesitated a moment. "They can wait still. Tiny Nat is more important. The Andolan Council are only my benefactors." He fell in step with Bet.

Bet set Pooch-kin on the ground once they cleared the town's edge. She considered telling him to stick close, but after the battle with the Mastives in the Dead Woods, she realized the Chook-chook could more than look after himself. Still, she kept a watchful eye on him just in case.

She hung back, not increasing her pace, letting Bathezine put some distance between them. When she was sure he was out of earshot, Bet stole a look at Errel. "What does Bathezine have against Andolans? I mean, really have against them. Not the *oh, they're a snooty bunch* stuff he says. But really."

"You could just read his mind and find out," Errel said jokingly.

"You know I don't have that Talent. I only sense intent, emotion, that kind of stuff. And even if I did, I wouldn't use it on my friends." She gave him an admonishing look.

"You're only a step away from developing that Talent," he said. Bet didn't reply. Errel hopped over a fallen log and Bet casually did the same. The lush forest surrounding Illguard flourished with firs and pines of every sort Bet knew of, and more than few she had never seen. Dogwoods bloomed with white flowers the size of her hands. Shaggy purple junipers glowed in streaks of sunlight sneaking its way through the canopy of tall yews.

After strolling several yards in silence, Errel cleared his throat. "I believe Bathezine holds a grudge because of the war. The Andolans chose to stay neutral through much of the conflict. We heard little of the war in the citadels of Andola, and what we did hear was filtered through the Council."

"You didn't know about the destruction?" She looked back at Pooch-kin, who had stopped to grab a beakful of grubs from beneath an upturned slab of bark Bathezine had kicked over. She waved for him to catch up.

"We did. I guess most knew, but it wasn't until near the end, when sentiment within the Andolan Council rose to the point of involvement. By the time the airships made ready, Fealist-Marsh had done her work and the conflict ended. Though the Andolans provided ample resources to assist in rebuilding much of the damage, there are those who still carry resentment, Bathezine being one of them. To be honest, after hearing the accounts of those involved and the hardship they endured, I can't say that I blame them. Many good people turned Foul in that time, and many more died."

Bet looked ahead at the Ursian, watching him disappear into a thick copse of old growth. She knew he had suffered falling to the Foul, but his heart was good; it was in the right place. She had skirted the edge herself and wondered if she would have seen the destruction and death of so many if she, too, would've fallen.

"I tried to keep that in mind when dealing with him before you came," Errel said, interrupting her thoughts. "But he can be very…disagreeable."

Bet snorted a laugh. Bathezine did have a way of rubbing just about everybody the wrong way.

"But seeing how he took to you, and his obvious love for you, made me look at him differently. Whether he be Fair or Foul in his heart, I'd stake my life on saying he is well on his way to the redemption he seeks. Whether he believes it or not."

They reached the darkened wood where Bathezine had disappeared and stopped. Bet watched Pooch-kin hop through the tall grass, finally catching up with them. "I don't know much about the Fair and Foul, but I believe you're right. We just gotta make sure he sees that we believe in him no matter what lays in store for us."

Errel nodded with an upturned smile. "You're wise beyond your years, Bet. Your story will make a good read when we finish our journey."

Six

The trio pushed their way through the dense undergrowth and into the shadowy wood, spotting Bathezine kneeling before the hollowed-out trunk of an old cedar. Bet held out her padded bag, and Pooch-kin hopped in without complaint. He knew Skin-cats hunted under the cover of the thick growth and had no desire to test Bet's ability to sense approaching danger, even though she had proven quite adept at doing so.

Bathezine looked up when Bet rested her hand on his brawny shoulder. "Snares and trip lines are still in place. Least nothin' could get to him that-a-ways." He rubbed his hand along the edge of a thick slab of bark, inspecting the recessed tree hollow.

"How much longer will he be in the cocoon?" Bet peered in the hollow beside the Ursian, looking at the three-foot-long grayish-green pod, which she thought looked like a large, unripe almond shell.

"Don't know, really. Guess it's dependin' on how long it takes to regrow his wing. Seen him do it before. Took about a week, but he was pretty beat up then. Took canon fire and…" Bathezine looked away, not saying any more.

"How'd he fit in something so small?" Bet asked. It was the first time she had gone to check on her friend since he and Bathezine had disappeared shortly after returning to Illguard.

Bathezine shrugged as he stood. He took the bark slab and placed it in front of the opening, neatly hiding the contents from any curious eyes or predators looking for a quick meal.

Errel grabbed a handful of dry lichen and sprinkled over the seam between the bark and the trunk. "I don't know much about Vivicon physiology, but I think the shell is his carapace. He must be much more flexible than he appears."

"Do you think it would be all right if I checked on him? You know, get a sense of how he is?" She adjusted the bag straps against her neck, smiling down at the Chook-chook.

Bathezine and Errel exchanged looks. Bathezine waved his arm. "Don't see what it can hurt."

Bet inhaled and closed her eyes. She hadn't reached out to touch an individual's presence since that day in the Waste. She had kept her mind open, feeling for any vague or hidden dangers, but aside from the pulses of life and death of forest creatures, there had been none. Her thoughts drifted away and she immediately felt the strong life-force of Tiny Nat in his unconscious healing state. His mind was strong, vigorous, but there was no conscious awareness. The hive mind was still there, but it was distant, connected but not. The sensation made her feel disoriented, as if her consciousness swirled in a vat of primordial ooze. The feeling became too much to bear, and nausea roiled in her gut.

She pulled her thoughts away and stumbled backwards into Errel, who caught her under her arms, holding her upright. Bet shook her head, swooned, and her stomach lurched.

Bathezine was by her side in an instant. Taking her chin in his hand, he studied her eyes. "You okay, girl?" Concern crossed his shaggy brow.

Bet waved him off, giving him a weak smile. "Yeah, yeah." She coughed an insincere chuckle. "Tiny is doing fine. I just wasn't prepared for what I felt."

Bathezine and Errel asked what she meant in unison.

"Well... He's there, but not. I mean his mind is present, but it's like his body is, I don't know, liquid-like, but thick. Kind of like a bowl full of gelatin. If that makes any sense. He's fine, though." She shook her head once again, let out a whistling breath, then patted Pooch-kin to reassure him she was fine.

"I think we're done here," Bathezine said and put his thick arm around Bet to make certain she was fine. "You sure Tiny's okay?"

"Certain of it. Whatever's happening is supposed to be happening." Bet stood upright, shivered off the spinning sensation, and started walking back the way they had come. "C'mon. Let's get back. I could use some of that pudding at the Dining Inn."

"Can't say I disagree with you there," Bathezine said, licking his chops. "Best idea I've heard in an age."

Bet took two steps, stopped, looked at the fragmented blue sky peeking through the tree tops. A strange fatigue washed over her. Her head swayed and her vision went gray. Her knees buckled, and she collapsed to the forest floor. A deep, dark pulse pushed all thought away, and darkness overtook her.

Seven

Bathezine rushed through crowds of workers, cradling Bet in his arms, barking at people to move aside. He jumped on the boardwalk, barreling his way through the front door of the Dining Inn, and darted upstairs to Bet's room.

Errel hurried to the stairs and stopped as Le'lel, the chips dealer, met him. "Close the table and get Mandi-lyn. She's at Wumple's, upstairs, with Babbers."

Although Handover's Dining Inn had suffered significant damage during the raid, Le'lel, the reptilian Lasoom, and Walt, the Andolan host, had made substantial repairs, enough to reopen the restaurant and game room to provide relaxation for the hard-working townsfolk in the aftermath of the attack. Only a few rooms had escaped damage upstairs, one of which was Bet's.

Le'lel rushed out the door with snake-like grace. Errel saw to the few patrons, apologizing for the inconvenience. Once the last of them was gone, he hung the closed sign and bounded up the stairs to assist Bathezine.

Errel hurried along the second floor hall, bumping into Walt, who was carrying a pail full of nails, ready to resume repairs on two twenty-three, where the fire had stopped. Rooms two twenty-four and beyond had been a total loss.

"Take a break. In fact, go see to helping with the airships. I'm sure the Council would appreciate another Andolan's assistance distributing supplies."

Walt rubbed the back of his hand against his sweaty forehead. "You mean not to see them?"

Errel reached for the knob on Bet's door. "Eventually. But Bet needs me right now." His eyes darted from the other's face to the door.

Walt scrutinized Errel. "I hope she's worth angering the Council."

Taking his hand from the door, Errel moved close to Walt and lowered his mouth to his ear. "This girl may be the keystone keeping the structure of our world standing. So yes, Walt, she is worth it. Events you're not aware of are quickly unfolding. I don't even understand most of it right now. But I've sworn myself to her protection—the Council knows my oath cannot be broken."

Walt took a step back. "Then, Knight of Andola, see to your quest. I only ask that you charge me with your duty in your absence." He lowered his head and placed his right fist against his forehead.

"You are so charged, brother. Wear it well."

Walt lifted his eyes to meet Errel's. "Will you take up the sword for your oath?"

"I fear the time will come that I must." Errel went back to the door, but turned back to Walt and rested his hand on his shoulder. "For now, keep this knight thing to yourself."

Walt nodded with a half-smile.

Errel went to the foot of the bed. Bathezine sat next to Bet, holding her limp hand in his. Pooch-kin nuzzled near her face, cooing his soft noises. "She hasn't stirred?"

Bathezine shook his head. "Hasn't so much as twitched. Like she got knocked on the crown and's out cold."

"Might be that the stress has finally gotten to her. The things she has gone through since crossing over…it would've done anyone of us in." Errel pulled a chair close to the bed, lifting it to avoid the legs scraping against the bare wood floor. "It's possible that touching Tiny Nat's mind was one too many stones for her to bear."

"Maybe," Bathezine shrugged. "One thing I learned this past week is, things that ya think are, ain't always is."

Errel scrunched his eyes. "You're going to have to help me with that one. I'm not sure I follow."

The Ursian blew his mustache through pursed lips. "Thought it was as plain as the blue on your face."

Errel gave him a dubious look.

"What I'm saying is, when ya came and told me 'bout some flit of a girl being a newcomer and was sayin' my name, I figured it was some kinda coincidence. Maybe Mokep the Black sent her on account I forgot to pay a fine for haulin' rocks on the city roads. Though I don't remember doin' it, doesn't mean it didn't happen. Then she told me 'bout Anna."

"Who was Anna to you?" Errel shifted to the edge of the chair. It was rare that Bathezine ever spoke of his past, let alone anything that might be considered insightful.

Bathezine scratched under his chin. "Back at the end of the war, I was stuck in the Din. And that ain't a good thing. A person of my appearance tends to stick out like a fish in a candy store."

"I could imagine," Errel said, trying to picture a trout between a display of gumballs and one of sugar snaps. He didn't think a fish in a candy store would matter to a voracious Ursian, and shook away the image.

"I spent my days on the outskirts of towns, avoiding the Dalverians— inquisitors as most know 'em."

Errel opened his mouth to say he knew what Dalverians were, but thought better of it.

"One day I come across a human girl, no older than Bet is now, I 'spect. I knew at once she was like me...like us. She was the first one I'd seen that wasn't being hauled in a worm-iron carriage to face the Tribunal. She hid it well, better than any I'd known in the war. But I knew. She was an

Oragoth, like Bet. She had knowing about her, too."

"What do you mean? Like the Talent of insight?"

Nodding his head, Bathezine continued. "Yeah…yeah. 'Cept it was a bit different. I know Talents are different for everyone. But Anna always found the Gateways. Without being told, mind ya. She'd lead other strays like me to the crossings, but'd never go herself. She wouldn't go without her brother."

"Bet told me a little about her. Her brother wasn't of the Whist." Errel stretched his legs out, his arms folded, waiting for the Ursian to continue.

"True. The fella fought for the king, a conscript." Bathezine adjusted his position, carefully laying Bet's hand across her stomach. "I couldn't just leave her. She needed help. We found others, but soon enough, there weren't no more to find. She said it was time for me to go on account a big bear-man wasn't inconspicuous in them parts. I was all set to trundle off, when Dalin, her brother, finally showed. Missin' a leg from the fightin'. He told her 'bout the tribunals and said they were closin' in on the last of the Users—a brother and sister, holed up somewhere near Hammerton."

"You couldn't leave then. She still needed your help."

"Yep. I stuck around a little longer. But by the time we found them, it was too late. We hid in a stock yard across the way from the old house they was holed up in. Helpless as clams without a shell. They set fire to the house. And we was 'bout to leave…" Bathezine sat up and leaned his mouth close to Errel. "Then Anna said she felt another inside the home. An infant."

Errel's eyes widened. "You don't think? What did you do?"

"Rescued the kid." He was about to elaborate when Mandi-lyn burst through the door.

"What happened?" the Flursh asked, her voice an alarmed whisper.

Errel and Bathezine locked eyes, then looked at Bet.

Eight

Bet became aware of the blackness holding her. She could feel it surrounding her body. She was floating in it, and its cold, gelatinous form oozed into every crevice of her being. She opened her eyes, but the dark was complete. At first she thought she had gone blind, and then she thought she had died. Her mind told her neither was true. She tried to move her arms but couldn't budge them. Her body was in sleep paralysis, and she knew immediately that she was in another state of consciousness.

Her mind raced, trying to find purchase on something in her dream, or vision, or whatever she was in. There was nothing for her mind to grab hold of. Panic began to rise. *What if it was the Reacher? What if he had already completed the Staff of the Din and he had imprisoned her the way he had Fealist-Marsh?* She shook the thoughts away the best she could, but the idea remained. Bet tried to bring the serenity over her that she had used during her confrontation of the Reacher. The peace crept over her, slowly replacing the panic in her chest.

When all but the smallest traces of fear had passed, she tried to think through her situation. *Was it something Fealist-Marsh, the Omia Temporian, was doing to her?* Bet stretched out her senses. No, it wasn't Fealist-Marsh; there was a wrongness in the state she was in. Was it the Reacher? She had touched the Reacher's mind before. Although she didn't feel right, this was nowhere near the pure malevolence she had felt before.

Letting her mind sink deeper into the serenity, she felt the weight of the darkness holding her begin to lift. Blurs of gray and dark shapes started to form as Bet struggled to regain her sight. Amber light infiltrated the dark, illuminating a dimly lit room. The light swirled, merging with gray much the way it had when she had Travelled to the Din. The sensation disoriented her. Bet shook away the dizziness. The dark shapes became solid. She recognized one immediately; King Dalverious, standing with sword drawn, his back against an unseen wall.

As the shapes continued to take form, she saw Putrice Malweather hanging in the air, her body twisting and contorting as if being wadded up like an old scrap of paper. The woman's body erupted into a shower of ash, replaced by something unseen, a void in the fabric of reality. Bet knew at once it was the Reacher.

Panic overtook her once more. She spun and saw the old man, Harrelle, chained and hunkering in the corner of the shapeless room. Bet reached out for him, knowing that whatever the Reacher had done to Putrice, the same or worse was in store for the man who had helped her escape. She had to save him. She had saved Pooch-kin while Travelling before, and she would do the same for Harrelle.

As she moved closer, her arms felt heavy and sluggish; it took all of her effort just to raise one hand. Her hand hovered over the man, so close she could almost feel his body heat. Doubt washed over her. Picking up a small Chook-chook was one thing, but in her present state, how could she lift a fully grown man? She bore down, focusing on her strength, raised both arms, and the images disappeared.

The blackness returned briefly, and in the next moment she found herself standing in a forest of dead trees. The sky swirled in bright colors causing her to squint from the blinding light. Instinct told Bet she had returned to the Whist, but she also knew she was still in an altered state. She examined the trees, first thinking she was back in the Dead Woods. She realized she wasn't. The trees in the Dead Woods would've been burnt; these were simply dead. The branches were devoid of all foliage, and they stood gray and lifeless.

Taking a tentative step, she noticed a large stone building just past the tree line. She narrowed her eyes as she continued to walk. The structure, which to her looked like an ancient keep crumbling from neglect and the ravages of time, carried an aura of something teetering between life and death. Guessing she was there for a reason, Bet pressed forward, her legs moving easily, free of the sluggish sensation she had felt in the company of the Reacher.

Clearing a cluster of dead growth, she spotted a large wooden door bracketed with wrought iron hinges. It was secured with a polished brass knob, which felt out of place on the dilapidated building. Bet examined the lock, bothered by the newness of the mechanism. She reached for it, and a sudden chill coursed through her body. Her mind began to swirl, and her legs trembled, growing weak. Brittle sticks cracked from somewhere nearby, breaking under heavy footfalls. She turned toward the sound, but the world spun around her. She reached out with her thoughts, trying to get a sense of what was coming. Her legs gave way beneath her weight, and just before the blackness took her once again, she felt a presence within the building, a presence she knew couldn't be in the Whist.

Nine

Bet's eyes blinked open to find Mandi-lyn's whiskers bobbing across her forehead. Without thinking, she raised her hand, batting the Flursh away. She looked at the concerned expression of her friends and heard the reassuring coo of Pooch-kin as he nuzzled near her ear. "What happened?" Her throat felt dry and raw, as if she hadn't drunk in days.

"That's what I was trying to discern before you pushed me away," Mandi-lyn said, her whiskers bouncing furiously.

Bathezine knelt beside the bed. "You passed out in the woods. Like someone clocked you on the head. We brought you back to your room." He nodded toward Errel.

Bet squeezed her eyes tight and cleared her throat. "Thirsty," she rasped. Errel hurried out to get a glass of water. When he returned, Bet drank without a breath then sat up, bringing Pooch-kin to her lap. "Thank you," she said. Errel gave her a tight-lipped smile and nodded.

Mandi-lyn leaned close, her whiskers still twitching wildly. "Do you mind?" she asked, not eager for another swat.

Bet shook her head, apologizing for slapping her friend.

The Flursh took her hand, examining her palm and wrist. "Do you remember what happened?"

Bet shifted more upright, stretching her back. "Not really. I remember checking on Tiny Nat and then…nothing. Just the darkness." She turned her attention to petting Pooch-kin.

Bathezine stood and returned to the chair. "That's it? Did you have one of your vision things? A dream or somethin'?"

Bet continued to stare at Pooch-kin, remembering trying to save Harrelle. Her heart felt heavy. She was certain the old man would die in the hands of the Reacher, and she knew it was because he had helped her. "Something. It was like a dream, or like I Travelled. The Reacher was there, but I couldn't see him. It was like he occupied an emptiness…if that makes any sense." She raised her eyes and met Mandi-lyn's. The two held each other's gaze until the Flursh blinked and looked away.

"What else can you tell us?" Mandi-lyn asked, touching the broken vessels on Bet's cheek.

"Why don't ya give her a minute? The girl's been through a lot lately. Maybe she just needs some rest." Bathezine put his hand on Mandi-lyn's shoulder, easing her back. "Give her some breathin' room."

Mandi-lyn looked at the Ursian's hand then shrugged it off. "Her visions are important. We need to know what happened while the memories are fresh."

"It's okay, Bathezine. Really. She's right. Whatever information we can get from this will only help us, if it wasn't just a dream." Bet looked at Pooch-kin, trying to puzzle out what she had seen through a haze of lingering disorientation. She flinched as Mandi-lyn touched her cheek again.

"Go on, then," Mandi-lyn said and began rummaging through her knapsack.

"When I saw the Reacher, or didn't see him, it was in a room. Like a dungeon or something. He killed Putrice, the mistress of the farm I lived at before crossing over. I don't know why. I also saw Harrelle. I tried to help him, but couldn't."

Errel sat on the other side of the bed. "How could you've helped him? Did he know you were there?"

"No." Bet shifted uncomfortably. "I just tried to reach for him. But the vision shifted and I was someplace else."

"Where'd ya end up?" Bathezine asked, reaching into Mandi-lyn's bag and stealing a nut, which earned him a sharp look from the Flursh.

Bet scratched her head and met Bathezine's eyes. "Before I get to that, there's something more." When all eyes were fixed on her, Bet continued. "When I was in the dungeon, I saw King Dalverious. I'm not sure why he was there. But I got the impression he was in league with the Reacher."

"How do you know?" Errel asked. His eyes met Bathezine's.

Bet shook her head. "I don't *know*. It was a feeling—a strong feeling."

"It makes sense now," Bathezine said. "The Reacher can cross the divide. If he completes the Staff of the Din, then the king can finish what he started."

Errel shook his head. "We don't know that for certain. Perhaps the Reacher is using him for some other means."

Bathezine looked at him doubtfully. "I wouldn't flip my chips on it."

"Either way, it's an alarming development." Errel gave Bet a reassuring smile. "What else did you see?"

"Just an old dead forest and a broken-down castle or something. None of it really made any sense at that point." She described what she had seen, carefully omitting the presence she had felt within the old keep.

"Well, there's more than one dead forest in the Whist, and it'd take us the better part of a lifetime to track them all down to figure out if there's a reason for ya seeing it." Bathezine stood and began pacing the room. "Anything else?"

Bet looked at Mandi-lyn. "This Travelling, or vision, was different. I didn't do it of my own accord. It was like I was being forced to do it. And before you ask, the answer is no. I don't know who made me do it. My only guess is Fealist-Marsh. But if it was, she didn't let her presence be known to me."

Mandi-lyn didn't seem overly concerned by Bet's account. She spoke while opening a small stoneware jar. "There are many things that even the greatest thinkers among us don't know. Perhaps your insight will open new doors to our understanding of the Talents."

"Well, there's my purpose, then, huh?" Bet said while looking at the jar.

"Perhaps," Mandi-lyn answered. "Now, about this mark on your cheek; where did it come from?"

Bet's expression turned serious. "It's nothing. Putrice, the one the Reacher killed, used to slap me...for disobedience. And she thought just about everything I did was disobedient."

Mandi-lyn scooped a paste form the jar. "You're glad she's dead, then?"

Bet's eyes widened. "No. I mean, I don't mourn her death, but I didn't want her dead." She leaned away from the Flursh. Truth was she wasn't sure. But after what she felt in the vision, she wasn't sure everything she saw was real.

Mandi-lyn's round dark eyes told Bet she knew the truth. "This paste will help heal the broken vessels."

"What is it?" Bet thought it odd that the scar of Biscuit Head's brutality would flare up after the vision. She wondered if what she'd felt at the building was real.

"Willow bark extract. It holds great healing properties. It will clear that nasty mark quicker than I could. Healing broken vessels and capillaries is very time consuming, and I would have to immobilize you. This will work just as well." Mandi-lyn rubbed a healthy portion on Bet's cheek, causing the girl to wince. "Most of it will dry up and flake away, but enough will remain to do the job. Don't wash your face for a week."

Old Babbers pushed through the bedroom door, followed by Le'lel. "Are you okay? What happened? What'd I miss?"

Mandi-lyn gave Le'lel a scornful look. "I told you to keep her there."

"She became...confrontational," Le'lel said, tucking his three-fingered hands behind his back. "She threatened to take my fingers."

Bathezine snorted. "Told ya that woman's scary."

"I'm fine. Just one of those vision things." Bet smiled up at Babbers, always happy in the presence of her friend.

"We'll fill ya in later." Bathezine took a step back at Old Babbers' withering glare.

"You'd better." She looked at Bet and smiled, adding a wink.

"Even beat up, you're mean as hellfire." Bathezine blew through his mustache. "You 'bout healed up? We got things to do as soon as Tiny emerges from his cocoon thingy."

Mandi-lyn stood, walked to Babbers, and ran her hand along the woman's side. "Close. One more session ought to be enough."

"You touch me with your stubby pink finger again, I'll bite it off," Babbers growled none too serious.

Mandi-lyn pulled back. "Neither will be necessary." She turned away and snatched the bag of nuts away from Bathezine, and motioned toward Babbers. "Those are mine. Touch them again and I'll sick the woman on you."

Old Babbers smiled. "And I'll do it."

Bathezine growled. "Now they're ganging up on me."

"Catch her and put her on the bed," Mandi-lyn said to Le'lel.

"Catch who?" Babbers asked just as Mandi-lyn touched her between the eyes, putting her to sleep instantly.

Bathezine laughed. "Deceitful critter, aren't ya?"

Mandi-lyn looked back at the Ursian. "Don't you forget that, the next time we play chips."

Ten

Surrounded by her friends while sitting together at a big round table in the Dining Inn, Bet beamed a contented smile. It was the first time since arriving in the Whist that she was able to truly relax. Even knowing that they would soon embark on another, and most likely dangerous, adventure couldn't dampen her spirits. Playful teasing, usually directed at Bathezine, and laughter filled the room as the group put aside all thought of what was to come to enjoy a meal together.

Bathezine sat with his back to the door before an ever increasing pile of licked clean dinner plates, while Errel sat across from him, complaining that the Ursian would empty his food stores.

"You said I could have whatever I wanted," the big bear-man laughed through his long mustache and beard littered with the remnants of his multi-course meal.

"Better hide your bowl, Pooch-kin, before that bear eats that, too," Errel said.

Pooch-kin looked up at the Ursian and hovered over his bowl of seed and meal-worms protectively. This elicited more laughter from the group, even from the usually stoic Mandi-lyn.

Walt brought Bet a second serving of pudding, causing her smile to broaden. She glanced around at the others, happy for their company. But as much as they had become like family, she realized she knew very little about them. She cleared her throat, hoping what she was about to ask wouldn't spoil the mood. "In the little bit of time I've been here, I've grown to love you all like family. But, everything has been about me. I mean stuff like where I'm from, how I got here, all of that."

"Well, you kinda brought us all together," Old Babbers said from the girl's side, reaching out and patting her back.

Bet smiled again. "I guess so, but I want to know more about you—all of you. You know, like where *you're* from. Do you have families someplace? Stuff like that. If that's okay."

The others traded looks with one another. When no one spoke, Babbers sat forward. "Yeah. We know your life story so I guess it's fair. And since no one else is chomping at the bit, looks like I'll get things going. I was born right here in Illguard. I lost Mama when I was too young to remember, and Pops raised me. He was a good man. Taught me everything I needed to know to get by in life. Did some fightin', roamed around a bit, and pretty much just've run the Supply Hut. And you all are the closest thing to family I got. Next." She ended her brief biography with a smile.

Bet looked around the table, a little disappointed by the brevity. "How about you, Mandi-lyn?"

Mandi-lyn pulled the corner of her hat over her eyes. "I'd rather not."

"C'mon, just a little bit. Where were you born? How'd you become the Charge of Danthbrook?" Bet lowered her head to peek under the hat.

The Flursh chittered the equivalent of a growl. "Fine. I was born in the hills of Gashburrow. One of six in the litter. I am the only survivor of my litter mates."

"What? Your mom eat the rest of ya? Isn't that what hamsters do?" Bathezine remarked with a laugh.

Mandi-lyn grabbed a nut and threw it at the Ursian, who caught it in his mouth and chomped on it with a wide smile. "This is why I don't talk about myself," she said.

Bet smacked Bathezine on the shoulder.

Bathezine rubbed his shoulder. "That hurt, girl."

"I'll do worse if you don't apologize." Bet raised her hand again.

He gave Bet a double-take. "I'm sorry. I didn't mean no harm. Just funnin' with ya."

"I wouldn't know how to act if you didn't behave like an ass every moment of the day." Mandi-lyn's whiskers bobbed in amusement to show she wasn't too offended. "No, my mother didn't eat the others. We were born at the end of the war, and there was a famine in those parts. The following year's litter fared much better. When I reached the age of one, I went to the Citadel of the Gray and studied to become a Charge. After my studies, I was assigned to the Halls of Danthbrook and furthered my studies in arcane history. I've been on a pilgrimage of knowledge ever since."

"See? That wasn't so bad," Bet said, motioning toward the Flursh. Mandi-lyn gave her a look to show she didn't quite agree.

"And that pilgrimage includes cheatin' at cards?" Bathezine remarked in jest.

"A Charge doesn't earn a salary. I have to eat," Mandi-lyn shot back.

Le'lel hissed to show he wanted to go next. Bet motioned for him to go ahead. "We Lasoom are hatched and leave the nest immediately. Though we do not have what you would call family, we forge powerful friendships. I have done so with Errel Handover, and I hope to do the same with all of you...even the Ursian."

"Why is it always me?" Bathezine barked.

"If you don't know, that might be why," Mandi-lyn chittered a laugh.

Bet ignored the pair's bickering. "I am happy to call you friend, Le'lel."

"Then it will be so until our time ends." Le'lel bowed his head, flicking his tongue.

"How about you, Bathezine?" Bet asked.

The big Ursian shook his head. "Nah, I wanna hear Errel's tale. I'm sure his is a lot more interestin'."

Errel raised his brow at Bathezine's comment. He shifted in his seat, sitting with perfect posture. "If you insist. Though Andolans usually only share life stories at betrothing ceremonies. But I've already traveled that path. I was born and spent most of my three hundred sixteen years in Andola studying and training. My wife and I had no children, and Andolan law requires a live birth within the first five years for the marriage to be legal. The marriage was annulled. After the war, I left and ended up here. Tired of my travels, I purchased the inn and transformed it into the burnt shell you see today." He raised his hands, presenting the room with a smile.

"What about your family?" Bet asked.

Errel's smile faded. "We don't see eye to eye…on many things."

Bathezine rested his chin in his paw. "What about Walt? Don't see too many Andolans in the county, let alone two."

"Walt was my page…I mean attendant. He was sent to convince me to return to Andola, but became charmed by the rustic lifestyle."

"Page?" Bathezine snorted. "You nobility or somethin'?"

Errel averted his eyes. "Let's just say that caste culture was one of the things I didn't see eye to eye on with family and leave it at that."

Bathezine shrugged after giving Errel a long stare. "How 'bout you, bird?"

Pooch-kin looked up from pecking at the remains of his meal. "I'm four. I was hatched at the farm. My mother and father were eaten, my eggs have all been eaten, most of my brothers and sisters were eaten or taken while still in the egg. I escaped the farm after my mate and coop family were taken. I crossed into the Whist to find Bet, whom I now consider my sister."

Bet gave the group a summary of what Pooch-kin had said, causing the group to reconsider their meal choices.

Pooch-kin chirped again. "Don't change your diets on my account. I eat worms and bugs; I'm sure they don't appreciate it, either. It's simply the way life is."

Bet translated once more, and Le'lel shook his head. "I am an Oragoth as well. You, little Chook-chook, are a very noble bird. I vow to never eat fowl again." He placed his hand against his chest and bowed.

"Thanks?" Pooch-kin said, unsure how he felt knowing he had been on the Lasoom's menu before the conversation.

Bet gave her friend a scratch. "It's appreciated, Le'lel. Now, Bathezine, you're the only one left."

"I'd rather not." Bathezine grabbed Bet's empty pudding bowl and began absently scraping at what was left with his finger nail.

Bet stretched out her hand, and Bathezine gave her back the bowl. Raising an eyebrow, she set the bowl aside and took his hand. "Like it or not, we're family now. But family should respect each other's feelings. And Bathezine, if you don't want to share, you don't have to. I understand. You've been through a lot."

Bathezine looked up from staring at an empty plate and met the others' eyes, each expression showing him that they did indeed care for him. He let out a long breath. "Ain't much to tell, really. I's born, ma took care of me and my brother. Galendine was his name. When I grow'd up, I became a gendarme, kinda like a sheriff, as you'd call 'em. Had a wife once… Cherlos, a pretty, golden-maned thing, she was. Kind as anyone you'd ever know. We had a few cubs: Lana, Amith, and Daphne. Good kids, the lot of 'em. Anyways, the war started and, being a gendarme, I's called to service. Ended up in the Scout regiment. That's where I met Tiny. While I was off in Hath, the king's forces came through my hometown. There wasn't much left by the time I got word and made it home. I reckon that's when I really took to fightin'." He paused, clearing his throat. "After I was through with the warrin' I bought Jangol from Tiny, and he's been my family ever since. 'Til I fell in with this lot, I 'spose."

The circle of friends sat in silence. Bet got up and went to Bathezine, wrapping her arms around his broad shoulders. "I'm sorry. I shouldn't have made you talk about it." She kissed him on his fuzzy cheek.

Bathezine patted her head. "Nah, I reckon you was right. I ain't told nobody 'bout it. Not even Tiny. Life is just life. We all got our reasons for livin' and dyin'. But be sure, girl, I ain't gonna let it happen again. If'n I have to bite the head off the king myself, I ain't gonna let it."

Errel sighed and looked at Bathezine. "Where was your home?"

Bathezine scratched at his chin, his face becoming as serious as Bet had ever seen. "Caverdon."

Old Babbers drew a breath between her teeth, and Mandi-lyn stiffened.

Bet's faced wrinkled in concern. "What? What happened there?"

Errel looked to Bathezine, and then to Bet. "You see, Bet, when King Dalverious' forces moved into the region of the Whist, they rarely confronted the defenders head on. They would send a smaller force one direction and send a larger force another way. They would attack defenseless villages, towns, never where they could meet any organized resistance. Whole communities were devastated. For whatever reason, they were exceptionally brutal on Caverdon. Their artillery shelled the hillside community until even the hill the town was built on ceased to exist. Atrocities like that were why…they were why I left Andola. I hoped for the Council's blessing, or at least to convince them to get involved. They eventually did, not at my behest, and not soon enough."

Old Babbers got up and went to Bathezine, slapping him on the shoulder. "Listen, you ornery old bear, you got us now. We're together for a reason. And when Tiny gets done doing his thing in the woods, we'll get this taken care of. But don't expect me to give you a family discount at the Hut when this is over." She smiled and slapped him on the other shoulder again.

"Thanks, you old she-devil. Wouldn't expect otherwise." He took her by the shoulder and gave her a friendly shake.

"Ain't giving you no hug either. Don't want fleas." Babbers pulled away, giving the Ursian a smile.

"Fleas?" Bathezine protested. "You're sittin' next to a Flursh and you're worried 'bout me givin' ya fleas?"

Mandi-lyn looked down her nose at Bathezine. "I'll have you know I have never had a flea in my life, not one. Can you say the same?"

Bathezine scratched behind his ear. "Maybe one or two has crawled on me in my day."

Mandi-lyn was about to comment further when a pounding came at the door.

"We're closed," Bathezine yelled.

Errel got up, shaking his head at the Ursian. He opened the door to find several Andolans standing on the porch, dressed in crisp black uniforms. His face quivered as he forced a smile. "Father?"

Eleven

Seven Andolans, wearing scimitars and side-arms at their hips, and various badges rattling across their chests, entered the Dining Inn with booted heels stepping in perfect unison. Errel moved back to allow the procession in, bringing his fist to his forehead in salute. "I wasn't expecting the Council to send *you*, of all people."

"This is a military exercise. We received word of a Creedan attack on Andolan property. We have come to deal with the tribe directly."

Bathezine scooted his chair back, making sure the legs scraped loudly on the wooden floor, and stood. "Late as always. Creedans have already been dealt with. Looks like ya made the trip for nothin'."

The commander's blue skin darkened and his nostrils flared. "Who is this Ursian?"

Errel stepped between them before Bathezine could say something unfortunate. "This is my friend, Bathezine—a former soldier in the war against the king. What he lacks in manners he makes up for in fidelity." He motioned to the Ursian. "Bathezine, this is my father, Commander Payv Handover."

Bathezine snorted. "Like I said, Creedans been handled by the lot of us." He waved his arm at the circle of friends and returned to his seat.

Payv gave him a dubious look. "Is this true?" he asked and turned to Errel.

The younger Handover placed his hands against his hips. "Bathezine is many things, but a liar is not among them. That particular tribe of Creedans shan't cause us more trouble."

"It was our understanding that it was more than a singular tribe. You know the law. Any attack on Andolan persons, or property, by any entities, shall be dealt with as a whole. All parties are considered to be equally guilty. It is not open for debate."

"I'm not debating law, father, I'm simply telling you they have been eliminated. Though I don't see how the eradication of an entire species lends itself to the Fair. Genocide is the way of the Foul." Errel shook his head, turning away from the procession. He spun back, his face on the edge of anger. "I have no love for the Creedans. But Thorn Eagles and Mastives were both involved in the attack, as well. Do you mean to drive them into extinction, too?"

"Thorn Eagles are simply tools of war, but the Mastives shall also face repercussions," Commander Payv said, placing his hand on the hilt of his scimitar, an Andolan gesture showing that his commitment to conflict was his vow.

Bet scooted back, pounding her fist on the table. "No. The Mastives were manipulated. They didn't attack of their own accord. They've suffered enough. I won't allow it."

Commander Payv stared down at Bet. "Mind your tongue, child. You have no say in Andolan affairs."

"Actually, father, she has the greatest stake in this. It was her that the Creedans were after," Errel said, rounding the table to stand by Bet's side.

"The Reacher controlled them," Bet said, looking to the others for support. "And he's coming back, and he'll be bringing King Dalverious' army with him if he can. If you want a fight, you'll have it."

Payv's eyes shot daggers at Errel. "You need to educate your friends on manners, or seek better company."

"There is much you do not know, father. And I have sworn my oath to protect her and those you see at this table. As you well know, that oath cannot be undone." Errel placed his hand on Bet's shoulder, giving her a slight squeeze.

Payv sucked a breath. "You have sworn the oath of your knighthood?"

The statement caused a stir amongst the others. Bet looked at Errel, eyes wide with question and surprise.

"I have. Walter will see to my affairs in my absence during this quest. He has already accepted his charge." Errel brought his fist to his forehead in salute.

Payv paced the floor, stealing glances at the other Andolans, his expression changing from anger to concern, and finally relenting to calm. "Will you carry the sword of Handover to defend your marker?"

"I will use all means available to me."

Commander Payv lowered his head, studying the floor. He raised his eyes, meeting Errel's. "So be it. As dictated by our custom, you should have the resources of Andola available to your quest. But," his eyes narrowed, "seeing as how you abandoned Andola *and* our customs, I cannot guarantee such aid."

"I never abandoned Andola. I swore an oath to protect, not only the federation, but all beings with equality. An oath both you and the Council seemed to have forgotten."

Payv raised his hands, indicating the room. "And yet we are here."

"Protecting Andolan interest, as you said." Errel moved from Bet's side and stood before his father.

Father and son stared at one another for several heartbeats as the others watched in tense silence. Payv relented. "We shall take your charge under consideration." He raised a finger. "But not before you explain who this Reacher is, how King Dalverious has the means to cross the divide, and who this girl is that you would be willing to lay down your life to protect."

"I will tell you all that I can tell you," Errel said, his stiff shoulders relaxing a bit. "There will be no papers. Much of what is to come must be kept secret, but this is of the utmost importance. Not just for the girl, but for all of the Whist."

"Very well," Payv said after some consideration. "Come to the airship and we will discuss this matter further." With that, the entourage turned to leave, each giving the fisted salute to Errel as they left.

With the commander gone, Bathezine stood and stared at Errel eye to eye. "Knight, huh? Just when I thought ya couldn't get no more snooty."

Errel let out a heavy sigh. "Don't even start with me, bear."

"Well, don't expect me to go fetchin' your mount or bowin' down or nothin'. And I ain't takin' orders from ya neither." Bathezine plopped back in his chair, looking the table over for more food.

"We'll see about that," Errel said with a smile. His face grew serious as he looked at the door. "I'll be back. And try not to eat everything in the kitchen while I'm gone."

"Ain't makin' no promises." Bathezine reached for a piece of sugar loaf on Babbers' plate, earning a slap on his paw. "You wouldn't do that if I was a knight, too."

Babbers raised her hand, threatening another slap. "I'd do it if you were an emperor."

Errel shook his head. "This is why I didn't tell you," he said and then left.

Twelve

Bathezine sat on a rotted tree stump waiting for the night sky to give way to the first hints of what promised to be a dreary morning. His breath came in rasps after three hours of nighttime target practice. Before nightfall, he had sent Babbers to the forest to set targets in various parts of the woods. He woke shortly after midnight, gathered his blow-pipe and quills, and a bundle of newly acquired shuriken, smaller than his previous throwing-star—he was now favoring multiple weapons over his bola, which had proved to be cumbersome in the battle of the Waste—and headed out, leaving Bet's protection in the capable hands of Babbers.

The heavy scent of rain approaching from the north masked Babbers' trail, making it difficult to track the set targets. He didn't mind. After the conflict at the Waste, he felt his skills as a tracker and warrior had slipped, and with what was to come, he knew he needed to be his sharpest if he wanted to survive and protect his friends.

His nose and ears twitched, taking in the sounds and smells of the forest. The sudden snap of a small branch deeper in the woods brought him to his feet. His lips curled back over his teeth, tasting the air, trying to get a fix on what had caused the disturbance. He couldn't catch a scent. The noise had come from somewhere near Tiny Nat's hollow trunk. Bathezine looked to the sky. The dark violet had begun yielding to morning, but he would have to wait to check his targets. Whatever was near his friend would have to be dealt with first.

He moved quickly and silently, padded feet carrying him over forest litter impossibly quietly for a creature of his size. He stopped, trying to catch the scent of whatever had made the noise. Nothing presented itself. Doubt washed over him. Maybe it was just a cone falling from a tall pine. A second crack of wood told him his suspicions were correct. He tasted the air once more and caught the scent of a human, there and gone again. He moved once more, slower this time, drawing a shuriken, in case it was another vapid, masking its presence, like the one they had encountered in Paskersville.

Bathezine crept through the woods, a silent predator stalking its prey. The sharp twang of the tripwire near Tiny Nat's nook rang through the muted night air. He sniffed, caught a brief smell of rosewater. He thought it odd; a tracker or assassin wouldn't wash in anything that cast such a scent. Throwing the cautious approach aside, he dashed through the underbrush, intent on catching or killing whatever had set its sights on the helpless Vivicon.

He rounded a cluster of trees and spotted a dark shape in the early morning gloom. He held the blade between thumb and finger, ready to throw, then the figure vanished. His head jerked in surprise. "What in the four corners of hell was that?" He sniffed again. Whatever it was definitely smelled like rosewater. Bathezine crouched low, intent on springing at the assassin if it showed itself again.

"What are you hiding from?" a tiny voice came from his side.

Bathezine let out a startled growl and fell to his backside. He looked up to see the bright smile of Misty, the kid from town, beaming in the dank light. "What are you doin' out here, kid? I coulda hurt ya," he snarled, half angry and half embarrassed at being caught off guard.

"The bug man is waking up. I wanted to see. Watch out, some dope put wires on the ground around his nest." She smiled again and tip-toed to the stump.

"How would ya know that? And ya shouldn't be out here. It's dangerous." He got to his feet, not bothering to dust himself off, and followed the girl.

"There's nothing dangerous out here unless you're a mouse. Even then, the snappers aren't awake yet and the owls have gone to bed." She sat down, cross-legged, in front of the stump, placing her hands on her lap.

Bathezine sat beside her, watching. "There's Skin-cats."

"What about them?" Misty asked, sounding perplexed.

"Skin-cats. They eat mice."

The girl seemed to take in the knowledge, and nodded. "Then the mice should be careful."

Bathezine sat silent for a moment and then looked at the girl. "So how d'ya know Tiny's waking up? And he's a Vivicon. Not a bug-man. He wouldn't like being called such."

"I heard him. I've been listening since you hid him away. Why didn't you put him in a closet instead of way out here by himself?"

"Too dry indoors. Needs the moisture. And I take it you're an Audiad?" Bathezine reached in the pocket of his tunic, pulling out some dried fruit. He handed a piece to the girl.

"Yeah, I hear well. I woulda put him in the closet and covered him in leaves and stuff. It's safer than the woods."

"His choice. And I like the woods," Bathezine grumbled. His anger at finding the girl alone in the forest subsided, and he had to admit he liked the company. He had seen her around town a few times, but owing to his gruff nature and general aloofness, had never spoken to her or many others, for that matter. "Shouldn't you be in bed?"

"Yeah. Shouldn't you?" she asked without looking at him.

"I'm an adult and don't have a bedtime. And nobody would worry about me if'n they found out I's gone."

"They're all asleep. And watch..." The girl disappeared in a blink. A moment later she reappeared, still in the sitting position. "I'd be back in bed before they'd know."

"Hmm," Bathezine said, tugging at his beard. "That's an impressive Talent. But don't go usin' it for fun n' games. Gotta exercise control when you have such a Talent."

"What's the point in having a Talent if you can't have fun with it?"

Bathezine opened his mouth to counter, but didn't find the words. *Why couldn't a kid have a little fun with her Talents?* "Well, just be careful," he finally said.

"Shh. He's breaking out."

The Ursian looked at the old stump and got to his feet, tugging at the back of his trousers from sitting on the moist ground. He walked around the area undoing the trip lines, rolling the wire into a ball. He dropped the wad beside Misty and motioned for her to stand back. "He might be a little groggy. Don't wanna surprise him."

The girl took a few steps back, then came forward again, looking around Bathezine's big leg.

The first rays of dawn shone through the tree tops, illuminating the morning haze with pale yellow light. The forest began to come to life with wood-knocker squirrels pounding their armored skulls against tree hollows, rousing the other diurnal woodland creatures. The pair listened to the wet snap of Tiny Nat's cocoon cracking apart. Bathezine took a step back with the girl's arms wrapped around his leg. He looked down, shook his head, and snorted. For some reason, the girl didn't irritate him. He wondered if Bet was making him soft.

"I'll be back," whispered Misty. "Mama and daddy Spiller are awake." She vanished before Bathezine's eyes.

"Lucky I don't have that Talent. I woulda kept disappearin' 'til my days runned out." He sat back on his haunches, scratching at the dirt in thought, waiting for his friend to appear.

A stirring came from within the hollow, and Bathezine prepared himself for Tiny's reemergence.

"I'm back," Misty whispered from Bathezine's side, causing the big Ursian to jerk.

"You need to work on that. Scares the tar outta me every time."

"Don't be such a scaredy-bear."

"I ain't a bear."

The piece of bark in front of the hollowed stump shook. Bathezine stood and pulled the large slab aside. Inside, he saw Tiny Nat curled up, his body wet and ghostly white. The Vivicon sat still, his thorax expanding and compressing as he breathed the morning air. Bathezine picked up Misty and moved a few yards away. "Watch. This is kinda neat."

Tiny Nat emerged from the cramped stump on bent legs, with his arms curled against his body. He stood motionless for another minute, his thorax rising and falling. He lifted his head, twisting this way and that, cocking it from side to side. A milky film covered his sightless eyes. After another minute or two, he stood, his exoskeleton creaking and cracking as he extended himself to his full height of seven feet. The effort seemed to tire him, and he stood still for a few more minutes.

Misty began to say something, but Bathezine put his finger to her mouth. He pointed to his eyes and then at Tiny Nat, telling the girl to watch. She nodded and moved closer to the Ursian for warmth against the morning chill.

Sunlight beamed through the trees in advance of the coming storm clouds, and danced off dew droplets clinging to the grass and leaves. In a burst of movement, Tiny Nat sprang to the top of his hideaway, standing fully erect, just as a sunbeam illuminated the old stump. He shook and quivered, and wings, much longer than his previous set, expanded outward, filling with blood and the heat of the morning light. His wings wavered and expanded, taking in the warmth, and waves of color washed over his body from head to foot. The milky white film covering his body began to dry, and after several minutes his entire body became a deep yellow, almost orange in color.

"That's another reason he couldn't go in a closet. He needed the sunlight. Though how he knew the light would be right where he needed it to be is beyond me," Bathezine whispered to the girl.

Tiny Nat turned his head to the sound of the Ursian's voice. "Bathezine? Have you watched over us this whole time?"

"From time to time. Good to see you, my friend. You're looking better than ever." Bathezine stood, brushing himself off, motioning for Misty to stay at his side.

"Who is the other one?" Tiny asked.

"Girl's name is Misty. A local kid. Guess she's been watchin' over ya, too."

Tiny Nat's head bobbed slowly. "It is appreciated, but unnecessary. We will forage to gain strength and join you soon." He expanded his iridescent wings and took flight, joined by a dozen other Vivicons hiding in the treetops.

Bathezine's eyes widened, surprised by the appearance of so many Vivicons. "Did you know they was out here?"

Misty shook her head. "Nope."

"Hmm. Well, that's that. We should head back." He stooped over, picking up the ball of wire.

"You were right. That was neat," Misty said with a beaming smile. "I'll race you home," she said, then disappeared.

Bathezine stared at where she had been. "That ain't a fair race," he grumbled, and went to check on his targets.

Thirteen

Bet sat at a table in front of a plate of cinnamon apples with a side of oatmeal, talking with Old Babbers, who was demonstrating various movements of fighting techniques she had learned over the years, and when to use them. Pooch-kin sat on the table, offering advice on when to hide and when to run, which was all the time.

"I'll keep all of that in mind," Bet said to him. "But for now I should learn how to defend myself for those times I can't run."

Pooch-kin simply clucked a reply.

Bathezine pushed through the front door, ending the morning lesson. "I'm starved," he said, dropping his rolled-up targets and satchel of throwing stars on the table.

Babbers rolled her eyes at Bet. "We'll finish up later," she said, then pulled the roll of targets across the table. "How'd it go out there, bear? You were gone longer than I expected."

"Not too bad. Eighty percent or so this time." He puffed his chest proudly. "And Tiny's awake. That's what took me."

"Tiny is awake?" Bet said, not masking her excitement. "Where is he?"

"He's out doing Vivicon things. He'll be by later on, when he's done doing, well, whatever Vivicons do." Bathezine walked to the kitchen and was promptly ushered out by Walt.

"I'm under strict orders to keep you out of the kitchen," Walt said, guiding Bathezine toward the table.

"Orders? Whose orders?" Bathezine barked.

"Mine," Walt barked back. "Now go. Sit."

Bathezine marched back to the table and unfurled a target, showing it to Babbers. "Why're all the targets shaped like an Ursian?"

Both Babbers and Bet laughed. "That's one of your better shots," Babbers said, pointing at the head on the Ursian shape. "Got it right between the eyes."

Bathezine tossed the sheet aside and sat with a growl. "Next time, I'll paint the targets, and they'll all be the shape of she-devil of a woman. And I won't miss a one, you can count on that." He turned his head toward the kitchen. "Where's the food? Person could starve waitin' 'round here."

Walt pushed through the swing doors, came to the table and dropped a plate in front of the Ursian.

Bathezine studied the plate's contents of a pile of white mush and various greens and berries. "What's this? Call this a meal?" He picked up a berry and tossed it in his mouth.

"It's steamed potato mash, spinach, poor-grapes, figs, and thrash-berries. I researched Ursian physiology. I prepared this meal with optimal Ursian health in mind." Walt stared down at Bathezine tight-lipped.

"My health is optimal enough. I want honey turnovers, and sweet cakes. You know, real food."

"That's what you get. You can go back to Beds and Foods and get *real food* there if you'd like." Walt reached for the plate.

"Bah," Bathezine snarled, watching his meal go. He reached up and took the plate back. "I'll take my chances with this."

"You're welcome," Walt said and went back to the kitchen.

Babbers stared at Bathezine for a moment. "What's got your shorts all in a knot? You're more cantankerous than usual."

"Yeah. What's bothering you?" Bet echoed, frowning at her friend.

Bathezine stuffed a handful of potato mash in his mouth, grimacing at the taste. "Ah, ya know. With Tiny up and at 'em, means we're gonna have to head out before we know it. And it's just... I'm kinda, ya know, likin' this." He waved both arms at the others.

Bet sighed. She was enjoying it, too. Real friends, real laughter, family; everything she never had before. She took Bathezine's meaty paw of a hand. "As much as I hate everything we've been through and will go through, I wouldn't change it. We have each other now, and the sooner we see this to the end, the sooner we can, maybe, have a normal life. I can get a place around here and take care of animals, Babbers can run her shop, and you— you can argue with her until you run out of words."

"He'll never run out of words to argue with," Babbers quipped.

Bathezine pulled his eyes from his plate. "I ain't workin' for her, if'n that's what you're suggestin'. I'd sooner cut off my own ears."

"Then you can help me with the animals, and Jangol won't have to haul rocks anymore." The idea made her think of Anna and Dalin. She hoped, when it was all over, she'd see them again, and maybe they would be her surrogate parents. It was a long shot, she knew. Normal didn't seem to fit in with anything in her life. She pulled her hand away, wiping the sticky remnants of potato she'd picked up from Bathezine's hand on her napkin. The friendly smile on her face melted away. "Regardless, now that Tiny Nat is up and back to normal, I think we should head to the Caves of Moth sooner rather than later. I have a feeling we shouldn't wait much longer."

The Ursian took his plate and shoveled the food into his mouth all at once. "Reckon you're right," he said through a mouthful. "Eatin's better on the road, too."

"How soon do you want to leave?" Old Babbers asked, inspecting Bathezine's shuriken for damage.

Bet pushed away from the table and helped Pooch-kin to the floor. "As soon as Tiny is ready, I guess. Are you feeling well enough to travel?"

Old Babbers patted her ribs. "I'm fightin' fit. I'll head to the hut and see what's left as far as supplies. We're gonna need another wagon, I know that much." She walked to the door, patting Bathezine on the head as she passed by.

He looked at the unfinished plate of food left by Old Babbers, and snuck a peek at the kitchen door. "No sense in wasting it." He reached for the dish and ate greedily, licking the plate clean.

Bet gave him an admonishing look. "I'm going to take a bath. Who knows when I'll get another? You should do the same."

"Nope. Took one 'bout two weeks ago. That should hold me for a bit."

"Well, at least comb the crumbs out of your mustache." She walked away, waving for Pooch-kin to follow. "C'mon, before he eats us, too."

Bathezine watched her go. He lifted his long mustache, examining the crumbs. He plucked a morsel of food stuck in the hair and plopped it in his mouth, then turned his attention to what was left on Bet's plate.

Fourteen

Old Babbers walked down the board walk and spotted Errel leaning against a post, looking lost in thought. "Hey there, Handover. You're lookin' a darker shade of blue this morning. I take it your meeting with your father didn't go so well?" She leaned against a hitching post and glanced to the sound of the first hammers pounding in the morning air.

Errel looked up from examining his finger nails. "I guess you could say that." His eyes drifted to the airship hanging over the edge of town.

"What, they still think Bet isn't worthy of protection? If that's the case, you know what I would do." Babbers flashed a crooked smile.

Errel glanced at her. "I can't feed them to the hogs."

Babbers laughed. "No. That's reserved for feisty Creedans. I'd tell them their opinion ain't worth spit on a hot rock. Doesn't matter what they think. You do what's right. And watchin' after Bet is what's right."

"I already did. Though not in such colorful language, but I got the point across." Errel took a breath. "I will see Bet to the end of what may come with or without the blessing of the Council. I have resources regardless of what they think they hold over me."

The first drops of rain began to fall. Babbers pulled her hat off and craned her head back, feeling the droplets dot her face. "Speaking of resources, I gotta get to the Supply Hut. You wanna come with me?"

Errel shook his head. "Later. Right now I have to check on one of my resources."

"Oh? What is it, a big pile of money?" Babbers hopped off the hitch.

"No. But I think you'll like it. In fact, I know you will."

"Now you got me curious. Maybe I'll wait on the hut."

"Let me get the dust off first. I'll see you in a bit." He walked away, giving her a half wave.

Old Babbers watched him walk for a few moments before heading in her own direction.

～～～

"Fiskers!" Babbers snapped when she entered the back office of the Supply Hut. "I need a new wagon, and travel supplies, and weapons, and some heavy coats."

A young man with sandy brown hair hanging in clumps of curls beneath a sun-bleached work hat spun around in a swivel chair, casting his narrow brown eyes up at Old Babbers. "Do you want tracking dogs, too? How 'bout a canoe, and maybe two-dozen Golden Swan eggs?" he asked sarcastically, then turned back to the ledger he had been working on, and his cup of tea.

Babbers stared at the youth blank-faced. She slapped him on the back playfully. "I don't remember sass being on my list. Really, I don't know where you get that attitude from. Who ya been hangin' around with?"

Fiskers shot her a sideways glance. "I've spent most of my life toiling it away here for you."

"Toiling away?" Babbers shot back. "You sound like an old man, not some seventeen-year-old punk."

"Punk?" he laughed. "Good to see you back on your feet. Does this order mean you're going out on another adventure?"

"Something like that. How does our inventory look? I noticed the shelves are a little bare." She took the ledger from beneath the cup, spilling a little tea on the cluttered old desk.

"The supply ships haven't offloaded most of what they brought. And most of what they have goes directly toward the rebuild. We'll know more tomorrow." He took the paper back, wiping off the spilled tea before setting it down. "How long will you be gone for?"

"Don't know." She threw her hat on a dilapidated wooden crate that passed for a filing cabinet. "I suspect a while."

"You don't plan on coming back half dead again, do you? I could use some help around here." He swiveled around again, placing his booted feet on a box near the desk.

Babbers rummaged through a few boxes on a crowded shelf. "Didn't plan on being half dead the first time out. Thanks for the concern, though." She scanned the cluttered office, biting her lip. "Hire a couple of the local kids; keeps them outta trouble." She pushed Fiskers' feet off the box and pulled back the lid.

"I doubt working here will keep anybody out of trouble." He stood and looked out a grimy window.

"Kept you outta trouble," she said, pulling out another box.

"More like got me in more trouble," he mumbled. "We do have one wagon left. But it needs a new wheel."

"Ah-ha! Found 'em," Babbers exclaimed, pulling out a pair of fingerless leather gloves. She slid the gloves on, made a fist, and three blades sprung out of each at the knuckles. She made a few boxing moves in the air. "Wanna have a go?"

"No, thanks." Fiskers scooted past the woman, who continued bobbing and weaving in an imaginary fight. "I have a wheel to replace."

Old Babbers extended her fingers, and all but one of the blades retracted. "Need to oil that," she said, examining the glove.

"Anything else you need, boss lady?"

"Nah. Just what I said. I'll go light a fire under those lazy Andolans and see if we can get restocked before I go."

"You do that," he said, grabbing a tool box from the ground outside the door, and headed out back to work on the wagon.

"You're a good kid, Fiskers. Don't know what I'd do without you," she shouted after him.

"You might actually have to work," he shouted back.

Fifteen

King Dalverious entered a wide, brightly lit white room buried deep beneath the citadel. Electric lights illuminated two white marble tables standing end to end in the middle of the room. On each table lay a segment of the Staff of the Din. Two men dressed in dark blue linens wheeled in a metal cart behind the king, carrying an unconscious old man, Harrelle.

"Put it alongside the second table." Dalverious watched them do as instructed then dismissed the pair. He inhaled deeply and waited. Moments later a wisp of black appeared near the far corner, twisting, growing larger until the Reacher's wraithlike form hovered over the sterile white floor. The king watched him, steeling himself. It unnerved him seeing the unnatural blackness in contrast to the room, making the specter seem even darker.

The Reacher floated over the tables, letting a tendril drag along Harrelle's forehead. "Awake," he hissed.

Harrelle's eyes opened and he reached for his glasses, which weren't there, as if awaking in his bed. His arm jerked back, chained to the long metal cart. He lay there in only the modest remnants of his undershorts, shivering uncontrollably. "Where am I?" he asked in a hoarse voice. He licked his lips for moisture.

"You are on the precipice of a great undertaking," the Reacher said, sounding proud and strangely parental. He turned away, placing the facet given to him by Bet on the table between the two segments of the staff.

"You will help me achieve that which I have so desired. And in doing so, you will bring security in service to your king."

Harrelle blinked, focusing on King Dalverious. "Rot in hell. I'll never help you."

The Reacher let out a disturbing laugh. "Whether you want to or not is irrelevant. In fact, your defiance is much more entertaining. Willing sacrifices are so dull." His white eyes fell on Dalverious. "Your Majesty, if you will."

Without hesitation, the king stepped beside Harrelle, drew a surgical blade and a small silver cup. "Stay still," he said as the old man bucked and squirmed, trying to free himself. Dalverious made a quick cut on the man's outstretched arm just above the wrist, quickly putting the cup underneath to catch the flow of blood, ignoring the old man's cries of protest and pain. When the cup filled, he placed it on the table in front of the Reacher.

The king turned back to Harrelle. He took a jar of ointment from beneath the cart, and taking a small scoop on his finger, smeared it across the open wound then grabbed a roll of bandage and wrapped the wound closed.

Harrelle panted and groaned, giving the king a look of hatred mixed with confusion.

"That wasn't so bad, was it?" the Reacher said, sounding half amused. "The first time can be so traumatic. But no worry, the next eleven times will be no worse. No better, but no worse."

Harrelle spat a curse at the two and fought harder against his restraints.

"Careful now, don't reopen that cut. I don't want you bleeding to death before I'm done with you." A slender arm of black smoke extended out and grazed the old man's face. "Sleep."

The king walked to the door, opened it, and motioned for the two men in blue to enter. One wheeled the cart away, while the other quickly wiped the spilled blood from the floor. After the men left, Dalverious stepped to the other side of the table, watching the Reacher examine the stone. "Eleven more times?"

The Reacher's eyes shifted from his examination to the king, then back. "This is the joining piece. The living blood must be given time to bond, to work its way through the stone, becoming one with each tiny fragment."

"He's an old man. What if he doesn't survive? He could have a heart attack from the stress."

"I will see that he lives."

Dalverious paced the floor. "Do we have eleven days? If this girl finds Fealist-Marsh, they could find the pieces of the other staff. You should've killed her when you had the chance."

"If I could have killed her, I would have. And do you truly believe that this child can find in eleven days what has taken me years?" A wave of gray washed over the Reacher's form.

King Dalverious' brow wrinkled at seeing the ripple of gray. *Was that doubt?* "If Fealist-Marsh helps her," he said in a low voice.

"We've been through this. If Fealist-Marsh were to reveal her location, I will know and I will destroy her." The Reacher dipped a wavering finger in the blood and stirred it slowly. "No more questions. I have work to do."

The lights flickered out, leaving the king to fumble his way to the door.

As the king touched the handle, the Reacher spoke, "Quell your doubts, King Dalverious, lest they make you an unsuitable ally."

The king exited quickly, closing the door behind him. He leaned against the wall, listening to the barely audible chants of the Reacher performing his ritual from the room beyond. "Doubts. He should speak." He pushed away from the wall and stormed down the hall. It was time to talk to his inquisitors.

Sixteen

Pooch-kin stood on the bed watching Bet sort through the contents of her satchel. He sniffed at the various pieces of debris that fell out when she dumped everything out at once. Finding a dead beetle, which had come from the inside of the old tree, he snatched it, made a hacking noise, then spit it on the floor.

"You don't like dead bugs?" Bet laughed, picking up the piece of quartz she had used to dupe the Troojian wasp.

"Freshly dead, yes. But that was a dried husk." He snuffled through the debris once more, finally gave up on finding anything of use to him, and settled on a pillow.

"I'm sure there'll be plenty of fresh bugs along the way. Just, you know, don't eat too many in front of Tiny Nat." She held up the quartz to the light, remembering the wasp attack.

"Seeds and nuts it is." He watched Bet examine the stone. "I don't think you'll need that anymore."

Bet snorted a laugh. "I guess you're right. It's funny how something as simple as rock can carry memories."

"Rocks can't think. They're rocks."

"I know rocks can't think, goofy bird. I mean, I look at this and remember that day. If Bathezine hadn't gotten to me when he did, if I didn't have the elixir to counteract the venom, I'd be dead. Same for the stone we found in the creek. The only reason I took it when I ran away was because it reminded me of you and our time in the forest. When I thought you were dead, it was the only reminder I had of you. It was something to hold on to." She looked at the waste basket by the nightstand and tossed the rock in.

"Memories are best carried in your heart, my friend. There, they can never be lost or forgotten, and can be kept no closer. That's how I keep my family alive and with me." Pooch-kin ruffled his feathers, changing to the color of his deceased mate. "See? She is gone, but always with me."

Bet stopped her rummaging. A tear coursed its way along her cheek. She crawled on the bed, and placed both hands behind Pooch-kin's ears. She leaned forward and put her forehead against his tiny head. "I love you, little brother. You are the only rock I need."

Pooch-kin looked up, his bright blue eyes meeting Bet's. "And I love you, featherless sister. Just don't give me to the Reacher like you did with the other rock."

Bet's shoulders shook with laughter. "You're a brat, my little feathered brother." She rubbed his crest playfully and got back to her work.

She put the things she needed aside; the pouch of coins given to her by Anna, a couple of iron bearings, the bottle of stamina elixir, and the flint given to her by Harrelle. She held the flint for a minute, remembering the trouble she had when she'd first tried to use it. She thought of the old man. They weren't happy memories. He was the tool Putrice had used to deal the punishment when a slap wouldn't do. She thought of the lashings Harrelle would give her; while severe and painful, they never scarred her, not physically, anyway. She had to wonder if he had held back. While he was old, he was a man and still had strength in him. Had he used it, the punishment would've been much worse. She remembered how he'd never made eye contact with her until the last day, when he'd helped her escape. Bet didn't really know why he had helped. Judging by what he said during their brief conversation that rainy night in the woods, she guessed it was an attempt to atone for past sins. She remembered her vision and struggled with the guilt.

Bet gripped the flint in her fist, deciding to keep it with her. The next instant, her body went rigid. Images flashed through tunneled vision. The fleeting images were of the farm, the woods, rain. Next came an iron carriage, the inquisitors, the large man with the red ribbons in his black beard. Then came a city, followed by the dungeon she had seen while Travelling, and the Reacher standing beside the king. She saw a white room, and a knife in the king's hand. She heard the old man's scream, and saw his blood dripping into a cup. Finally, she saw the facet of crystal. Her vision moved within the stone and she watched as the blood oozed through the rock, coursing its way through tiny fractures too small for the eye to see.

She broke free of the visions, gasping for air, and trembling. Sweat poured off her brow, and her sight returned. She spotted Pooch-kin standing on the bed, with wide eyes, chirping wildly. "What happened?" she asked through fits of breath.

Pooch-kin shook his head. "I don't know. You stopped moving, and then your body began to shake."

Bet wiped her forehead and pulled at her clothes, which were drenched with sweat.

Bathezine and Le'lel burst through the door. The Ursian looked at Bet and crossed the room in two steps. "What happened, girl? Are you all right?" He took her by the shoulders, looking in her eyes.

"I...I don't know." Her breathing began to slow. *A vision? Was it of something that had already happened, or of things to come?* She gathered her thoughts, fighting the last chills rolling through her body. She looked at the flint in her sweaty palm. "Mandi-lyn. Get Mandi-lyn."

"You heard her. Get the Flursh," Bathezine barked at Le'lel, who hurried from the room. "You're okay. I'm here. I ain't gonna let nothin' happen to ya." Bathezine guided her to the other side of the bed. He fluffed a pillow and sat her back. She shivered once more, and Bathezine took a throw blanket from the foot of the bed and laid it across her lap. He wiped the sweat from her face. "You're all right, you're all right. You wanna tell me what happened?"

Bet shook her head. "Wait for Mandi-lyn."

Bathezine patted her leg and got her a glass of water.

A few minutes later, Mandi-lyn walked through the door. She looked around the room cautiously, her whiskers bouncing in spastic twitching, then climbed on the bed, sitting at Bet's feet. "With as often as I get summoned, I'm beginning to think I should nest in your room."

Bet half-smiled. "You might be right. I'm sorry."

"No need for apologies. Tell me what happened." Mandi-lyn took a book and pen from her bag and sat waiting.

"I don't know, really. I was cleaning out my bag, and the next thing I know I had some kind of vision or something."

Mandi-lyn's whiskers went still. "Was it of the past or future?"

"I don't know for sure. I'm certain some was of the past, but the rest—I just don't know."

"How long did it last?" Mandi-lyn scribbled furiously.

Bet shrugged. "The images came so quickly."

Pooch-kin chirped from Bet's side.

Bet's eyes narrowed in concern. "Pooch-kin said it was only seconds. It felt longer, though."

"Tell me what you saw."

Bet recounted what she had seen, leaving no detail out. "What do you think?" she asked when finished.

Mandi-lyn studied Bet for a moment, tapping the pen on her notebook, seemingly lost in thought. "I can't say with any certainty. It sounds like a vision of past events. But these things are very rare, and owing to that, rarely studied. What were you doing when it began?"

"I was cleaning out my bag." She looked at the pile on the bed, then at her hand, and showed the flint to the Flursh. "I was holding this. It belonged to Harrelle."

Mandi-lyn sniffed the flint. "Are you certain it was blood you saw in the stone?"

Bet nodded. She motioned for Pooch-kin to come to her lap.

"It may be that the Reacher is using a blood sacrifice to reconstruct the staff. If so, this is a very dark Talent, but I won't pretend to know how the staffs were constructed. What does your instinct tell you? The voice of the Crickshaw within you—what does it tell you?"

Bet closed her eyes and slowed her breathing, searching her mind for the knowledge the old tree had instilled in her. "The blood. The blood is like…it's like a glue, bonding the pieces together. It doesn't make any sense. Or does it?" she asked, reading the concern in Mandi-lyn's eyes.

The Flursh shook her head. "I don't know. I wish I did. I will study my scrolls. An answer may present itself there. But what I do know is that we must go to the Caves of Moth. Immediately. I fear further delay may not be in our best interest." Mandi-lyn scooted closer to Bet, taking her head and running her whiskered nose along Bet's forehead and temples, checking for any injury.

Bathezine stared at Mandi-lyn. "Is she okay?"

"She has no physical injuries." She got up and went to the door. "I will gather my things. We leave tonight."

"Figured as much." Bathezine patted Bet's leg once more, and gave Pooch-kin a scratch behind the ear. He looked at Le'lel.

"I know," the Lasoom said. "I will find the others and tell them at once."

After Le'lel left, Bathezine stood and tugged at his beard. "You was holdin' the old man's flint, were ya? And you were thinking on him?"

Bet only nodded.

"Sounds like you found yourself another Talent. I heard tell of a man who could hold a person's things and tell you where they were. He made a good detective, from the stories I heard. It's a rare Talent, girl. Seems you get the pick of the litter when you find a new one."

"I'm not sure that's always a good thing," Bet said, only half joking. She looked at the flint and tossed it on the pile of things she'd keep. She pulled at her sweaty shirt and stood. "If you don't mind, I need to freshen up."

Bathezine watched her close the bathroom door behind her, then looked at Pooch-kin. "You did good, bird. Callin' me like that. We'll keep her safe."

Pooch-kin chirped his affirmative.

"That we will, Pooch-kin. That we will."

Seventeen

Night had fallen by the time Old Babbers had gotten the freshly repaired wagon loaded, and hitched up Alice the Fleet Ox. Alice stood beside Jangol, and the two snorted at one another in a rumble of conversation.

Bathezine stepped from beneath the porch of the Dining Inn turning his head up to the steady drizzle of light rain. "Couldn't a picked a better time for hittin' the road."

"I'm not sure if that's sarcasm or not," Old Babbers said from the bed of her wagon. "You want a hat to keep the rain off?"

"Ursians don't wear hats," Bathezine grumbled, carrying a crate of food to his ride.

"That wasn't sarcasm, then." Babbers rolled her eyes. "Any sign of Tiny yet?"

"Nope. I ain't big on leavin' without him. But Walt said he'd tell him when he shows. If he shows, that is."

Babbers cocked her head, staring at Bathezine. "I'm sure he's fine. He's probably just tending to hive business or something."

"Just hope he didn't have a change of heart after what happened in the Waste." He pulled back a canvas tarp covering the wagon bed and dropped the crate in.

Old Babbers came to his side. "Tiny made a vow to protect Bet. And from what I know, a Vivicon's word is as good as any signed paper. He'll come along soon enough."

"I know. After all we've been through, I wouldn't blame him for preferrin' to see to his ferries. You know, instead of havin' his wings plucked." Bathezine was about to say more when he let out a startled growl.

"Where ya going, bear-man?" Misty asked, appearing on the driving bench behind Jangol.

"Gah! Don't do that, kid. Can't you walk up to somebody like every other livin' being?"

"It's funny to see you jump," Misty snickered. Her snicker turned to laughter when she heard Babbers laughing as well.

"It wouldn't be funny if I was armed. Be careful. You could get hurt doin' your thing. Remember that." Bathezine turned his attention to fastening down the tarp.

"I'll try. Where ya going?" Misty hopped from the seat and held up the tarp, making it easier for Bathezine to run the rope through the eyelet.

"We're goin' away for a bit." He ran the end of the rope through the eye.

"Where to?"

"Away. Far away," Bathezine said, trying unsuccessfully not to sound short with the girl.

"I wanna come," Misty said, hopping to the corner of wagon, holding up the edge once again.

"Ya can't. It's dangerous, and you're a kid."

"It's dangerous here, too, with all those monsters that came, and the birds burning the houses down."

"We took care of that, so it ain't dangerous no more. This is grown up stuff. It ain't for kids. 'Sides that, your parents will miss ya." He jerked the rope through the next eye, beginning to lose his patience.

"The red-haired girl ain't a grown-up. Is she going, too?"

Bathezine growled. "That red-haired girl is more grown up than me half the time."

"That's not hard to believe," the impetuous girl said, drawing another laugh from Babbers, who was feeding Alice a carrot.

Bathezine took the tarp from Misty's hand. "Like I said, it's dangerous. And it's late, and it's rainin', and you should be in bed already, not standin' out here in the cold, pesterin' me."

"I'm not a pest," Misty said in a small, sad voice. Her body sagged.

Bathezine's shoulders slumped. He squatted down to look at the girl eye to eye. "You're right. You're not a pest. And I 'preciate your help. But you can't come with us. It's gonna take everything I have to protect Bet, the red-haired girl. And I don't want you getting hurt. You understand?"

Misty looked at the ground, drawing a circle in the mud with her bare foot. "Yes. I understand."

"Good. Maybe one day, when I'm all done with what I gotta do, and with your parents' permission, I can take you on a trip haulin' rocks to Paskersville." He did his best to give her a friendly smile.

"Paskersville smells funny."

Bathezine's chin fell against his chest. "Then maybe you can come with me across the Plece River, if'n I have a delivery there. Sound good?"

Misty stood silent for a moment. She looked up at Bathezine with earnest eyes. "Promise?"

"I Promise."

Misty's eyes lit up. "Okay, it's a deal." She held out her hand to shake Bathezine's.

Bathezine snorted and shook the girl's small hand. "Deal. Now go get in from the rain."

The girl nodded. She turned and started to run across the road but stopped midway and looked back. "You promise, right?"

"Promise," Bathezine said, raising his right hand.

Misty beamed a smile at him and then disappeared.

Babbers came around the corner of her wagon, shaking her head at the Ursian. "You're getting soft in your old age, bear-man."

Bathezine stood upright and glared at Old Babbers. "I ain't a bear. Immunuh check on Bet."

"Immunuh ain't a word," Babbers said.

The Ursian took a big breath. "I'm going to check on Bet. Is that better?"

Old Babbers laughed again. "It's entertaining when you're cross. And you're always entertaining."

Bathezine waved her away. He walked to the door, stopped for a second, then stepped back.

"I don't care, it's safer for you to ride in the pouch. And look, it'll be drier, too. It's raining," Bet said pushing through the door. She carried her satchels across her chest, a belt of pouches, fully stocked with iron balls and pea gravel bags, and a pack on her back, looking somewhat like an explorer off to discover ancient ruins. She pulled down the brim of her hat, and shook her shoulders, adjusting the fit of a new long coat given to her by Old Babbers. She looked at Bathezine and pointed to the Chook-chook. "Tell him it'll be safer in his carrier."

Pooch-kin chirped at Bet and hopped past her.

"I doubt it's like being in an egg. And how would you even remember being in the egg?" She motioned at Bathezine again.

"He's your bird. And if he don't wanna ride in a sack, he don't wanna. Can't say I blame him." Bathezine winked at the bird.

"He's not *my* bird. He's my friend, and I'm just trying to protect him."

"I'm tryin' to protect you, too. Ya want me to put ya in a sack?"

Bet put her hands on her hips. "Fine. You have a point," she said after a few moments of contemplation.

Le'lel came out behind Bet, and Bathezine looked him over. "You ain't bringing no weapons?"

Le'lel showed the Ursian his claws and bared his razor sharp teeth with a hiss, and walked past him. He crawled into Babbers' covered wagon.

"Guess you have a point. Where's Errel?" Bathezine stuck his head inside the door. "Hey, Andolan, you comin' or what?"

Walt came out of the back room behind the reception desk carrying a duffle. He looked outside at the rain and handed the bag to Bathezine. "He'll be out momentarily."

Bathezine dropped the bag on the boardwalk, crossed his arms over his broad stomach, and waited.

Moments later, Errel Handover exited the back room, dressed in black fatigue pants, with long boots rising nearly to the knee. Two bandoliers containing rows of small canisters crisscrossed his chest beneath a long black coat. A leather scabbard containing a long sword hung from his left hip, and a cutlass hung from the right. He wore an unadorned, black bycoket hat. He strode across the room and stood before Bathezine. "Let's hear your criticism of my attire before we leave. Get it out of your system now."

Bathezine threw him a mock-hurtful look, giving his dress the once over, his eyes coming to rest on the bycoket at the top of his head. "Hat looks like a bird beak. And ya kinda look like you're headed to a ball expectin' a fight. But other than that, I got nothin'."

Errel shook his head slightly. "You're letting me off easy." He walked to Babbers' ride. Its cover made it look like a smaller version of a Calistoga wagon.

"Is this what a knight of Andola looks like?" the woman asked, examining him in the amber glow of the Dining Inn's light. She looked at his swords and bandoliers, and her eyes traveled over him from head to toe.

"It's what this knight looks like," Errel said with a short bow.

Old Babbers flashed a crooked smile and gave him a playful slap on the arm. "I like it. Shall we?" She motioned toward her wagon.

Errel grabbed his duffel from the boardwalk and followed her.

"Anybody seen that Flursh?" Bathezine yelled. He turned back to Walt. "Remember, tell Tiny where we're headin' if'n he shows up."

"Mandi-lyn's already in my ride studying her scrolls," Old Babbers yelled back. "Now let's get going, bear-man."

Bathezine looked at Bet. "Ya wanna ride with Old Babbers? Seems that's the popular ride since she has the cover."

Bet held up a canvas roll, shaking her head. "I've got this to keep me dry." She climbed on the driver's bench and waited for Bathezine.

Bathezine climbed next to her, leaning close. "Can ya do your sensin' thing and see if Tiny's anywhere near?"

Bet nodded. Her eyes lost focus as she stretched out to sense their friend. She closed her eyes, her head twitching slightly. She made an almost imperceptible nod and opened her eyes. "He's safe. He's busy doing Vivicon things. I'm sure he knows we're leaving." She looked at the roof tops and her gaze fell on Misty, watching them from a second-story window. She motioned toward the girl.

Bathezine followed her gaze and snorted a laugh. Misty waved wildly and he gave her a two-fingered salute. "You all set back there, bird?"

"I'm safe and dry. Though I'm not looking forward to the jostling to come in your rickety old wagon," Pooch-kin said from beneath the tarp.

Bet wrapped herself in her roll. "He said he's fine."

"That was a lot a chirpin' for sayin' he's fine." Bathezine shook the reins. "Giyyup, Jangol. We'll rest at daybreak."

Old Babbers followed Bathezine's lead, and the caravan headed east into the darkness.

Eighteen

"Whoa, whoa. That's enough for tonight." Bathezine pulled back on the reins, stopping the Rhinodon out of habit. Jangol didn't need the physical reminder to do what he already knew.

Bet raised her head from Bathezine's shoulder, rubbing her hand across her face. She looked at the sky, noticing the first hints of another gray morning. "How long have I been asleep?"

"A few hours. Jangol needs a rest. And so do I." He slowly crawled off the bench, groaning about his stiff back.

Bet stretched and threw off her cover. She hopped down and rubbed her hands together for warmth. With just enough light to see, she noticed a line of trees to the side of the muddy road, which to her seemed much too uniform to be forest. She decided to take a look, and started walking.

"Where ya goin'?" Bathezine's voice rang through the morning air.

She threw her hands in the air. "Personal business. Is that okay?"

"Don't go too far. Stay close."

Bet shook her head. "I can take care of myself, in case you hadn't noticed," she muttered, and started off. When she reached the tree line she saw it wasn't a forest, though the forest was doing its best to reclaim the land, but rows and rows of old pecan trees. Saplings, brush, and weeds told her it wasn't an active farm. She pushed past willowy branches of wild jasmine and stepped into the ancient grove.

Her feet crunched and slid over untold years of nutshells. She picked up an empty shell, then another, in search of treats to bring Mandi-lyn, knowing her love for such things. But she could only find one; all the others were empty casings. She put the nut in her coat pocket. "Of course the wildlife would get to them. This must be a bounty for them." She cast the empty shells aside and walked deeper into the grove.

After walking for a minute or two, she decided to head back to the others. A cracking noise coming from behind made her stop. Bet turned to look. Between the dim light and morning mist, she couldn't see much. She shrugged it off and continued walking. Another crack from somewhere nearer made her stop again. She squinted toward the sound and saw a faint shadow move behind a tree. Bet let her senses stretch out and felt the presence of an animal, though she didn't know what kind it was. Judging by the abundance of eaten pecans, she decided it wasn't a predator and kept walking. Several cracking sounds from all around her made her wonder if it was a predator come to feed on the pecan eaters. She let her senses flow again and felt several animal minds. Not just several, but dozens. They began to show in her mind like light creeping over a vast landscape. They didn't seem hostile, but they were agitated.

"No harm meant," she said, quickening her pace, hoping to keep the creatures' agitation from turning to anger. "Just passing through. I'm leaving now."

The cracking noise turned to a low chatter, and Bet began to understand what they were saying. *Trespasser.* Her quick pace turned to a run, but her moccasins betrayed her and she slipped in the loose piles of empty shells. Quickly standing, she started to run again, but saw multitudes of dark figures surrounding her, scurrying down the trees, moving closer, chattering incessantly the word *trespasser.*

Bet went for a weapon, but thought better of it. The creatures didn't seem intent on causing her harm. She took a few more steps, but stopped as they finally came into view. Dozens of bi-pedal, two-foot-tall creatures, looking like a cross between a squirrel and a pig, with bushy gray tails and fur, and upturned pink noses, came toward her. Tiny, tufted and pointy ears twitched this way and that, as the chattering turned to whispers, still saying *trespasser*.

She raised her hands. "I'm not a trespasser. Not intentionally, anyway. Now if you'll excuse me." She took a step, but the squirrel-pigs closed in.

A slightly darker gray one came forward. "Trespassers or thief," the creature chirped.

"I'm not a thief. I'm just passing through."

The lead squirrel-pig moved closer and began sniffing her pants, running its nose up her leg.

Bet remembered the one pecan she had found and slowly began to lower her arms, hoping it wasn't pecans it was looking for, though she had a feeling it was.

The creature sniffed higher, its nose finally reaching her pocket. Its dark round eyes grew wide, and it stuck its fore paw in her pocket. It pulled out the pecan and spun to show the others. "Thief," it yelled, raising the pecan in the air.

A chorus of the word thief rang out repeatedly, and their bushy tails twitched with wild spasms. "Thief, thief, thief," the creatures chirped, mixed with an occasional call of trespasser.

"I'm not a thief," Bet yelled back.

"Kaggy," the leader called out. "Take thief to Kaggy."

"What? What's a Kaggy?" Bet felt the mood turn from agitation to something on the edge of violence.

The creatures surrounded Bet, nudging her back, deeper into the orchard, repeating the calls of *thief* and *Kaggy*.

Bet let herself be guided, fighting against her own agitation. She let a trickle of serenity wash over her to keep her agitation from turning to anger.

The mob pushed her along, eventually coming to a stop before a large oak surrounded by smaller pecan trees. Bet looked around and spotted movement on a limb in the oak. The chattering turned to a whisper.

A rotund squirrel-pig, twice the girth of the others, hopped from the limb, landing on two feet with ease. It carried a gnarled old branch in one hand as it strode toward Bet with an air of confidence, but also with a hint of caution.

"Kaggy," the leader said to the plump creature. "Trespasser, thief." It handed the branch-wielding squirrel-pig the pecan.

The chubby critter sniffed the pecan, then glared at Bet through narrowed eyes. "Thief! Our nuts. Not your nuts." The chorus of 'thief' rang out once more.

Bet looked around, trying to figure out a way out of her predicament. "I apologize. I didn't know they were your nuts. Just take it back and I'll be on my way."

"Thief," the fat creature yelled again. "Our nuts."

Bet gritted her teeth. "I know they're your nuts *now*. Take it. I'm sorry."

"Our nuts. Not your nuts, thief."

"Okay. I get it. They're your nuts. Just take it and let me go." Her serenity was starting to give way to annoyance.

"Our nuts." Kaggy raised the pecan in the air. "Thief take our nuts." The crowd of squirrel-pigs started shouting again.

"All right," Bet shouted. "You have your nut back. I don't want your stupid nuts."

Kaggy sniffed the pecan and threw it aside. "Our nuts."

"This is going nowhere fast," Bet mumbled. "Okay, I'll tell you what. I'm going to go now. Have fun with your nuts." She turned her back on Kaggy, and tried to walk, but was blocked by the horde of tiny creatures.

"Throw thief in pit of bad nuts," Kaggy announced and the horde began pushing Bet forward, chanting "pit" over and over.

"This isn't funny anymore. And I'm starting to get mad." She wasn't sure what the pit of bad nuts was, but she was sure it wasn't good. She reached for her pouch of pebbles just in case she couldn't resolve the situation peacefully.

They were pushing her ever closer to the unseen pit when a roar rang out in the distance. The mob of angry squirrel-pigs grew silent and turned to face the sound, their bushy tails turning rigid. A second roar echoed through the orchard, followed by the distant crunch of pecan shells. A nervous chatter began to move over the horde.

A third roar screamed out, closer this time, and the small creatures began to chirp wildly. "Bear, bear, bear," they yelled and began to scatter in every direction.

Bet watched the exodus and spotted Kaggy toss his gnarled little oak branch aside and scramble back up the tree.

Bathezine charged through the mist, bearing his teeth and growling, followed by Le'lel and Old Babbers.

Bet saw the Ursian leading the others and let out a long breath, not wanting to hear the impending reprimand.

Bathezine's snarl turned to an admonishing look. "You can take care of yourself, huh?"

Bet threw her head back. *Here it comes. I'm sure I'll get a good long lecture on this one.* "You heard that? Well I can...mostly. I guess I'm glad to see you. How'd you know?" She glanced at Old Babbers, who wore a half-cocked smile.

"You can hear their yappin' for a mile. We was watchin', waitin' for the right time. It's a hoot watchin' Snickers scatter like that. Ain't done it since I was a cub." Bathezine put his arm around Bet and started walking her back.

"They're called Snickers?"

"Yep. Or Nutters, on account of their penchant for nuts."

A squeal from behind made Bet spin around, thinking the Snickers had mounted a counter-attack. Instead, she saw Le'lel holding a Snicker by the scruff over his unhinged open mouth. "Le'lel. No. They just wanted to protect their nuts. Let it go."

Le'lel looked at Bet. His shoulders slumped and he closed his mouth. He dropped the creature, which ran away chittering something profane in its language. "There goes my breakfast."

"C'mon, Le'lel. We'll get you some pecans on the way back," Old Babbers said and started laughing.

Bet looked at her sideways. "Not funny."

Nineteen

Bet did her best to avoid eye contact with the others when she got back to the wagons. She went directly to Pooch-kin, who was standing on the driver's bench waiting for her. He sniffed her when she climbed beside him. "You smell like…like a squirrel," he said, rubbing his beak on the bench.

"You too?" Bet sniffed her clothes, realizing she was covered with the scent of Snicker musk.

Bathezine came beside the wagon, still carrying an amused look. "There's an old weigh-station 'bout a mile or two up the road. We'll stop there for a bit, and eat, and rest. Give us a chance to dry up. We'll head out around mid-morning." He climbed up, and Pooch-kin crawled on Bet's lap.

Bet looked at the brightening sky. Clouds hid any hope of sunlight, but at least the rain had stopped. The wagon jerked into motion, and Bet let her gaze fall on the Ursian. "Sorry 'bout that."

Bathezine scratched his nose. After a few moments of silence, he patted her on the knee. "No trouble. It was darn funny seein' them critters scatter like that."

Bet sniffed a laugh. "Yeah, it kinda was."

Another minute passed before Bathezine stole a glance at the girl. "But, Bet, ya gotta remember, there's lotsa things here ya don't know nothin' about. Dangerous things. Those Snickers weren't nothin'. If ya showed any kinda fight, they woulda runned off. But there's plenty a things that won't. Ya can handle yourself real well. Ya even done better than most of us coulda at times. That ain't always gonna be the case. So when I tell ya to stick close, I ain't tryin' to be overprotective, or smother ya. I'm just watchin' out for ya."

Bet leaned her head against his beefy shoulder. "I know, I know. I've never had that, really. In the orphanage, it was like we were just, I don't know, merchandise—items on a shelf waiting for the right buyer. And at Malweather…It wasn't even that. Takes some getting used to, I suppose."

Bathezine nodded. He lifted his arm, tentatively at first, and then wrapped it around her. "I know. You've had a tough go of things. But I can tell ya this, ya turned out to be a damned fine person by my reckoning. And once we get all this adventurin' done with, we'll get that spot of land and have a nice place and a nice life, and have nothin' to worry about 'cept takin' care of those critters, and we'll have butterscotch puddin' for dessert every day."

Bet smiled and scooted closer. "I'd like that, Bathezine. That sounds nice."

~ ~ ~

They rode in silence until they came around a wide bend in the road, on the side of which, hidden by trees and overgrowth, they saw a rundown old building. Rusted metal siding clung to the frame, bent and folded as climbing ivy did its best to pull it free under its weight. A warped and faded wooden sign stood atop an equally warped tin canopy hanging over a driveway carpeted by weeds of every sort, where freight haulers once stopped to weigh their load before heading to or from Illguard, Fiverton, and other towns. Empty windows and door frames, now devoid of glass and the boards that followed its absence, announced the years of neglect that had fallen on the abandoned check point.

Jangol's slow trot became a slow walk as he looked back at Bathezine to make certain they were stopping. Bathezine nodded and the wagon came to a halt.

"Alpha Bar Weigh Station," the Ursian announced. "They'd fine ya for being an ounce overweight if old man Masterson was working. And he almost always was."

Bet hopped down, followed by Pooch-kin. "What happened to it?" She walked under the awning, examining the rusted metal posts and equally rusted door frame. She thought the place looked like a tetanus infection waiting to happen.

"Weren't much need for it after what happened in the Waste. Don't need to weigh freight if'n there ain't no commerce." He stepped on the wood drive-up scale and bounced a few times, listening to the faint squeak of a spring underneath. "Seems sturdy enough still. Jangol, pull up under cover to keep out of the rain."

Bet looked at the gray sky. "It's not raining."

Bathezine ignored her and peered inside the building. He pulled what remained of the door open, which squealed in protest. A moment later the rain started again.

Old Babbers drove Alice under the cover, too. "If an Ursian says it's gonna rain, it's gonna rain," she said, climbing down from the driver's seat.

Bet stepped under the shelter. "I'll remember that. Is that a Talent, predicting the rain?"

"Nah. Ursians just know. Probably have an extra bone in their thick skulls that tells them the weather."

"I can hear your insults, woman," Bathezine said from inside the station.

"It ain't an insult if it's true." Old Babbers nudged Bet, who agreed with a sideways nod.

"Grab a couple of bedrolls, girl. It's clean enough for nappin'," Bathezine's voice echoed off the empty walls inside. "And grab some grub."

Bet got what he'd asked for from the wagon and went inside. Her feet crunched on an array of dead insects and things she'd rather not know. Cobwebs hung thick toward the back of the wide room, and she could hear the scurrying feet of the denizens of the decaying building, disturbed by the intruders. She decided Bathezine had a very different definition of *clean enough for nappin'* than she did. "I'm not really tired," she said, wrinkling her nose.

Mandi-lyn entered and looked around. "Quaint," she said, not masking her disgust. She took a bedroll from Bet and spread it on the ground. "Sit with me, Bet. I need to talk to you."

Le'lel followed, and his tongue immediately began flicking, tasting the air. He went to the darkest reaches of the room and began hunting for wood rats.

Bet was about to protest, but she figured the reptilian Lasoom weren't vegetarians. She handed the food to Bathezine and parked next to Mandi-lyn.

Errel stuck his head through the vacant window frame. "Do you need a fire?" He looked at the space and shuddered.

Bathezine shook his head. "Nah. I like cold beans. 'Sides that, the smoke'll probably asphyxiate us."

Errel studied the holes in the walls. "I'm sure there's ample ventilation. I'll do my nappin' in the wagon." Babbers agreed and followed him.

Pooch-kin walked in and immediately turned around, and followed the others without saying a word.

"Snobby bird," Bathezine mumbled through a mouthful of bread.

"What did you want to talk about?" Bet asked, sitting cross-legged, facing Mandi-lyn on the roll.

"I believe you have uncovered a new Talent. It's a variation of the sight Talent, and not very common."

"So I've been told." She tilted her head at Bathezine. The Ursian had already fallen asleep after scarfing his food.

"He is correct. This Talent can prove useful in our search for Fealist-Marsh." She reached into a bag, pulling out an assortment of objects. "I want to try some experiments. If you don't mind?"

Bet shook her head. "I don't know. The last time wasn't a very pleasant experience. And I didn't try to do it. Maybe it was like the Travelling. Maybe somebody wanted me to see it."

Mandi-lyn's whiskers twitched, showing her impatience. "No. From what you described, it was most definitely a Talent. And you should know by now that once a Talent shows itself, it never goes away."

"I know. Wishful thinking, I guess."

"Good. Here. Take this." Mandi-lyn handed Bet a medal.

Bet looked at it suspiciously. "Did you lift this from one of the Andolans?"

Mandi-lyn's whiskers bobbed in amusement. "Now I want you to focus on one of the Andolans' faces. Take your time."

Bet closed her eyes and took a deep breath, concentrating on the line of Andolans in her memory who'd shown up at the Dining Inn, locking in on one. Almost immediately, her vision took her through a tunnel and she saw the inside of an Andolan airship. She saw a small room, which looked like sleeping quarters. She saw one of the Andolans tossing clothes aside, rummaging through drawers in a small hutch, his face a darker shade of blue. She felt his anger and frustration. She opened her hand. "He's really upset over losing this." She dropped the medal on the bedroll in front of the Flursh.

"Good. Good. Very good." Next, she handed Bet a pecan. "Now focus on a Snicker."

Bet looked at the pecan. "How do you get this stuff without getting caught?"

"Cause she's a sneak and card cheat," Bathezine grumbled between snores.

Bet fought back a laugh. She closed her eyes, repeating the process. She saw Kaggy, the plump old Snicker. He was sniffing the ground, then running his branch through the pile of empty shells. He stood and sniffed the air. His bushy tail quivered in agitation. Bet opened her eyes and tossed the pecan to Mandi-lyn, who caught it, cracked the shell with her large incisors, and ate the contents. "How could it possibly know that a single nut has gone missing?"

Mandi-lyn didn't answer. Instead, she held out a small box and opened it, handing Bet a tarnished silver ring. "Take this. Focus only on the ring."

"How do I do it without knowing who it belongs to?"

"This is part of the experiment."

Bet nodded. Her brow furrowed in concentration. She closed her eyes. A loud crash from the back of the room jolted her out of her focus.

"Quiet. Please, Le'lel. We are working," Mandi-lyn said, admonishing the Lasoom.

"Apologies," Le'lel said before stuffing a squirming rat in his mouth.

Bet did her best to ignore the sound of Le'lel's breakfast. She returned her focus to the ring. She closed her eyes, holding the ring tight, rubbing it with her fingers against her palm. The tunnel came. But this time it didn't end. Her vision followed it. And when it seemed it wouldn't end, a thick, almost viscous black wall brought her to a halt. A strange sensation washed over her body. She felt cold, fear, and a feeling that skirted the edge of peace. The sensation made her nauseous and the fear grew. Her eyes snapped open and she dropped the ring, trying to catch her breath. "I can't… I couldn't see anything. Just blackness."

Mandi-lyn's whiskers stopped moving, and her beady eyes stared at Bet. "You did well. Your Talent is actually very strong. You must develop it further."

"Whose ring is this? I couldn't see who it belonged to." She shivered and her breathing slowed.

Mandi-lyn put the ring back in the box and stuffed it in her bag. "It belonged to my mentor at the Halls of Danthbrook. It was bequeathed to me upon his death."

Anger flared in Bet. "You gave me a dead man's ring? Did you know what would happen? That was a horrible feeling."

"I didn't know what would happen or what you would see, though I had suspicions. But you have proven the strength of your Talent. I have a feeling more Talents are to come."

Bet huffed for a moment longer until curiosity got the better of her. "What I saw, what I felt, was that the afterlife?"

"If there's truly an afterlife, no one could know. What you felt was the end of life. The end of his life. The boundary between life and death." Mandi-lyn pulled her notebook out and began scribbling. "You did well."

Bet stood, shaking her head. "I need some air." She stomped out of the room.

With Bet gone, Bathezine rolled onto his side, propping his head on his hand. "You shouldn't ought a done that. She skirted the Foul before, and it's dangerous for her. We gotta protect her, keep her safe."

Mandi-lyn pulled her eyes from her writings. "It may be her who keeps us safe. I have a feeling she is much more than we thought."

Bathezine sat up, stuffing a bite of sweetbread in his mouth. "I was a-scared you'd say somethin' like that."

Twenty

Mid-morning came, and true to his word, Bathezine got the band of travelers underway. They rode for several days, following the road along the Twist River. The rain had passed, making their journey much more pleasant. Bet constantly asked questions about the wildlife she spotted along the way, which, after a while, began to irritate her Ursian companion. So much so, she switched wagons with Le'lel so he and Bathezine could trade stories about their time at the gaming tables. Bet studied with Mandi-lyn while riding, and trained with Old Babbers in the art of defense while camping. When her inquisitive mind got the best of her, and she felt the itch to explore, she made sure not to stray too far from camp, keeping Bathezine's advice in mind.

No trouble found them. The only hint of danger that crossed their path was a small hunting party of Mastives. The massive creatures gave them a wide berth. Judging by the scorch marks Bet saw on one of their legs, she guessed they were survivors of the battle on the Waste, and weren't eager to confront more blasts of fire. Bet touched their minds to reassure herself and her friends the Mastives had no ill-intent. With their minds free of the Reacher's influence, they were relatively placid creatures, but wary of the travelers.

They drove southward over low, sparsely wooded hills until arriving at the edge of a deep and wide depression where the road cut away, heading west. Mandi-lyn stuck her head out from beneath the canopy of Old Babbers' wagon and cried for the team to stop.

The group dismounted their rides, all except Mandi-lyn, who went as far as the driver's bench. Bet walked to the edge of the depression, which stretched far into the horizon, meeting with distant purple mountains. "What is this place?" she asked, looking down a steep slope that terminated in juts of angled stone and dead gray trees, protruding above a haze, far below. A hint of sulfur floated in the air.

Mandi-lyn, Le'lel, and Bathezine sniffed or tasted the air respectively. Errel placed his hand on the hilt of his sword as if expecting an attack. Old Babbers casually folded her arms, leaning against Alice's shaggy side, and Pooch-kin circled the ground at Bet's feet, foraging for bugs.

"It is an ancient caldera," Mandi-lyn finally said, "from an eruption long before written history. Somewhere in there lay the Caves of Moth."

Bet swallowed and stepped away from the edge. Her senses told her there was life within the maze of rock and trees, but it was indistinct, as if a veil covered its presence, masking it from her Talent. There was something else within the caldera—a vague impression of a mind, strong-willed yet chaotic, dancing on the fringe of insanity. A shiver coursed through her body. "What else is down there?"

Mandi-lyn's bouncing whiskers grew still. "Many things, or nothing. Mostly legend or myth, or rumors. Only a few have ideas of what Moth is. Fewer know that it is an Ancient One."

"Do you know what it is?" Bet moved closer to Bathezine.

"Not with any certainty. As I said, most of what we know is based on myth or even superstition." Mandi-lyn looked at Bathezine. "We should make camp here. We will need to decide who will accompany Bet."

"I will," the group said almost in unison.

Errel cleared his throat. "The wagons won't be able to make it. Unless you know of a road down." He looked at the Flursh.

"None that I know of." Mandi-lyn rummaged through her knapsack, pulling out a looking glass.

Babbers snatched it from her hands, put it to her eye, and surveyed the landscape.

"Anything? A road, a path, something we could use?" Errel asked, not eager to send Bet down with less than a full company of support.

Babbers pulled the scope from her eye, closing the telescoping lens. She shook her head with a doubtful frown. "If there is, I can't see it. That smoke or dust, or mist, or whatever it is, hides just about everything."

Bathezine scratched angrily at his beard. "What about that half-witted crow? He could just fly ya to where ya need to be. Any sign of that bird?"

Bet shook her head. "Haven't seen him since we got back to Illguard. And I can't sense him. He can block me. Remember?"

"Yeah, yeah. What about Tiny?" The Ursian's voice sounded desperate.

Bet averted her eyes. "He'll be along. I'm not sure how far behind he is."

"Fine time for him to be havin' a hive gatherin', or whatever they do." Bathezine looked at the cloudless sky with the first hints yellow and orange creeping in from the west. His body sagged. "Well, no sense in frettin' over it right now. We're losing daylight. Might as well make camp."

The others guided Jangol and Alice to a clear spot across the road beneath the gnarled branches of two withered old black oak trees. Bet stood looking at the vast caldera, trying to get a sense of what was hidden from her. Despite her best efforts, no answers came. She knelt beside Pooch-kin, scratching his ears.

"What's wrong?" the little Chook-chook asked. "Other than knowing you have to enter a place of myth and legend, that is."

Bet snorted a laugh. "Thanks for putting me at ease."

"That's why I'm here."

She ruffled his red-orange crest. "I don't know. I can't get a sense of what's down there. It's almost like I'm purposely being blocked. All I get are vague impressions, but they're somehow familiar, like fleeting memories from a dream. And no matter how hard I try, I can't grab a hold. They're being dangled in my mind, just out of reach."

"With the dreams you have, I'm not surprised. Do you think this impression is from one of your dreams or visions?" Pooch-kin glanced at the haze in the caldera.

"Maybe, but even then, it feels like the memory is being repressed." Bet watched the haze as well, noticing the tree tops disappearing beneath it. She looked at the sky and realized the mist was rising as the sun fell. She turned to where the others were making camp, wishing the camp was farther away from the caldera.

"Maybe you should ask Mandi-lyn."

"Maybe…I don't know. I get the feeling she isn't telling me something." Bet watched the Flursh for a moment. Mandi-lyn was carrying a small box from the wagon bed. She stopped and looked at her. Bet held her gaze for a second longer and turned away.

Pooch-kin lunged for a grasshopper, but missed. "Do you trust her?"

"Yeah," Bet said without hesitation. "But she knows something, or at least thinks she does."

Pooch-kin watched Bet. "I'm going down there with you."

Bet stood and frowned. "No. I don't think you should. And don't argue with me. I have a bad feeling about this place. You have to trust me on this one. Now come on, let's help make camp."

"What am I supposed to do to help? I have no arms," Pooch-kin said, following after her.

"I don't know. You can be the sentry. Check the area for snappers."

"There you go with the snappers again. Why is it always snakes?"

Twenty-One

Bet sat silently by the fire, roasting a squash on a stick. She watched tendrils of mist creep across the road. The image reminded her of the Reacher as he extended his smoky black hand to nab the facet of the Din from her hand. The mist carried the scent of decay, similar to rotting vegetation, but not quite. Everyone sat on crates or the ground, equally silent. The sounds of crackling wood and working jaws, crunching various meals, were all that could be heard.

Mandi-lyn scratched her head under her tricorn and cleared her throat. "I know we're lost in thoughts of what tomorrow holds, and since we are, we need to discuss who will accompany Bet to the caves."

"I'm going. There ain't no discussion about it. It's final," Bathezine said from Bet's side. He gave her a light slap on the knee.

"How many of us should stay behind to keep watch over our supplies? I'm thinking at least one, possibly two," Errel said. "And we've already been through this. All of us want to go with her. Does that hold true for you, Mandi-lyn?"

Mandi-lyn raised her eyes while gnawing on a gasher-nut. "While I am not eager to go, the research would be invaluable. As far as we know, no one has actually studied the area. No one even knows for certain what Moth is. We could learn much from encountering an Ancient One. In answer to your question—yes, I need to go."

Babbers tossed aside an apple core, and raised her hand. "We're gonna need to draw straws," she said while chewing the last bite.

"We ain't got no straws, and I ain't drawin' anyhow. Already established I'm goin'." Bathezine folded his arms across his chest, defying anyone who would tell him differently.

Le'lel's tongue flicked at the air. He looked at the crawling mist for a moment, then back at the group. "Then how do we decide?"

Mandi-lyn grunted her displeasure. "Fools," she said. Taking out her notebook, she pulled out a sheet of paper, tore it into smaller pieces, and wrote on them. "I have marked two pieces. Two of us will remain behind. If you draw a blank, you stay here. At the Ursian's insistence, he will not partake in the drawing." She pulled off her hat, dumped the pieces in, and handed the hat to Bet.

Errel stepped forward, and looking at Bet, drew his lot.

"Don't look at it until everybody has theirs," Bet said.

Le'lel went next, followed by Babbers and Mandi-lyn. When they returned to their seats, Bet nodded for them to open the folded papers.

Errel opened his and frowned. He showed the others the blank paper. "Sorry," he said to Bet, and crumpled the paper, tossing it in the fire in disgust.

Old Babbers opened hers and beamed a smile, showing the marked paper. "I'm going with you, bear-man."

"I ain't a bear," Bathezine muttered.

Le'lel and Mandi-lyn exchanged looks. The Lasoom opened his paper, showing the others the mark. "I will protect you with my life or death on this venture."

Mandi-lyn took her scrap and followed Errel's lead by tossing it in the fire. "It has been decided. Bet, you must remember every detail. It is of the utmost importance. Promise me this."

"I will." She stared at Mandi-lyn for a second, then looked at Pooch-kin. She took her half-eaten squash, wrapped it in cheese cloth, and stuffed it in her bag. She stood up, cradling Pooch-kin in her arms. "Might be best if I get some sleep now. I have a feeling it'll be a while before I'll get a full night's sleep again."

Errel got up and went to the fire. "That would best for all of us. I'll douse the flame."

Bet spun around. "No. Don't. Let it burn through the night." She looked at the mist, which had surrounded the camp, avoiding the fire.

Errel's eyes followed Bet's. He reached for a chunk of coal, and igniting it in his hands, he tossed it on the fire, making the flame glow white. "Then I will make it burn hot."

Bet crawled inside her tent, setting Pooch-kin beside her bedroll. She took off her gear, and fluffed a knapsack of clothes she used as a pillow. Reaching for the laces on her moccasins, she pulled away, and stared at her shoes for a moment. Her brow wrinkled, thought better of it, then lay down.

Babbers crawled in a few minutes later, repeated Bet's actions, and looked at the girl's shoed feet. "Sleeping with your boots on?" She kept hers on, too, and fell back on the bed.

Bet turned out the light. "Is Mandi-lyn coming in?"

"Nah. She's studying her scrolls. She's done enough reading of those things, you'd think she'd have them all memorized by now."

"You'd think." Bet blew out a breath.

"What's troubling you? You've been acting spooked since we got here." She rolled on her side and looked at Bet through the firelight glowing against the tent door.

"I don't know. Something doesn't feel right," Bet said in a whisper, rolling on her side to face her. "And that's only part of it. It's like there's a veil over my Talent to sense what's down there. I get hints of things, but it's muddled and sorta confusing. It feels like it's intentional."

Babbers thought on it for a minute. "Maybe that's why nobody really knows much about this place. If you can't sense anything, maybe no one else can, either. You're still growing into your Talents. The fact that you can sense anything at all might mean that you're stronger than you might think."

Bet rolled to her back, putting her hands behind her head. "Maybe. I guess all of the Ancient Ones aren't as kindly as the Crickshaw was. But honestly, something feels…odd. I think whatever is down there is dangerous."

Babbers rolled to her back. "Probably, but when has anything not been, on this little adventure? Don't worry too much. You'll have me and that bear, and Le'lel, watching over you."

"That worries me, too. I don't want anything to happen to any of you."

Babbers muffled a laugh. "C'mon, girl. I took a punch from the Reacher-possessed Mastive. If that demon can't finish me off, I doubt much can. I'm tougher than I look."

Bet raised an eyebrow. Old Babbers was indeed tough, maybe the strongest among them, if not the fiercest. The word demon stuck in her mind. She hadn't told anybody that she had learned the true nature of the Reacher, that he was essentially the dark half of Fealist-Marsh. She wasn't sure why she kept the information hidden, even from Mandi-lyn. She wondered if they would abandon their quest to find the Omia Temporian if she told them. Whatever it was, she hoped to find more answers from this Moth person. "I don't know; you look pretty tough to me."

"Ah, you're just saying that," Babbers said, nudging her. "Now quiet your head and get some sleep."

Bet opened her mouth to say something else, but Babbers' heavy breathing told her she was already asleep. "I don't know how they fall asleep that quick," Bet whispered to Pooch-kin.

"Maybe you should figure that out," Pooch-kin said. He nuzzled next to her and matched Babbers' quick sleep.

The corner of Bet's mouth raised in a smile. "Maybe I should."

Twenty-Two

A guard threw a cup of water in Harrelle's face. "Drink, old man," the large man armed with daggers yelled when finding that the prisoner hadn't drank anything or eaten his food for the second day in a row. He reared back to slap him, but Harrelle didn't flinch. Seeing he couldn't intimidate the man, the guard knocked over the tray of food and turned to leave. He took two steps, but stopped, as if frozen in place.

"Now how can he eat if his food is on the floor?" The Reacher formed in front of the door as if it was poured from an invisible ewer.

The guard tried to open his mouth, but couldn't make the tiniest of movements.

"I guess you'll have to eat it instead." The Reacher made a motion with his wispy arm, and the guard fell to his knees. "Eat...all of it."

The guard scurried on hands and knees, grabbing each morsel of diced meat and vegetables, stuffing them all in his mouth and swallowing, barely chewing. He looked up at the ghostly form.

"I said all of it."

The guard searched the floor, finding the spoon.

"Eat it!" the Reacher demanded.

The man pushed the spoon down his throat, gagging and choking. Gasping for air, he looked back at the Reacher with bulging eyes.

The black form floated closer. "Just one more bite."

The guard took the flimsy tin tray, folded it in jerky movements, and began forcing it down his throat, compelled by the Reacher's will.

Harrelle, who had been watching the proceedings, turned away, sickened by the ghastly sound.

The Reacher's white eyes stared at the twitching body of the dying man. He turned to Harrelle. "Such rude behavior on his part. Wouldn't you say?"

The cell door swung open and King Dalverious entered. He looked at the dead man lying in a contorted heap on the floor. "What happened to him?"

"He was impolite to my guest." The Reacher gestured and the guard's body lifted into the air. A flick of his smoky arm sent the body flying against the corridor wall outside the door.

"This is the third one you've killed this week. These are good men. They—"

"Good men don't disobey orders and mistreat a shackled prisoner. If you want to keep your *good men* alive, I suggest you reinforce the rules." The shadow grew larger and loomed over the king.

King Dalverious raised his chin, doing his best to show he wasn't intimidated, and was even defiant, though he was neither. "I shall speak with the captain of the guard." He spun on his heel to leave.

"Have another tray of food brought at once, and fresh linens." The Reacher's eyes narrowed, seemingly taking pleasure in issuing orders to the king.

Dalverious' shoulders jerked almost imperceptibly. He left without looking back.

The door slammed shut at the Reacher's whim. He hovered near the old man, then lowered down to meet his eyes. "You can eat and drink willingly, or forcefully. The choice is yours."

Harrelle jerked against his chains. "If I'm going to die anyway, I'll choose how I die."

"You can't starve yourself in a week's time. And if you become dehydrated, the blood will only flow slower. You can suffer a long and painful death, making us cut deeper to get what I need. Or, as I am not entirely without mercy, I can allow you a quick and painless death. Again, the choice is yours."

Harrelle looked at the multiple bandages around his naked arms and legs. "Rot in hell, demon."

A light rap came on the steel door. The door swung open by the Reacher's will. A guard entered, carrying a tray of food and cup of water. He placed it on a small table near the bed and quickly exited, never looking at the specter hovering near the old man.

The Reacher lifted the cup. "Drink."

Harrelle took the cup unwillingly. His eyes glared hatred at the creature who controlled his will. He took a long drink, emptying the cup, coughing as he tried to resist.

"Good. Now eat." The Reacher brought the tray near, and Harrelle took a bite of food involuntarily.

Harrelle chewed, fighting against the pressure in his mind telling him to eat. He closed his eyes tight, willing himself to stop. He stopped chewing, opened his eyes, and stared defiantly at the dark form wavering in the amber light before him.

"Swallow," the shadow hissed.

Harrelle curled his lips and spat the food at the Reacher. The mashed meat flew through the Reacher's form, landing with a splat on the stone floor.

The Reacher grew still as he stared at the old man. "Impressive for one of the Din. Not even King Dalverious can resist my will."

"I was once on the Tribunal. I have been trained to resist the will of Users." Harrelle sat panting on the bed, the effort pushing him to the edge of exhaustion.

The Reacher let out a sickly laugh. "Amusing. You share the overconfidence of your inquisitors. But you will do as I say." A dark arm sprang out and entered Harrelle's eyes. The old man's body went stiff. "Now you will eat. I need your blood rich."

Harrelle began eating with vigor, in rigid, unconscious movements.

The Reacher let go of the man's mind when the meal was finished, and slid away. He hovered near the door, and a flash of gray washed over his amorphous form. "She approaches. Interesting." The Reacher vanished.

Twenty-Three

Bet slept restlessly. In her sleep, she desperately tried to reach Fealist-Marsh, with no effect. She fell into a dream of the orphanage, with images of no particular importance. The dream transitioned to her and Anna walking in tall grass, with a host of animals languidly grazing, and birds of every color flying overhead. Pooch-kin, fluttering on tiny wings, leaped in the air, snatching an insect midflight. The two laughed and looked at each other. Anna's mouth moved, but Bet couldn't make out the words. Bet asked her what she had said. Anna's face grew serious. "Something is near."

In her dream, Bet's face grew concerned. An image of something small and dark flashed before her. She realized what she'd seen wasn't a dream, but something near their camp.

Bet sprang up, grabbing her weapons without thought.

Babbers was up immediately. "What is it?"

"Something's out there. It's small, not much bigger than Pooch-kin." She squatted, moving toward the tent flap.

"An animal?" Babbers asked, her hatchet already in hand.

Bet stretched out her senses. "No. It has a purpose. It's not looking for food." She peeked outside and saw something move on the edge of the mist, highlighted by the dimming fire. She gripped an iron bearing, waiting for it to move into the light.

A blur of something large and dark crossed the firelight, and in a heartbeat, snatched the tiny creature. The creature squealed in protest.

She smiled at Old Babbers. "Bathezine got it." The two exited the tent, joined by Errel and Le'lel.

"No. Down, down. Put me down, beast," the creature screeched.

"I'll put you down in the fire." Bathezine moved toward the flame.

The creature wriggled in the Ursian's grip. "I meant no harm. No harm."

"Bathezine, wait. No." Bet stepped closer. She looked at Old Babbers. "What is it?"

"A Pidge," Mandi-lyn answered before the woman could. "They rarely come near camps or settlements."

"Yes. Listen to the girl, beast," the Pidge squealed.

Bathezine looked at Bet, who nodded. "It means us no harm," she said, motioning for him to set it down.

After being dropped by Bathezine, the Pidge's bulbous eyes, set on the side of its head, looked at each of them, and the weapons that were trained on it. "A message. I bring a message." The Pidge lifted an insect-like arm to a small pouch it wore around its skinny neck.

The group raised their weapons, ready to strike if the creature produced a weapon of its own.

Tiny bucked teeth showed from a narrow slit of a mouth in an apparent attempt of a smile. "Such big beasts to be scared of me, so small." Small, feathered antennae danced at the top of the Pidge's broad head.

"What's your message and who's it from?" Bathezine asked, keeping his hand resting on the handle of his chain mace.

"Not from whom, from what." The Pidge pulled what looked like a small ball from its pouch. "The message is for the girl. It comes from Moth." It tossed the ball at Bet's feet.

Bet stooped down, examining the ball. On closer inspection, she saw that it was no ordinary ball, but an eye. She pulled her hand away, and gave the Pidge a questioning look.

Babbers put her hand on Bet's shoulder. "Careful. You don't know what it is."

The Pidge made a little hop. "It is safe. Safe to touch."

Bet's eyes drifted back to the eye. Her hand hovered over it for a second. Sensing no danger, she snatched it up. For a moment nothing happened. Then the eye grew warm in her hand. An electric sensation buzzed through her fingertips, and sparks of static danced over the eye. The static grew, turning to tendrils of blue electricity, knocking Bet to her backside. The charge grew, crackling in the night air, but Bet felt no pain. A quiet moan came through the sound of the static charge, turning into a voice that seemed to come from every direction at once.

"Bethany," the disembodied voice said. "Only those who desire to see me may come. You and the Charge of Danthbrook may pass. You may enter at dawn. If Bathezine Cormorder, Errel Handover, Le'lel of Husk, Babitha Gainfell, or Pooch-kin follow, they will die, as will you. Heed my warning." The snap of electricity grew louder, and the eye exploded in a flash of white light.

Silence fell over the group. "Silly beasts, you fear the wrong thing," the Pidge said and darted away, disappearing in the mist.

Bathezine ignored the fleeing creature. "Babitha?" he said to Old Babbers.

"Is that all you took from this?" the woman shot back.

He snorted, and his eyes went to Mandi-lyn. "What was that? I ain't never seen nothin' like it in all my years."

"A message," the Flursh said flatly.

"I know what it was," he growled. "What do ya think? Is it a trap?"

Mandi-lyn crawled down from the wagon, her whiskers bouncing frenetically. "I think we must take it at its word, lest you end up a message yourself."

"What do you mean?" Old Babbers asked, her face a mixture of question and fear.

"The eye. I've read of such things. It is a type of alchemy, if you will, which endues the tissue of a deceased creature with the psychic energy of the user to convey images, or in this case a voice. This would explain why no one has seen Moth. None have lived to tell." Mandi-lyn sniffed around Bet, then went for her notebook. "She seems to have suffered no ill effects."

Bathezine threw his hands up. "Need I remind you that the Pidge lived? She ain't goin' down without me."

The Flursh looked up from her writing. "Perhaps the Pidge is a servant to Moth, either willing or unwilling."

"Servant or not, I'm goin'. And If I don't, ain't nobody goin'."

"Bathezine," Bet said in a calm voice. "You can't go. I won't let you. Moth said we will all die if anyone else comes. This is my task. Fealist-Marsh gave it to me. I gave up the piece of the staff to keep us safe and buy us some time to find her. And if you go, and we die, it would've all been for nothing. The Reacher will come, and there will be no one to stop him."

Bathezine kicked at the dirt. He scratched his ear, put his hands on his hip, and then scratched at his ear once more. "Don't go using logical arguments against me, girl. It ain't fair play."

Bet went to the hyper-frustrated Ursian and took his hand. "Think about it. If he wanted to hurt me, he wouldn't have said anything, and just killed us when we went down there."

"Reckon you have a point. Don't mean I have to like it." He stared at the ground.

"I'm not asking you to like it. I don't like it. None of us do. But it's what has to be done if we're to have any hope of ending this." Bet tilted her head, looking up at Bathezine's face.

"I don't like it when you sound more grow'd up than me," the Ursian relented. "It's spooky."

"I have the knowledge of a thousand-year-old talking tree in my head somewhere. It's an unfair advantage." She put her hand on Bathezine's shoulder. "We'll get through this."

The tension left Bathezine's body. "Still don't like it."

"I'll be fine. I'll have Mandi-lyn with me. Remember, she's a sneak. You said so yourself."

"She's also a card cheat. And unless this Moth is a gambler, that won't do you much good."

Errel walked around the fire, giving Bet a stately smile. "You are beyond your years, young miss." He bowed formally.

Bet raised an eyebrow at him. "I'm not sure I like this knight thing."

"Sorry, it's the sword and hat. It makes me act up to the nobility I'm supposed to carry."

Bathezine barked a laugh. "Makes ya act like ya got an even bigger stick lodged up your arse, ya mean."

Errel did his best to ignore the Ursian. "Know that we will not move from this spot until you return. And if you don't, I will risk death to find you."

Bet raised a skeptic brow. "Let's hope it doesn't come to that." Her gaze took in her friends around the campfire. There wasn't a thing in the world she wouldn't do to protect them, and she knew it went both ways. In an odd way, the message from Moth came as a relief. At least they would be out of harm's way. She looked at Mandi-lyn, who continued to write in her journal, knowing it wouldn't be the same for her.

"Get some rest," Bathezine said. "There's still a few hours 'til daylight."

"I'll do my best." She exhaled and went back to her tent to find Pooch-kin waiting for her. He didn't say a word, but crawled straight to her lap when she sat. This time she took off her moccasins and crawled under her blanket.

Old Babbers came in a moment later and did the same. "You okay?" she asked, pulling her blanket up to her chin.

Bet shook her head. "No."

"You scared?"

"Yeah," she said through a small voice, as if admitting it made her weaker.

"That's not a bad thing. Fear can help at times. You can either let it paralyze you, or use it to give you strength to fight."

"I'll keep that in mind," Bet said after letting a few seconds pass. Not feeling like talking, she cuddled next to Pooch-kin, and his quiet purring lulled her to sleep.

Twenty-Four

The group huddled near the campfire in the predawn gloom, eating breakfast in silence, enjoying the last few moments of fellowship. Jangol and Alice grazed in the field nearby, chomping noisily on grass while keeping an eye on the others. Old Babbers got up, went to her wagon, and returned holding a small knife in a leather sheath. "Here. You might need this." She handed the knife to Mandi-lyn.

Mandi-lyn looked at it and shook her head. "I have no need of a weapon."

"It's only a weapon if you stabbed something with it. Think of it as a survival tool."

"I survive by running away, thank you."

"That's not always possible. And you'd better not survive by running away from trouble where Bet's concerned." Babbers' face showed she wasn't joking.

"I have no intention of doing so. We will run together or not at all." Mandi-lyn matched her serious tone.

"Just take it. It'll make me feel better knowing you can defend Bet if need be." Babbers pushed the leather-bound blade into the Flursh's hand.

Mandi-lyn sighed and relented. "If you insist."

Bet sat her plate on the ground and looked to the first traces of daylight peeking over the distant eastern mountains. "Time to go," she said without preamble. She had spent the past hour in near silence, trying to break through the veil that hid what awaited them on their trek into the caldera to no avail.

Old Babbers checked Bet's gear, making sure all was in order. Bet said brief farewells, saving Pooch-kin for last. She kneeled close to her friend. "If something happens to me down there, I want you to stay with Bathezine. He'll take care of you."

Pooch-kin chirped mournfully. "Nothing will happen to you. I believe that."

A thin smile crossed Bet's face. "Let's hope you're right." She looked at the rapidly approaching morning light.

Pooch-kin followed her gaze, crawled into her lap, and rubbed his beak against her nose.

Bet couldn't help but laugh a little. "I love you, my friend."

Mandi-lyn came to Bet's side. "Moth said dawn. We shouldn't test his word."

Bet stood, steeling her resolve. "I'll see y'all soon," she said, trying to sound more upbeat than she felt. She headed toward the edge of the caldera, willing herself not to look back. Her friend's pained expressions would make it that much harder.

She took her first cautious step over the precipice, making sure loose soil wouldn't send her tumbling down the slope and end her journey before it began. Satisfied, she headed down, sliding occasionally on wobbly stones, but otherwise without trouble.

Mandi-lyn followed close behind on all fours, moving easily down the slope. She carried a single pack, choosing to leave her scrolls under Errel's protection. She would sometimes scurry ahead of Bet and wait, not wanting to get separated from the girl.

They reached the mist-covered bottom in no time, arriving at the first of many jagged up-thrusts of rock. The haze engulfed them, limiting their vision to only a few yards.

"This will take a while if this mist doesn't ease," Bet said, groping forward between dead gray trees and columns of stone.

"My whiskers will lead us through. Follow me." Mandi-lyn hopped in the lead. Bet followed, keeping her hand against the Flursh's back, letting her guide them through the fog.

They traveled for over an hour with no relief from the blinding haze. Bet tried several more times to get a sense of what might live in the caldera, but gave up after getting no stronger connection with her surroundings. If anything, it had gotten worse. "Hold on. I need a drink." She leaned against a tree and took a swig from her canteen. She offered a drink to Mandi-lyn, who refused it.

The Flursh squatted, peering into the mist, her whiskers a blur of motion. "Drink on the move. We shouldn't linger."

"Can you get a sense of what's down here with your whiskers?"

"No. I have a feeling there are creatures hiding out of sight, but I can't smell them."

"Me too. If something jumps out at us, we won't have time to react." Bet stumbled forward, kicking up clouds of dust. Her eyes narrowed, and she purposely kicked at the dust again. "It's strange, don't you think?"

"What is strange?" Mandi-lyn asked, creeping forward.

"The dust. You'd expect that, with all of this fog, there'd be moisture. Doesn't fog form when there's moisture in the air, and cool air meets warm? This mist, or whatever it is, feels dry. Almost like it's sapping the moisture away." Bet took another sip of water at the thought.

"Yes. You are mostly correct. But atmospheric phenomena are not my area of expertise. I will make notes for others more versed in meteorology. And I remind you, we are in the bed of an ancient volcano. One wouldn't expect much moisture."

"You said this erupted before written history. There should be water. It should probably even be a lake. Plus, remember all those dead trees? There had to be water here at some point," Bet said, more to keep her mind off a growing feeling of wrongness that had been growing as they wandered deeper into the caldera.

Mandi-lyn chattered her teeth in irritation. "I'm more concerned with what's to come than the geology of this region."

Bet rolled her eyes. "Just sayin'. What if the geology has something to do with the fog? What if Moth controls it? What if what we think is a mist is a toxic gas? That would explain the dead trees."

Mandi-lyn turned to Bet. "Listen, whatever the cause and effect of the fog is doesn't matter at the moment. We are in it, and there is little we can do about it. We are still breathing and still alive." She started walking again.

"For now. If I can't sense any danger, how long will we stay that way? I'm beginning to think that the fog is what's blocking my Talents." She ducked beneath a low hanging branch she hadn't seen until the last moment.

"If that were true, it would be entirely unprecedented…at least on this scale. Not even an Omia Temporian could achieve such a thing."

Bet stretched out her senses once more, trying to get a feel of any life, thoughts, or intentions, with no results. "Nothing," she said, pulling away from Mandi-lyn.

The Flursh turned back to face her, clearly irritated. "What do you mean?"

"I can't sense anything or anyone. Not even you," Bet said, her voice on the edge of trembling. Her eyes grew wide. She took an iron bearing from her bandolier, holding it for a second. The weight seemed doubled. She threw it with all of her strength. No hum of flight came. All she heard was the bearing thump against something solid, then plop to the soft dirt. She fell to her knees, fear stealing her strength. "My Talents really are gone."

"That's ridiculous. Talents, once shown, cannot go away. Look," Mandi-lyn said, drawing the knife Old Babbers had given her. She poked the tip of her own finger, wincing at the pain. She sheathed the blade and began chittering over the bleeding cut. After a minute of the healing chant, she showed her finger to Bet. "See? All is fine."

Bet stared at the wound. Her eyes moved to meet the Flursh's. "It's still bleeding."

Mandi-lyn jerked her hand back and tried to heal the cut once again, with no effect. She tore a swath of fabric from the lining inside her bag, quickly wrapping the wound. Her dark round eyes fell on Bet. "We may be in for some difficulty."

Twenty-Five

Bathezine paced along the rim of the caldera, stopping every few steps. He stared at the haze below, then resumed his energetic stomping.

"Wearing a hole in the ground isn't gonna speed up time," Babbers said, sitting on a crate, sharpening a blade. Pooch-kin sat by her side, watching the antsy Ursian.

He snapped his head at Babbers. "Well, it ain't gonna slow it down, neither." He continued pacing.

"It's slowing my time down plenty. They've only been gone half the day, and you're already driving me crazy." She examined the blade she was working on. Satisfied, she picked up a Kukri knife from a box of weapons and began sharpening its curved blade.

Bathezine looked like he was about to say something he shouldn't, but relented. "You're right." He walked from the edge and sat on the ground next to her. "How long do ya figure they'll be gone?"

Old Babbers shrugged. "That's a big hole in the ground out there. Could be a week, maybe two. Maybe longer." She reached in the box, pulled out a pistol-grip crossbow and tossed it to Bathezine.

He turned the weapon over in his hands, examining the wood stock. "How long do we give her? And this ain't got a string."

She tossed him a ball of heavy twine. "Restring it and it's yours. And I don't know how long. Reckon we'll know when the time comes."

"If'n the time comes, I'll go lookin'. No sense in anyone else riskin' death. Y'all have businesses to run. I ain't got nothin' but rocks to haul. Makes the most sense."

Old Babbers punched the big Ursian on his meaty shoulder. "Shut up, bear. Nobody here is more important than the other. We all swore an oath to Bet, and we all came along knowing it might be a one-way trip. So quit acting like your life ain't got a purpose. If worse comes to worse, we go together. And if worse comes to the absolute worst, we'll leave this world knowing we did all we could."

Bathezine rubbed his shoulder. "I getcha. I'm just a-scared of losin' her. And that hurt." He rotated his arm, trying to work out the ache from the punch.

"I'll punch you someplace more tender next time. Keep that in mind." She pointed at the crossbow in his lap with the knife. "Fix that thing, and we'll set some targets."

Errel sat next to the pair, holding a potato. He cupped his hands around the spud, and a flash of fire escaped between his fingers. "Here, have a bite to ease your mind," he said, tossing the potato to the Ursian.

Bathezine caught it and stuffed it in his mouth in one motion. A second later, he dropped the crossbow and snagged his canteen. "Hot, hot."

"Try taking bites next time." Errel laughed, along with Babbers.

"Laugh it up, Babitha," Bathezine said, flashing a toothy, potato-filled grin at the woman.

"Call me that again, and I'll hogtie you and kick you down that crater myself." Babbers gave him a look that told the Ursian she was only half kidding.

Bathezine swallowed hard and lifted his head toward Errel. "The woman scares me. Honestly."

"Rightfully so," Errel said, giving Old Babbers a half-smile and a wink.

Le'lel returned from surveying the grassy field and sat his lithe frame next to Bathezine. "The hunting is sparse. Seed mice are hardly worth the hunt."

"You want a potato?" Errel asked, flash cooking another.

"Yes, please. I will have a potato. Uncooked, if you will."

Errel shrugged and motioned to a sack near the fire pit. He tossed the cooked potato to Old Babbers.

The group sat around, engaged in idle chat. Pooch-kin crawled on Bathezine's lap, further calming the big Ursian's nerves. A shadow passed over the camp, escaping everyone's attention except the Chook-chook's.

Pooch-kin stared at the sky, losing the dark form in the midday sun. "Did any of you see that?"

Le'lel glanced at the Chook-chook while swallowing his third potato whole. "See what?" The others looked at him and he motioned toward Pooch-kin.

"A big bird. I thought it was Her-Gad-Ishu." Pooch-kin continued looking up.

Le'lel translated, and the group scanned the cloudless sky.

Bathezine shrugged. "I don't see nothin'. Probably a Scab Vulture, thinkin' we was a meal."

Errel kept his eyes on the sky. "We haven't seen any animals large enough around here to support such a large scavenger."

"Probably just passing through," Old Babbers said. She returned to her work.

The band of travelers spent the next few hours trading stories and working on making the camp more secure and permanent. Bathezine had repaired the crossbow, and he and Babbers went out on the grass-covered knolls, setting targets and practicing their aim. Pooch-kin sat with Le'lel, telling him of his adventures and demonstrating his camouflage techniques by blending with the yellow grass, the gray oak trunk, and various other things. The Lasoom was considerably impressed.

As they sat, the shadow swept over once again, and Pooch-kin leapt to his feet. "There!"

Le'lel did the same and spotted the large dark form high above them. "I see it. Errel," he called, pointing to the sky.

Errel hurried from beneath the canopy of the oaks and followed Le'lel's finger. "I see it, too. I can't tell if it's the crow, though." He ran to the wagon, grabbed the looking glass, and tracked the bird. "It's definitely a crow, but I couldn't tell if it had three heads."

"I'm sure it was Her-Gad-Ishu. Who else could it be?" Pooch-kin said, with Le'lel translating.

Errel called for Bathezine and Babbers, who came running at once. "What is it? Did you see Bet down there?" he huffed, seeing the looking glass in Errel's hand.

"Nothing so interesting. But I believe your friend the crow has come to join us." He handed the telescope to Old Babbers.

"Hey, crow! Get down here," Bathezine shouted, waving his hands wildly. His arms dropped as the bird disappeared into the distance. "Stupid crow."

Babbers thumped Bathezine on the back. "He or she, it, they'll be back. Does anyone know if it's male or female?"

"I dunno. Male, I think." Bathezine twisted, shaking off the thump. "And quit hittin' on me, woman. That hurts."

She double-clutched her fist, and the small blades sprung from her glove. "Lucky I don't use these."

"Hellfire of a demon. If I didn't like ya, I'd wallop ya back."

Babbers laughed and scratched under her hat. "You're right. I'm sorry. Guess I'm nervous. And when I get nervous, I have a tendency to punch things. No harm intended." She smiled up at him and rubbed his back. "And I like you, too, bear-man."

"I ain't a bear. And if'n you're so nervous, why don't you make those knife-glove things more useful. Make 'em so you can shoot the blades, too."

Old Babbers raised an eyebrow. "Good idea." She went for her tool kit and got to work immediately.

Pooch-kin chirped. "He's coming back."

Everybody looked at the sky and saw the crow swoop in from the eastern sky. He circled overhead, finally alighting on the highest limb of the oak.

Bathezine stood with his hands on his hips. "Get down here, bird."

The three heads conferred with one another, and the crow fluttered to the ground.

"It's about time. We coulda used some help while you were out being useless," Bathezine growled.

"We were gathering information," Her said.

"Intelligence," added Gad.

"There was a cornfield and we were hungry," said Ishu.

Bathezine threw up his hands in frustration. "Well, while you were out stuffing your beaks, Bet's found herself in a new mess. I have half a mind to pluck some tail-feathers."

"If you had half a mind, you'd be twice as smart," Ishu cawed.

"Already with the insults," Bathezine grumbled and turned away.

Old Babbers set her work aside and went to the crow, giving the Ursian a scornful glare. "I never had the chance to thank you. If it wasn't for you, I probably woulda been mashed underfoot on the Waste."

The three heads bowed. "Our pleasure," they said in unison.

Bathezine faced the bird. "You're right. Couldn't a done it without you. But we could use some more help."

"That's why we're here," Her said.

"Have you been in contact with Fealist-Marsh?" Errel asked before the two other heads could chime in.

"Who?" asked Ishu.

Errel took a breath, forcing patience. "The purple lady."

"Violet," said Gad.

"Lavender," added Ishu.

"Yes, one and the same. Have you? Bet hasn't had contact with her since the battle on the Waste."

"Only once," Her said. "The dark one has nearly completed the Staff of the Din. If she shows herself, he will find her."

"The dark one?" Errel asked. "You mean the Reacher?"

"One and the same," Ishu said, mocking the Andolan.

The others exchanged fearful looks. "You mean she's a-scared of him?" Bathezine asked.

The three heads shook vehemently. "No. She is merely at a disadvantage until Bet frees her," Gad said.

Bathezine pointed toward the Caldera. "Well, Bet is doing her best to learn how to do just that. She's gone to find Moth."

Her-Gad-Ishu hopped to the edge of the crater. "Alone?" Her asked.

Babbers followed the crow. "No. Mandi-lyn went with her. Moth said if any of us went with her, we'd all die."

"Maybe you could do a flyover and check on her progress," Bathezine said, looking across the expanse.

"It would do no good," Her said.

"We can't see through the mist," said Gad.

"Too dangerous," added Ishu.

"Dangerous?" Bathezine growled. "Bet's down there. I need to know if she's all right. Fly low and see if you can spot her in that mist somewhere."

"We can't," Her said, sounding unusually agitated.

"The mist is created by Moth," said Gad with equal agitation.

"The mist suppresses the Talents of all who enter," Ishu added, sounding dire. "We die if we fly too low."

"Suppresses Talents?" Errel asked, looking at Bathezine and not masking his fear.

"Then she's defenseless." Bathezine turned in circles, not sure what to do. He made a motion toward the caldera. "I'm goin' after her."

Babbers snatched him by the back of his tunic and pulled him off his feet, back to the ground. "No. You'll get yourself killed. And that won't do anyone any good."

"Get off me, woman. I gotta help her." He brushed Old Babbers' arms off him and stood.

Errel stepped in front of the terrified and angry Ursian. "Listen to Babbers. You won't do anything other than get yourself and Bet and Mandi-lyn killed. Bet's strong without her Talents. And she's smart. We can't do anything right now. If Moth told her to come, I'm sure it won't do anything to harm her. There's no sense in it doing that. We have to trust Bet and what she's capable of. Mandi-lyn too."

Bathezine sat on the edge of the crater feeling more helpless than ever. "How can I just let her be down there knowin' she's defenseless?"

Babbers rested her hand on Bathezine's shoulder, giving him a reassuring squeeze. "Errel's right. The girl is strong. We have to trust her. We don't have a choice."

Pooch-kin hopped forward, chirping. "The mist avoided the fire last night," he said, with Le'lel speaking for him.

"Yeah, so?" Bathezine said.

"I have an idea on how to help. Follow me," Pooch-kin said and fluttered back to the camp.

Twenty-Six

Bet followed Mandi-lyn through the maze of stone and dead trees, staying as close to her as possible. The fog thickened as the daylight began to wane. They came to an impassable row of jagged rock, and had to double-back to find another way down the slope.

"How long have we been walking?" Bet asked, straining her eyes to see through the fog.

Mandi-lyn clicked her teeth. "It is difficult to say. I would guess no more than ten hours. Night will come sooner in the shadow of the crater walls."

"Should we find shelter and wait out the night?" Bet tried to remind herself she had gotten by just fine before discovering her Talents. But with the fog adding to her sensory deprivation, harmless shadows played in her mind like enemies in wait.

"Finding anything in this place is a fool's errand. We should keep moving."

"I'm starting to think coming here was a bad idea. Why would this Moth creature want us to come here blind and helpless?"

"Perhaps it is a test of our resolve. That is the only explanation I have. When you found the Crickshaw, you had to fight through the Floragads. This may be the same."

Bet thought about it. When she'd evaded the mushrooms the first time, her strength Talent had proved useless and she had only been aware of having the Oragoth Talent besides that. Her abilities hadn't helped her escape Malweather, either, until she threw the rock at the inquisitor. She searched her thoughts, trying to find the knowledge that had been given her by the old tree, hoping to find some hint to help them through. Her mind fell on the last time she'd seen the Crickshaw, burning in the woods. Through the sadness of the memory of seeing her friend die, she framed a thought. "Let's find a tree," she said, and pushed ahead of Mandi-lyn.

"A tree? There are plenty of dead trees. What will it do? Do you intend to climb above the fog?" Mandi-lyn hurried behind her.

A moment later, Bet struck her head on a low-hanging branch. She rubbed her head, thankful for the hat Old Babbers had given her that had saved her from another scrape. "No. I doubt the brittle branches could support my weight." She hung on the branch, snapping it off and falling to her backside. Bet rummaged through her satchel while sitting on the ground.

"What are you doing, child? You can snack later. We should keep moving."

"Aha," Bet exclaimed, holding up the flint. "Last night, back at camp, I noticed the mist was repelled by the fire. Maybe we can push it from us, or at least give us a bubble of clarity."

Mandi-lyn stared at Bet, her whiskers bouncing cheerfully for the first time since entering the caldera. "It may work."

Bet struck at the flint, drawing sparks, but none strong enough to catch the dead wood. "Give me a piece of paper from your notebook." She crumbled some tiny limbs, making a pile.

"No. I need it to document what we find." Mandi-lyn clutched at her bag.

"Do you want to be able to see or not? Memorize what you learn." Bet held out her hand, motioning for her to hurry. "Gimme one piece."

Mandi-lyn snorted in frustration and tore off half a sheet, waving the paper at Bet.

Bet crumpled it and struck the flint once more. The flame took, and she laid several small sticks on the fire until she was satisfied it was hot enough. Then she placed the tip of the branch on it. The branch received the flame at once, and Bet held it high. The fog around them began to retreat, and she took a deep breath, as if surfacing from a long swim.

Mandi-lyn pulled back her bandage and healed the cut she had given herself. "You did good, child. Very good."

Bet stretched her senses, feeling for any threat nearby, but the fog surrounding their bubble still masked anything more than a few yards away. She handed Mandi-lyn the burning branch and snapped off a few more with ease.

The burning branch burst into flames. Mandi-lyn cried out, dropping it, and Bet saw it turn into powdery ash almost before it hit the ground. She pursed her lips and blew out a short breath. "We'll try it again. Another paper, please." She held out her hand, not giving the Flursh the option to protest.

With the next torch lit, they started off at a brisk pace. Bet snapped off branches as they passed, relaying the flame from one to the other as each branch quickly burned away. She caught a sense of something alive at the edge of her awareness, but it moved farther into the fog before she could see it. She was about to tell Mandi-lyn, but the Flursh seemed to know it was there, as well.

Bet broke away branches until she held almost more than she could carry. She passed the next branch to Mandi-lyn, who lit it and dropped the other just before it burned away. Each torch burned for little more than a minute. Bet was having a hard time keeping up the pace and finding more fuel.

Mandi-lyn held the torch in front of them, moving at a brisk pace. "We're making good progress, but at this rate we'll have burned through every tree by nightfall."

Bet looked up through the gap in the mist and saw the darkening sky. "I think night is almost here anyway." As she continued looking up, she heard the distant caw of a crow. She focused her sensing Talent but couldn't get a fix on the crow's mind. She turned to Mandi-lyn and smiled.

"What's with the grin?"

"Her-Gad-Ishu is flying over. At least we have someone watching over us now." She lit another stick.

"Better hope he doesn't try to land. We'll all die," Mandi-lyn said, taking the fire.

Bet's eyes widened and she yelled as loud as she could, warning him away. "Let's hope he heard."

"I'm certain he's already spoken with the others. Let's move. We need to make it as far as we can before we run out of wood." Mandi-lyn broke into her best bipedal trot.

Twenty-Seven

Bet and Mandi-lyn traveled another hour before finally running out of wood. The pair hunkered beside a large rock after nightfall to rest and eat. "I'm uncertain as to how we're going to find Moth in this blind maze," Mandi-lyn said between nibbles of small nuts. She scribbled in her notebook with vigor.

"I don't know either, but I'm sure we'll find a way." Bet ate only a small portion of bread and fruit, not knowing how long the food would have to last.

"I have been keeping track of our steps. By my calculations, we are an eighth of the way to the center of the caldera. This is only an estimate, as the scale may be incorrect. See?" She lifted the book to show Bet.

Bet fumbled through her bag to find the small light Harrelle had given her. She was thankful for everything the old man had put in the satchel, knowing they wouldn't have made it this far without his well thought-out provisions. She turned on the light.

"You should keep that turned off. We don't know what comes out at night." Mandi-lyn blinked against the light.

"You're nocturnal. I can't see squat at night." Bet studied the roughly drawn map. "That's great, but we don't know where Moth is. He could be on the other side of the crater for all we know."

"Let's hope not. At our current pace, we will run out of provisions by the ninth day. We could do better if the fog lifts." The Flursh returned to writing.

Bet flicked off the light and leaned back against the rock. She squirmed, trying to get comfortable, finally giving up. It seemed every inch of the rock was covered in jagged edges. Several minutes passed before she spoke. "Did you see the creatures hiding on the edge of the fog when we had the torches?"

"I did," Mandi-lyn said, concentrating on her work.

"Do you know what they are?" Bet did her best to hide her impatience, acutely aware that whenever her Talents were blocked she became more irritable. She wondered if it was an effect of the mist or the frustration of losing her Talents. She had noticed the same thing in her Flursh companion.

Mandi-lyn closed the book with a slap. "I couldn't see them well enough, nor could I smell them. Whatever they were, they weren't fleet of foot. They haven't bothered us yet, so I doubt they mean us harm."

"Maybe they hunt at night," Bet said, half-joking.

"Your pessimism is unbecoming. Though I have to admit I have thought the same thing." Mandi-lyn sniffed the air. "We should sleep in watches. No more than an hour each."

"So no idea what they could be?" Bet asked, not feeling like sleeping yet.

Mandi-lyn sighed heavily. "They were too big to be a Pidge. All I've read are the rumors, and you can never know a rumor, you can only hear it."

"What are the rumors, then?" Bet shifted uncomfortably on the stony ground, feeling the evening chill. She pulled a pair of gloves from her coat.

"Some say they are Drullids, beings malformed by the Foul. Others say they are undead creatures, that Moth sucked the life from them and reanimated them to guard its realm. Both are nonsense, if I must say. Since there are no valid claims of anyone seeing Moth, there is no way to know what lives down here."

"The unknown breeds monsters," Bet said. She curled up on the ground. "You get first watch. Don't let anything eat us or drain us of our essence."

Mandi-lyn chittered. "You sound like Old Babbers—or worse, the Ursian."

"I'll take that as a compliment," Bet's voice trailed away.

"You shouldn't," Mandi-lyn said, but Bet had already fallen asleep. "If you are what I suspect, monsters will be the least of your worries."

Twenty-Eight

Her-Gad-Ishu landed near the campfire and clucked noisily until everyone gathered around. "Bet knows the fire repels the fog," Her said.

"That's why she told me to keep the fire burning last night, then," Errel said. "Your idea will work, little Chook-chook."

Pooch-kin chirped a derisive comment that Le'lel wouldn't translate. "He said that's good to know," the Lasoom said instead.

"She had torches of her own, but we haven't seen one for some time," said Gad.

Bathezine jerked his head toward the crow. "Did somethin' happen to her?"

"Her is right here," Ishu remarked.

"Bet, you idiot. Not the other talking head. Did somethin' happen to Bet?" Bathezine clenched his fist open and closed, fighting the urge to go after the girl.

Ishu cawed something rather rude in crow language. "Nothing has happened to them. It appears the trees are sparse on the path they're taking. She simply ran out of wood to burn."

"The wood burns quickly. As we watched them, they lit several torches. Most lasted only a minute or two," Gad added, clarifying Ishu's explanation.

Bathezine looked at Old Babbers, who was preparing torches, soaking the ends in lamp oil on the far side of the camp. "How's it comin' along? How many do we got?"

"I think we can get about a dozen out of the wood we got here. Even if we find more wood, the oil is about gone. This oil will burn for a long time though—several hours. It's hard to snuff out. You pretty much need to soak it in water to put it out," Babbers said, wrapping the end of the torch with strips of fabric she had pilfered from spare clothes.

"That'll have to do." Bathezine paced in front of the fire. "I'll take Jangol out in the morning and see if we can find more."

Babbers shrugged. "I'll save what's left of the oil then. When are you gonna take her one?" she asked Her-Gad-Ishu.

"Soon," Her said.

"When the moon rises," said Gad.

"So we can see," added Ishu before Bathezine could insist they leave that instant.

Errel walked toward the mist covering the road outside of camp. "We should test it to make absolutely certain this will work."

"Do your thing, fire-starter," Old Babbers said with a half-cocked smile.

"Fire-starter? I like that." Errel smiled back. He stepped into the mist, made a fist, then expanded his hand, trying to create a flame that wouldn't come. He swayed as he stood. Clutching his head, he stumbled back toward the camp. "That is a horrible sensation. It's like becoming suddenly blind. I felt ill, anxious, powerless and almost angry."

Babbers went to him, looking over his tall frame. "You all right?"

Errel nodded. "I'm fine. Much better now. Hand me that small piece of fire wood." He pointed at the round, not trusting himself to stoop over after the dizzying effect of losing his Talents. Babbers handed him the piece and he lit the end in the campfire. Errel walked back into the fog, and it retreated from the flame. He repeated his earlier motions, and yellow fire danced across his fingertips. He looked toward the others. "It works."

"Okay then," Bathezine said, pounding his fist against his palm a couple of times, feeling a little better about Bet's predicament. "The crow just made things a little better. You too, Pooch-kin. You did good. When the moon rises, they'd better be off. We should eat."

"Are you ever not hungry? You should get checked for worms," Old Babbers said. She went to one of their many food lockers and took inventory. "At this rate you'll starve us out in less than a month."

Bathezine followed her to the locker. "Better you than me." He snatched a pear and stuffed it in his mouth, noisily chewing the fruit with an open-mouth smile.

Babbers rolled her eyes, grabbed a can of beans and utensils, and went to the campfire.

Errel joined her in staring at the flames. "Losing my Talents was quite disconcerting. I wonder how the Din do it. Perhaps that's why they are such a warring type."

"What do you mean? You think not having Talents makes you aggressive?"

"In a way. The Din have to work harder, fight more to achieve a goal. I've seen it in the caste system. Andolans with minimal Talents can never rise above their station. Certain human societies have the same thing. It was one of my many disagreements with my father. That kind of treatment can lead to dissatisfaction, and aggression eventually enters the equation. In the Din, money and property take the place of Talents, and greed takes over. Those without them resent not having power, and those with power want more, to secure their station."

"Maybe. Makes sense in a way. But there are plenty of critters with no Talents here. I ain't ever seen a horse rebellion. Horses have never been known to have much in the way of Talents. And I've heard there are people in the Din who are happy with what they have, poor or not." Babbers handed Errel a plate of beans.

"True," he said between bites. "Perhaps it takes the spark of greed, or a particular mistreatment, whether real or perceived, to fan the fire."

Old Babbers contemplated the beans on her plate. "You know what I think?"

Errel lifted an eyebrow at her without answering.

"I think you're overthinking it. Some folks are just born rotten, and some ain't. Most of us float around the middle somewhere, trying not to fall too far one way or the other." She mopped up the bean juice with a chunk of bread.

"From my experience, I believe you're right. When I was a squire, my teacher, a knight himself, believed you must choose your path, good or evil, Fair or Foul. He said to balance between the two was folly. As part of his lesson, he once asked, 'Do you know what word you get if you mix fair and foul'?"

Babbers looked at Errel. "Four? What does the number four have to do with it? Foil? Did you have to wear flimsy metal suits of armor?"

"No," Errel said, closing his eyes and shaking his head. "Fail. He said you'll always fail."

"Phht. That's stupid. Of course you can balance between the two. If you're too nice, people take advantage of you. If you're too ornery, people hate you. Whether in the Whist or the Din, it's all the same. As a knight, you have to have a certain hardness of heart. Like if you're out slaying a dragon, or whatever knights do. You don't stop to consider the dragon's feeling before you lop its head off. You do what you gotta do. End of story."

"There are no such things as dragons." Errel's mouth creased into a slight smile. "I didn't say I disagreed with you."

"Moon's comin' over the hills. Best get a torch or two ready," Bathezine announced, interrupting the conversation.

"Yes, sir." Babbers handed her plate to Errel and went to the stockpile of torches.

Her-Gad-Ishu hopped to Bathezine. "The moon hasn't risen high enough," Her said.

"Just getting' ready." He took a torch from Old Babbers and stood just beyond the reach of the mist. He watched the moon, bobbing his head, as if he were counting the seconds until it reached its apex. "Ya ain't gonna catch your feathers on fire carryin' this thing, are ya? A crispy crow ain't gonna do them much good."

"We have carried a torch before," Her said.

"We will be fine," said Gad.

"Is that what you're hoping for?" Ishu asked.

Bathezine turned to them, his mustache lifted in a smile. "Not today."

Twenty-Nine

Mandi-lyn woke Bet for her watch and curled into a ball, falling asleep as quickly as Bet had. Bet listened to the Flursh's heavy breathing and felt her eyelids begin to droop. She shook her head and rubbed her face to stay awake.

She felt the ground, groping blindly until she found a small rock, and mindlessly drew unseen circles in the dirt. Looking to the sky, Bet noticed the fog grow a little brighter with the moonrise. It did nothing to help her see. If anything, it made it worse. She didn't know how she would know when to wake Mandi-lyn. She figured she would have to guess.

As she sat alone in the muted silence, her thoughts drifted to Anna and Dalin. She worried about their safety and wondered if they would come to the Whist once the Reacher completed the staff, hoping at least some good would come from her decision to give up the shard. She guessed Anna probably wouldn't want to give up caring for the animals unless she was forced to leave. Bet missed the warm comfort of their home and the kindness they had shown her. Her mind began to fill with worry for them, and she forced herself to think of something else.

The oppressive feeling of the fog made her mind wander to the claustrophobia of being inside the tree. She took a deep breath and tried to find the knowledge the tree had imparted upon her, hoping that recovering the knowledge didn't rely on her Talents.

Images of a growing forest, moving in fast-forward, flashed through her mind. Each millisecond was a day, and every second a season. The speeding images came to a stop, and she saw a young girl with violet skin, no older than five or six years, walk up to the tree. She watched the girl from the Crickshaw's point of view, high above her. The next instant, she was face to face with her. The violet-skinned girl smiled and placed her hands against the bark. Her face grew large, and her dark eyes flared to a luminous white. An image of an enormous white quartz monolith appeared quickly, then disappeared just as quick.

"Moth will instruct you on how to find this place," the girl said. The voice startled Bet out of her mind's eye.

Bet sat on the ground, taking deep breaths, shaken by the revelation. She knew at once that the girl was a very young Fealist-Marsh. "But how?" she whispered. "How would she know as a child that I would be looking for her?"

She stretched out her legs, wiggling her feet to get the blood flowing after sitting cross-legged for so long. The moonlight brightened the fog just enough to see her hands a few inches in front of her face. The thought of Fealist-Marsh knowing that Bet would meet the Crickshaw and Moth years before she was even born disturbed her on a base level. *Did it mean she was destined to be here? Or was it meant for no one in particular?* Either way, the idea bothered her.

Bet rubbed her hands together, and took off her gloves, feeling the heat of adrenalin coursing through her body. She took a calming breath, and relaxed. She'd decided it was time to wake Mandi-lyn when she heard the tiny hum of an insect pass by her ear. Being that it was the first life she had encountered since entering the caldera, other than the creatures hiding at the edge of the fog, she resisted the urge to swat it away.

The insect flew by again, and Bet felt the slightest weight on the brim of her hat. Not wanting to hurt the bug, she slowly brought her hand to her hat and felt the itchy legs crawl across the sensitive skin on the back of her hand. She brought her hand down and strained her eyes to see, just making out that it was a beetle of some sort. "I'm sorry, but without my Talents I can't talk to you."

"Hello, Bet," the beetle buzzed, causing Bet to jerk in surprise.

"How? How can I understand you? And how do you know my name?" Bet asked, hoping her Talents had returned.

"Your questions are unimportant. I have come to give you warning," the beetle hummed.

"Do you know where Moth is?"

"Quiet. I only have moments to live. The mist is for your protection."

"What? I don't understand. How can something that robs me of my Talents be protecting me?" Bet asked, feeling confused, almost angry.

"The mist hides your Talents. Do not burn it away. The Drullids hunt by sensing Talents. You have been fortunate as they have not yet found you. I cannot stop them. They are here for a purpose, and they will consume you if they find you." The beetle began fluttering on her hand.

Bet took the bug in her other hand, feeling it buzz against her palm. "What do you mean, *you* can't stop them? Are you Moth?"

"I am Moth. The mist is Moth. We all are Moth." The beetle buzzed violently and died in Bet's hand.

"Wait. I don't understand. Where is Moth?" She blew on the bug, hoping it wasn't dead, but it was too late.

Mandi-lyn poked her head over Bet's shoulder. "I heard its warning." She took the dead bug from Bet's hand, sniffed it, then let it fall to the ground.

"What do we do, then?" Bet stood, straining her eyes against the fog, wary of the bug's warning.

"We press forward. We have no other choice." Mandi-lyn adjusted her hat, and began walking. "Come. We should get moving."

From high overhead, they heard the caw of Her-Gad-Ishu. They watched in horror as a torch fell from the sky, landing less than ten feet away. Bet eyed Mandi-lyn. "This isn't good."

Thirty

Mandi-lyn rushed to the torch and grabbed it, tossing it only a few yards away.

Bet shook her head. "Let me do the throwing." She started for the torch but stopped when a Drullid stepped from the mist toward the light. Her eyes widened with a mix of horror and disgust at seeing the creature. Its six-foot frame, with sagging gray skin that seemed to drip across its hairless body, lumbered toward the flame. It stopped and admired Bet with round, coal-black eyes, tilting its equally hairless head as the viscous skin dripped down the length of a long, quivering proboscis hanging at the center of its wilting face. It dragged a three-fingered hand across its bulbous stomach, as if anticipating a meal.

"What do we do?" Bet asked, backing away from the Drullid.

"Get back into the fog." Mandi-lyn took her hand and ran back to the safety of the fog.

"Those are Drullids? I don't like Drullids," Bet said after running several yards back into cover. She rested her hands on her knees, panting, more out of fear than fatigue.

"It appears some legends are true," Mandi-lyn said. She took out her notebook and began scribbling notes.

"This isn't the time for taking notes. Moth said those things are killers, and not even he can stop them."

"We're safe as long as we stay in the fog," Mandi-lyn reminded her. She closed the notebook.

"What if we happen to bump into one in the fog? Who knows how many are out there?" Bet pulled an iron bearing from her bandolier.

"The fact that we haven't done so makes me believe we won't. Whatever the fog is, it blinds them. Perhaps they are dormant when blind. That would explain why we didn't run into them with the other torches. They burned too quickly for the Drullids to get a sense of where we were. Let's go." Mandi-lyn took Bet's hand again.

They walked for no more than a minute when firelight cut through the fog around them. Bet turned to find a Drullid holding the flaming torch. "Great. Now what?"

"We need to take the torch from it, and douse the flame." Mandi-lyn hid behind Bet. "Do what you must, Bet."

Bet looked at the Flursh, giving her a quick nod. She felt the weight of the bearing in her hand. It felt good, heavy and solid, almost comforting, like the return of an old friend. A feeling of anticipation washed over her as she drew back her arm. She threw it, and the ball hummed through the air with blinding speed, striking the Drullid in the center of its head. The creature dropped the torch, stumbled back, and fell. Bet inched forward, hyper-aware that if Moth couldn't kill the Drullids, she probably couldn't, either. But then again, maybe Moth didn't have a Talent for throwing. She stood over the Drullid, watching the oozing skin melt over the open wound. There was no blood, just a gaping hole in the middle of its forehead.

She grabbed the light, keeping a cautious eye on the creature. The Drullid's skin dripped over the wound, sealing it closed. It sat up with such suddenness, Bet didn't have time to react. Its arms reached out, grabbing her by the leg. She tried to pull away, but couldn't break free of the unexpected power of the creature's grip. She struggled forward, dragging the Drullid behind on its bulging stomach. Its grip tightened, feeling as if it were crushing flesh and bone. She screamed out and fell. "Do something, Mandi-lyn," she yelled, trying to twist free of the monster's grip.

"What do you want me to do?" Mandi-lyn fumbled for the knife at her belt. She pulled it free as another Drullid appeared from the edge of the mist. At the sight, she squealed and dropped the knife.

The Drullid holding Bet stood, dangling her by her leg, presenting her to the other.

Bet twisted and brought the torch up, pushing the fire in the creature's face. It swatted the fire from Bet's grip.

A long, needle-like appendage crawled out of the Drullid's proboscis, inching its way toward Bet's leg.

With her head on the ground, Bet reached with both arms and pushed off, swinging her body upright. She took the Drullid by the head mid-swing, twisted, and let gravity bring her back down. The Drullid's head spun in her grip, turning full-circle. Bet heard no snap of bone from the twisting of its head, which would have snapped the neck of any other living being.

The Drullid tilted its head left and right, then slammed Bet on the ground, never losing its grip. The second Drullid approached, colliding into the one that held her. In any other circumstance it would have seemed almost comical, but Bet saw that the collision wasn't by accident. The two Drullid bodies began to merge, melting skin folding over one another, arms and legs, fat stomachs and round heads becoming one. The creature's grip became stronger, and this time Bet felt her ankle snap.

A screech came from somewhere on the edge of the fog, and Bet watched as Mandi-lyn rushed toward her, grabbing the fallen torch and stabbing the double-sized Drullid in the torso. The creature slapped the fire away, and took Mandi-lyn by the throat in a blur of motion. Bet watched helplessly as the Flursh tried to shake free, gagging and coughing as the Drullid began to choke the life from her.

Bet focused on the Drullid's mind to convince it to set them free. But its mind was like a slab of stone; no thought, no emotion, just a single-minded purpose to devour the essence of its prey. Mandi-lyn's dark eyes bulged as she grappled against the grip, trying to break free.

Frustration, fear, and anger coursed through Bet's veins as the Drullid's appendage, crawling from the proboscis, poked and prodded, seeking a soft spot to puncture her skin. She knew both of them would die. Her anger turned to rage, and her vison turned white as it had when fighting off the Floragads in the Dead Woods. Heat surrounded her body, and all thought turned to the destruction of her captor.

"No, little monkey. It is not the way," the small voice of the Crickshaw said from the back of her mind.

She ignored the voice, and her rage flared into unconstrained hatred. She shook violently, as impending ferocity rose from within her. Burning hot pain shot through her hands, and gouts of orange and white energy burst outward, streaming into her attacker's body. The Drullid dropped her at once. Bet landed on her feet, not feeling the pain of her crushed ankle, continuing to pour the electrified fire into the creature.

Mandi-lyn fell free, gasping for air. She stared at Bet with wide, terrified eyes and crawled into the cover of the fog.

Bet kept up the assault. Fueled by unbridled hatred, she screamed, sending the Drullid into the air, surrounded and riding on fountains of energy. The creature's body twisted and stretched in wild gyrations until it exploded in a flash of light. Tiny droplets of gray flesh rained across the ground. The stream of energy disappeared, taking the fog with it, and Bet stood shaking uncontrollably. She heard the caw of Her-Gad-Ishu from somewhere high above, lowered her head, and collapsed.

Thirty-One

Bathezine held Pooch-kin close as he and the others watched the gouts of fire and electricity taking place in the caldera. A ball of bright light erupted, causing them to shield their eyes. A wild wind swept over the edge of the crater, rolled over the grassy hills behind them, then reversed its path, sweeping back into the caldera, and dissipating along with the fog.

Old Babbers ducked against Errel's chest, who wrapped his arm around her, holding his hat. Le'lel stood unflinching, watching the campfire bend beneath the waves of air.

"What in the devil's arse was that?" Bathezine asked, holding the Chook-chook tight. Pooch-kin squirmed against his firm hold. The Ursian looked at him and set him gently on the ground. "Sorry, bird."

"I have no idea," Babbers said, pulling away from Errel. "I've never seen anything like it."

Errel shook his head. "I don't know. I hope the crow didn't decide to land and Moth held to its promise."

"Don't say stuff like that." Bathezine walked to the edge of the caldera, scanning the moonlit landscape, fighting the worry in his heart.

Le'lel licked the dust from his lidless eyes with his long tongue. "The mist is gone," he said, telling them what they already knew.

A moment later they heard the call of Her-Gad-Ishu as he flew with speed across the expanse.

Errel stepped to Bathezine's side. "At least my theory was wrong."

They all watched as the big crow flew in, landing with haste. He ruffled his feathers, clucking a low nervous chatter. "The torch was a bad idea," Ishu finally said.

"What do ya mean?" Bathezine snapped. "Was there gas in the air? Did the gas ignite? What happened? Is Bet safe?"

Old Babbers put her hand on Bathezine's arm to slow him down. "Give them a chance to answer, big guy."

"We think the fog was there to hide them from something," Her said.

"The torch attracted whatever those somethings are," said Gad.

"Bet appears to have discovered an unknown Talent," Ishu said. "She fought the somethings off and incinerated them."

Bathezine shook his head, trying to get a grasp of what they had been told. "Are you sayin' Bet caused that blast?"

"From what we could see, yes." Her looked at her two companion heads.

"We don't know if she is safe. She collapsed after the release of energy," said Gad.

"We are unsure where Mandi-lyn is. The creature had them both and we only saw Bet after the bright light," Ishu added, lowering his head. "I like that Flursh."

Errel paced in circles, with one hand on his hip and the other scratching the back of his head. "Are you certain the blast wasn't created by Moth? Perhaps he was protecting them."

"The energy was clearly coming from Bet," Her answered.

"This energy, what did it look like?" Errel stopped pacing and placed his hand on his chin.

"Like fire and lightning together," Her said.

"It was white and orange, with streaks of purple," said Gad.

"Violet," Ishu corrected, drawing a stern look from Bathezine.

Babbers walked up to Her-Gad-Ishu, looking up at their beaks. "I know we've asked a lot of you, but can you fly back to check on her?"

Her-Gad-Ishu spread out his broad wings, flapping them once to make sure all was well. "We will go at once," Her said. The crow took flight and disappeared in the moonlit sky.

Bathezine watched the crow fly for a moment, then turned to the others. "What do you suppose this new Talent is?"

"I've never heard of such a thing," Le'lel said. "But my experience is limited."

"Maybe it's like Errel's pyro Talent. Except, you know, amped up." Babbers looked around the camp, her face growing concerned.

Errel shook his head. "I don't think so. With the electricity involved, if that's what it was, that would be like combining two Talents. Spark and Fire-tend are two very different Talents. And the explosion—I've never heard of anyone generating that much power. But then again, I've never heard of anyone being able to travel between the realms until recently."

Bathezine took a deep breath and stood looking out at the caldera. "Whatever it is, I hope that girl is all right."

Old Babbers continued to scan the campsite, looking under the wagons and behind crates. She grabbed a lantern, walked to her tent and looked in. "Pooch-kin? Are you in here?" No reply came, and she turned to leave when she heard a quiet sniff. She crawled inside the tent, pulled back Bet's bedroll, and spotted Pooch-kin looking like a feathery white lump, matching the blanket. "Hey there, little friend. Whatcha doing in here all alone?"

"It's my fault. I thought I had a good idea to protect Bet, and now it seems I may have gotten her killed." His little blue eyes were wet with tears.

"Hey, no." Babbers knelt in front of him. "It's not your fault. Your idea was great. Remember, she did the same thing. You two think alike.

Whatever may have happened down there isn't your fault. No one is to blame."

Pooch-kin shrugged his stumpy wings. "I hear your words, and I know they're true, but if she is gone, I feel I took a part in it."

"C'mon. You know better than that. Bet...she's strong. She's stronger than me, that bear-man, Errel, probably stronger than all of us combined. I have no doubt that she survived. And I'm sure she did whatever she did to protect Mandi-lyn. That's the kinda girl she is. Now quit your worrying. You know she's okay. Right?"

Pooch-kin nodded, his red-orange crest falling to one side. "I have lost everyone I have ever loved. I don't want to lose her, too. That fear lives in my heart. If she dies, I will join her in final death."

Old Babbers sniffed back a tear. "I won't let that happen." She scratched the Chook-chook behind the ear, the way she had seen Bet do it a thousand times, and looked at the yellow light of the lantern dance across the tent walls. "Do you really believe that we all die twice? I've heard it before, but I've never had a reason to believe it."

Pooch-kin looked her in the eyes. "I know we do."

"I wonder if that holds true for everybody."

"It may," Pooch-kin said. "I have a question."

"I might have an answer," Old Babbers said with a tender smile, still scratching his ears.

"How come you never told me you were an Oragoth, too?"

A cheeky smile crossed Old Babbers' face. "A girl's gotta have her secrets. I've got a few Talents I keep hidden. Now don't go blabbing it to everyone." She ruffled Pooch-kin's feathers.

"I won't if you tell me what other Talents you have." Pooch-kin let out a chirp of a laugh.

"Are you blackmailing me, little bird?" Babbers asked in exaggerated shock, with a small chuckle.

"If that's what you want to call it."

"You scandalous, devious little bird." She shook her head. "I like it. I'll tell you later, though. Now let's go out and join the others before they come looking for us."

Thirty-Two

Bet felt the darkness around her. It permeated her essence, crawling through her veins like insects invading her body, trying to devour her from the inside. The sensation felt like a sickly presence tugging at the goodness she kept in her heart. She could hear the Crickshaw's words, warning her about something she couldn't comprehend. The words sounded like useless babble, irrelevant to anything relating to her. Images flashed before her; images of death and destruction. She saw her friends, engulfed by flame, screaming silent accusations at her, eyes filled with anger or question. The images transformed, swirling into the shape of a long, blood-red staff. The vision switched once again to hordes of men running through unknown towns, firing weapons and killing all who stood against them. The images disappeared, and she welcomed the blackness that came with it.

A presence interrupted her respite, an ominous whisper, scratching through the darkness. The whisper crawled across her, hovering over her like an angel of death. "What are you?" the Reacher's voice asked.

Her eyes shot open, and the dark vision was replaced with pale moonlight. She closed her eyes against the bright light of the moon. As she lay on the ground, her breath coming in shallow rasps, she became aware of pain. Her hands felt like they had been dipped in a cauldron of boiling oil, her eyes as if someone had tried to gouge them out with a sharp stick, and her ankle like it had been crushed in a vice. She moaned, trying to speak, but her throat felt like she had swallowed burning coal.

"Stay still," a quiet voice whispered.

Bet lifted her head and saw what appeared to be a half-naked rodent gnawing on her ankle. She tried to pull away, but lacked the strength. She tried to scream, but only managed a hoarse cough.

The rodent's face appeared before Bet's. "You must keep quiet and stay as still as possible."

Her brow wrinkled in confusion. *Why do I have to be quiet? And why is there a big rat trying to eat me?*

The rat brought a canteen to Bet's mouth. "Drink slowly."

Bet sipped the water. She winced. The water felt like fire against her raw throat.

"Do you know who I am?" The rat's whiskers fluttered across her face.

The tickling whiskers made Bet smile, and a memory danced in her mind. She studied the rat's face, and realized it wasn't a rat. "Where's your hat?" Bet rasped.

Mandi-lyn's whiskers bounced in amusement. "You remember me?"

Bet nodded. "Your name is Mandi-loon. No, Mandi-lyn. Right?" Her voice was little more than a whisper.

"Yes. My name is Mandi-lyn. You've been badly injured, and I'm trying to heal your injuries. But I need you to stay still. Okay?"

Bet nodded in understanding and let her head fall back. She heard the Flursh making chittering noises near her foot, and she lifted her head and saw Mandi-lyn running her whiskers up and down her swollen leg. She lifted her hands to find her palms blackened and the sleeves of her shirt and coat gone up to her elbows, with edges frayed.

"I will get to those next. For now, lay back and try to relax," Mandi-lyn said, then returned to her healing.

Bet closed her eyes, trying to recall what had happened. She remembered the fog and a torch, and she remembered seeing the Flursh choking and hanging in the air in the grip of an unseen hand, but everything else was lost in confusion. Bet heard a crow's caw somewhere in the night sky and wondered why a crow would be flying at night, knowing they usually returned to roost at sundown. Nothing made any sense, so she tried to relax. She turned her head to the side, trying to figure out where she was, and saw something that made even less sense. She gasped and lifted her arm, pointing at what she saw.

Mandi-lyn was by her face in a heartbeat. "You really must stay still."

"What is that? How?" She pointed at what appeared to be a reflection of her and the Flursh in the distance, scarcely illuminated by the faint moonlight.

"It is a render. An image projected through thought. A Talent that is difficult to maintain, especially while healing. If the Drullids return, they will be drawn to that instead of us. So please, try to stay still." Mandi-lyn hovered over Bet's face to make sure the girl understood.

Fear washed over Bet. "What are Drullids? Where am I? What is this place?" She tried to sit up.

Mandi-lyn shook her head. "I hate to do this." She raised a pink finger and tapped Bet between the eyes, putting her to sleep instantly.

Her-Gad-Ishu swooped low over the render, cawing incessantly. Mandi-lyn shook her head in frustration and let the projection fade away. "Over here, bird," she called, trying to keep her voice low.

"Is she alive?" Her asked.

"Yes, but she is injured. I've made her sleep. You need to go before you attract more Drullids."

The crow soared in a circle overhead. "Are you injured?" asked Gad.

"Only singed. Bring something to wrap Bet's leg. Please leave now. You are putting us in danger."

Mandi-lyn watched the crow fly away, closed her eyes, and the mirror image of the two of them reappeared. She stood, and walked away from her patient, searching in the gloom for her hat. It was not far away, no worse for wear. She looked at the bare patches across her body, where Bet's display had singed the hair away, applying a healing touch where the skin was tender. Then she came back to Bet and sat beside her. She watched the sleeping girl, and reached out, touching her blackened hand.

"Poor girl. You are innocent to what looms before you. Though I now know, I must leave you to your blindness, lest it lead to our destruction."

Thirty-Three

King Dalverious stood before the door of the inquisitor's chambers, his hand hovering above the tarnished brass knocker. The inquisitors were the enforcers of the king's will against the Users. The people called them Dalverians, and the king hated the name. The term was used as either a show of respect for who commanded them, or, more often than not, a term of contempt for their king's enforcement of the rule of law. The common folk were so petty and ignorant. If they truly knew the disorder the Users had caused, they would want them eradicated as much as he did.

Yet the rule of law had prevailed. The Users were being hunted down, one by one, and those who harbored them were executed along with them. The king's inquisitors, though he preferred to think of them as what they were, executioners, had an uncanny ability to track them down wherever they hid. Some went as far as to suggest the inquisitors were themselves Users, that they could sense the enemies of peace using their abilities. Dalverious hoped that wasn't true. They were simply expert huntsmen, skilled in combat, and with no moral ambiguity to hinder finding their prey. They were also skilled interrogators. Some said they could sniff out a lie simply by looking at their prisoner.

The king didn't care about the rumors or myths surrounding his elite team of executioners. They were effective and unquestionably loyal to the crown, and they struck fear into the hearts of those they pursued. But there was one User who had no fear of them, and in due time, that lack of fear would mean his end.

Dalverious grabbed the heavy knocker and let it drop against the door. He stepped back, waiting for the slow opening. A series of latches and bolts banged from the other side of the door. The door creaked open no more than an inch, and then closed. The sound of chains echoed on the steel door. When it finally opened, a tall, thin man with long blond hair bowed his head. King Dalverious stepped in and waited as several locks slammed shut behind him.

The blond-haired man escorted him to the rear of the spacious room that lacked any decoration other than a small, circular, stone table. Dalverious glanced at a shallow onyx bowl sitting on the table, containing light gray ash known as the Testament. The sight coaxed a mirthless smile from the king as it always did; a teaspoon of ash was taken from the pyre of each User executed since the foundation of his inquisitors. His escort opened a heavy drape, and the king entered the common room.

A large man with a long black beard tied at the end by a red ribbon sat in a chair equal in size to the king's throne. He rose as Dalverious entered, giving him a curtly nod. The man stood and approached. His black attire, seven-foot frame, and barrel chest, gave the king the impression of the Reacher if he were a man of flesh and blood. This man intimidated all who encountered him—all but the king.

"High Inquisitor Awren Vanth, how was your hunt?" asked Dalverious.

The man looked down at him with eyes so dark beneath his bushy black brow that the whites were scarcely visible. "They fled to the Lorde's Mountains. The Scow boars have their scent. They won't stay hidden long," he said in a deep, rumbling voice. He turned his back on the king and returned to his seat.

An ordinary man would have been executed for the rude display, but Awren Vanth was not ordinary, and the king allowed him certain privileges, lack of decorum being one. "The one you hunt is an Oragoth; are you certain she won't turn the boars against your men?"

"My boars are well trained and have encountered her kind before." He reached for a chalice beside his seat and took a long draft of ale. "Have you come to discuss my boars, or is there another purpose for your visit?"

Dalverious watched the ale drip down his beard, glistening in the amber light of the wall sconces. "I have. Things have progressed quickly while you've been away. The barrier will be down within days. We must be ready."

Awren stared at the king for a moment. "Are you certain the demon will uphold his end of the bargain?"

Dalverious shook his head. "No. In fact I'm sure he won't. After he gets what he desires, that is. I'm reasonably sure he will kill us all. And that's where you come in."

The big man finished his ale, setting the chalice on the table gingerly, as if he were trying to control the violence rising within him. He motioned for another inquisitor to close the door in front of the drape. The man slid a large lead door closed with a snap and a hiss. "What am I to do with this demon? He cannot be killed, or else it would have been done long before now."

"Are you certain he cannot enter?" the king asked, looking at the lead door.

"He hasn't done so in the ten years of your alliance. Though he has tried."

King Dalverious nodded. "When the staff is complete, he will be a man of flesh and blood, like you and I."

Awren slammed his fist on the arm of the chair. "Then I will kill him in that moment. Too long he has had freedom in our realm."

"No," Dalverious said, shaking his head. "He must complete what has set out to do. The one who created the separation still lives. He intends to kill her. After that, do as you will. Though I warn you, he is formidable. I have seen firsthand what he is capable of."

"And the girl? She nearly killed one of my men."

"If you find her, do as you wish. The demon has lost interest in her, now that he has what he needs. She is inconsequential." Dalverious straightened his shoulders. "Do not tell the Tribunal what we have spoken of. You have complete autonomy in this matter."

Awren Vanth leaned back in his chair and watched the king exit the room. His face creased into a sneer. "If I find her? I would think Dalverious would know better." He looked at the blond inquisitor.

The blond man returned the look. "Instructions, High Inquisitor?"

"Send word to the trackers. Tell them to double their efforts. I want those two. I need bait."

Thirty-Four

The Reacher ran his ghostly hand along the white marble table, admiring the pulsating red glow of the Staff of the Din resting on a black silk cloth. Tendrils of black quivered in anticipation of the final bloodletting, which would bind the staff to him for all time. No more would he be hindered by his vaporous form. He would become flesh at last, and be free of the Omia Temporian. He touched the staff, longing to wield its power.

"King Dalverious, where is the sacrifice? They are late."

Dalverious stood by the door, tapping his finger on the hilt of his sword. He yanked open the door. Someone would pay for their dereliction of duty. He took two steps and stopped at hearing the echo of footsteps running along the corridor. He braced himself, knowing that a running guard rarely carried good news.

The running man rounded the corner and slid to a stop. "Your Highness, the prisoner," he said between breaths. "The prisoner is dead."

"What? How could this be?" He spun back and looked at the Reacher. White eyes glowed amidst a swirling tempest of black smoke. He started to approach the demon and pulled up short, not wanting to have the Reacher's wrath brought upon him.

"Bring the cup," the specter hissed and vanished.

The king grabbed the cup. Before leaving, he stopped and looked at the messenger. "Come with me." The two men took off at a run.

~ ~ ~

The Reacher twisted into existence in the center of Harrelle's cell. He swept across the room and stood over the old man's body. Blood leaked from an open wound on the man's arm, where he had managed to tear away the bandages with his teeth and reopen the incision. He placed his hand over the man's head, then brought it over the heart. "Did you believe that by dying you would prevent me from completing my work and save the girl? Noble, but foolish, old man."

King Dalverious threw open the door, with the other man following close behind. He looked at the pool of blood on the floor, and Harrelle's ashen body. "Is he dead?"

"Yes," the Reacher whispered. "But not dead enough. Behold what you would call a miracle."

The Reacher's wraith-like body rose to the ceiling and the torch light flickered wildly. His eyes swirled with every color in the prism. The vaporous form hovered over Harrelle like a cloud carrying the portent of a deadly storm. Tendrils of black mist caressed the dead man from head to toe. The Reacher's color-changing eyes turned bright white once again, and the fingers of smoke engulfed the man's head. The Reacher's body floated over Harrelle, undulating, swelling and contracting. Two streams of black shot from the Reacher, swirling in the air, then stabbed downward into the old man's lifeless eyes. The phantom twisted and turned, followed the streams, disappearing into the corpse, as if being sucked inside.

The king's escort made a startled gasp and stepped in front of Dalverious to protect him from whatever dangers would come from the possession.

Dalverious pushed the guard aside, drawing his sword out of instinct, though he knew steel couldn't protect him from this demon. He watched the old man's body contort and twist, until the arms and legs stretched out, breaking the chains that held him. The movements continued and repeated for several minutes until Harrelle's body fell limp on the bed. The king lowered his sword and watched the body, eyes narrow with suspicion.

The Reacher shot from the old man's eyes, and Harrelle sat up, screaming and gasping for air.

The king lifted his sword once more to defend himself against the undead.

The spectral form of the Reacher brushed his hand against the man's head, and Harrelle fell back, breathing easy through quiet moans. "It is not quite time for you to die. I still have need of you. But worry not, your time will soon come."

Harrelle turned his head back and forth, trying to see though the dark voids where his eyes had been. He tried to speak, only managing low grunts.

"Is he truly back from the dead?" Dalverious asked, his own eyes wide and haunted.

The Reacher spat a sickly laugh. "Spoken like a man of ignorance. True death takes several days once the body ceases functioning. He lives, though his mind is damaged. But no matter. He will get what he desires soon enough. Hand me the cup."

Dalverious sheathed his sword and brought the cup, keeping a wary eye on the reanimated man.

"Quickly," the Reacher demanded, when Dalverious didn't move fast enough for his liking. "Time runs short." He placed the cup below Harrelle's arm, and looked at the king, waiting for him to make the incision.

With the task complete, the king stepped into the corridor. He felt the coldness of the demon creep up behind him. "I will return to the drawing room at once."

"No need. I will complete the task alone. See that your men are ready. We move on the Whist at first light." He swirled back, looking at Harrelle, lying on the bed, still bleeding. He waved a shadowy arm, and the prison cell burst into flames, becoming a fiery furnace. "Now you may die."

Thirty-Five

Eerie blood-red light radiated from the Staff of the Din in the center of the darkened room, casting a pallid crimson glow across the walls. The Reacher stood before the staff, chanting indecipherable words punctuated by fits of low moans and chattering whispers. The amorphous form twisted with wild gesticulations, ending in calm, flowing movements.

He held the bowl of sacrificed blood over the staff, pouring small droplets along the length of the shimmering quartz. The Reacher emptied the bowl and began chanting in a low voice. "Bound to me, bound to thee, never broken but by three." He repeated the mantra several times over, his voice growing louder, reverberating off the walls, thundering, the vibrations shaking lights from their fixtures.

Sparks of light flowed over the staff, yellow, white, and red. The snap hiss of electricity filled the air, bouncing off walls and running over the floor in blue-white webs of energy. "Let what was undone be remade, bound by blood," the Reacher bellowed. He took the staff in both hands, holding it high above him. Lightning coursed through his incorporeal form, shaking him violently. The shadow writhed beneath the storm, screaming inarticulate noises. White light exploded from his body, incinerating the marble table before him. Silence fell over the chamber and all went dark.

Several minutes passed, and the staff began to glow once more. Red light pulsated like a disembodied heart, and the Reacher stood, studying his hands on the glowing rod in the darkness. The room sizzled with dissipating energy. The Reacher walked toward the door, slowly at first, as if feeling the ground for the first time. He reached for the steel handle, crushing it in his grip. He looked at the mass of bent steel in his hand. "Beautiful," he said, then let it fall to the floor. He placed his hand against the door, and with a thought, the heavy door exploded outward, crashing against the wall.

The Reacher stepped into the light of the corridor and lifted his hand, turning and waving it, admiring the charcoal gray skin. He looked at his muscular arms, letting his gaze fall to his powerful, animal-like torso and legs. He sucked in deep breaths of air, filling his body with oxygen. A movement at the end of the corridor caught his eye. "Step forward," he said, his voice low and deep.

A frightened guard peered around the corner, gun forward. The guard looked at the gray man standing naked in the hall, then at the staff he held, and brought his weapon to his shoulder. "Who enters the king's palace?" He cocked the hammer back.

"You have no need of weapons." The Reacher extended his arm, and the gun fell from the guard's hands.

The guard stood trembling, staring at the intruder. He made a motion to run, and the Reacher vanished, reappearing in front of the guard before he could take a step. Grabbing the guard by the chin, the Reacher dug long, curved, sharp fingernails into the soft flesh beneath the jaw. "Where do you run to, little man? Do not fear me, for I am your king's ally."

The guard stammered, staring into the Reacher's pupil-less white eyes, trying to find his words.

"It feels like it's been ages since I've eaten." The Reacher's black lips parted in a disturbing smile, exposing jagged white teeth.

"P-please. Please don't eat me." The man shook, unable to break free of the demon's grip.

The Reacher spat a saccharine laugh, looking the man over from head to toe. "You're not my type. Bring me food and summon your king." He released him, and the guard rushed away, set to carry out his orders with mindless obedience.

The specter turned flesh and blood strode down the corridor, running his hand along the stone wall. Coming to a torch, he ran his hand through the flame, pulling it away quickly. "What the old man must have felt."

He entered the darkened chamber and held the Staff of the Din before him. The Reacher eyed the staff greedily. "The things we will do."

Thirty-Six

Bet limped behind Mandi-lyn as they climbed a low rise. The jagged stones buried beneath the loose soil continuously dug into Bet's shoeless foot, slowing their progress. She stubbed her toe against an unyielding rock and threw down her walking stick. She sat, rubbing her aching toe. "Gimme my shoe. My toes hurt worse than my ankle."

Mandi-lyn's shoulders slumped. "The swelling has not gone down enough yet. If you put it back on, we will probably have to cut it off for the next healing session. Your ankle wasn't a simple fracture. Your bones were crushed."

"So you keep telling me. How about the next time Her-Gad-Ishu comes around, I have him bring a cart so you can pull me? It won't take any longer than me limping along banging my foot on every sharp rock between here and there." Bet held out her hand. "Give me my moccasin."

"We will do one more healing first. But you still have to take it easy. If you injure it again, it may become too damaged for me to heal." Mandi-lyn slid back down the slope to Bet's side, kicking up plumes of gray dust. "Lay back."

Bet did as instructed, while waving away the dust cloud. As she sat watching the Flursh healer do her work, her mind began to wander, as it had much of the past two days since her encounter with the Drullids. "You're holding back from telling me something, aren't you?"

Mandi-lyn looked up from her healing. "If you interrupt me each time

I work on you, you'll never heal."

"I remember everything now, up to seeing you being choked. You said I used a Talent like Errel's—I shot fire or something."

"Yes," the Flursh said in a curt tone, not lifting her head away from Bet's ankle.

"How come I can't do it now? I thought once you acquired a Talent it never leaves you." Bet looked at her hands. Mandi-lyn had healed much of the scorching, but traces remained. She looked at Mandi-lyn and her pink hairless patches where her orange and white fur had been singed away. "It was more than fire."

This time Mandi-lyn did look up. "Is that a statement or a question?"

"Maybe both. Your skin didn't look like it was burned. And I've never seen Errel black out from starting a fire. I remember a buzzing sensation. It was almost like getting stung by the wasp. A wasp sting feels like electric fire."

"I have never been stung or electrocuted. I wouldn't know." Mandi-lyn chattered over the ankle once more.

"Then whatever I did was more of a release of energy or something close to that."

Mandi-lyn sighed and looked at Bet. "All right. I have never seen, nor have I heard of what you did. It was akin to combining several Talents at once. And since you have shown no predilection to using such Talents, it was quite…shocking."

"What do you mean?" Bet wiggled her toes as Mandi-lyn healed the injuries from the multitude of times she had stubbed them.

"Talents usually come in categories. Not always, but usually. You seem to have an affinity for three groups—strength, psychic, and understanding. I have healing, psychic, and, one would say, knowledge. The energy you expelled would add a fourth to your Talents."

"Do you think I'm like Fealist-Marsh? That I'm a seventy-two?" Bet felt a tinge of fear crawl over her. She had no desire to carry such a responsibility.

All she wanted was to have the task end so she could live out her days on a ranch with Pooch-kin and Bathezine.

Mandi-lyn seemed to hesitate. "I don't believe you are an Omia Temporian. And a seventy-two is a bit of a misnomer. While Fealist-Marsh may embody all of them, there are some she can't use, and can never use."

"Like what? I thought she was an all-powerful being or something." Her mind flashed back to seeing a young Fealist-Marsh standing before the Crickshaw. She strained, trying to recall the memory, but it faded away, much like some of the knowledge the old tree had imparted on her. It both frustrated and worried her. She felt like part of her brain was still stuck in the Talent-muting fog.

"She is quite powerful, but no one is all-powerful. For example, if she were from an aquatic race, she may have the fire tender Talent, but no way to use it, as fire can't ignite under water. You, being human, can't be a Seeder; you would have to be a flora race."

"A cedar? That makes sense. How could a human also be a tree?"

"True. Wait…what?" Mandi-lyn shook her head. "A human can no more be a tree than a fish a bird."

"Right. So I can't be a cedar tree. I didn't know being a tree was a Talent."

"No. No, no, no. A Seeder. One who casts seeds. Not a cedar tree."

"If they cast seeds, why not call them a caster? Whoever named these Talents needs to keep homonyms in mind." A smile crept to the corner of Bet's mouth.

"A caster is a small wheel. It wouldn't make sense to call someone a wheel." Mandi-lyn saw Bet's smile, and sighed in annoyance. "You're playing with me. I'm trying to educate you and you're playing with me like a child."

"You're so serious, it's easy. Now I see why Bathezine gives you a hard time." Bet let out a small laugh, the first in many days. "You could just call them sowers."

The Flursh raised a stubby finger to protest, but seemed to agree with the name. "Don't pick up his bad habits," she said, trying to sound less serious. "The point is, you have acquired a Talent, or the ability to use Talents in a way I have never heard of. And like all Talents, it can be used for good or ill. I'm not sure which your display falls under."

"I did it to save our lives. I'm thinking it wasn't all bad...or ill." Bet seemed to remember the Crickshaw's voice warning her of something just before she blacked out, and wondered if in her haste she had overlooked something, or another way of achieving her aim. "I killed the Drullid."

Mandi-lyn shook her head. "No. While you slept, I saw the pieces of gray flesh crawling across the ground. Some joined other pieces. Whether they will create new Drullids or reform into what they were, I don't know. Regardless, we haven't seen them since. Perhaps they are wary of another encounter. Now let me work on your ankle. We need to move soon."

Bet leaned back and watched the Flursh work. Something gnawed at her gut. Something Mandi-lyn still wasn't telling her. She had felt it for some time, but refused to read her friend's thoughts. The words she heard before waking after the attack came to her. She remembered they sounded much like the Reacher. Bet leaned up on both elbows. "What am I? There's something you're not telling me."

Mandi-lyn continued to work for a few moments before sighing. "I've done all I can for now. You may put your shoe back on. Lace it tightly."

Bet grabbed her moccasin, happy to have it back. "Mandi-lyn, I need to know."

The Flursh looked at her, blinking her dark round eyes. "You are a girl with many Talents. You are strong and will likely become stronger. You have a part to play yet which I do not know, nor will I guess. There will come a time when certainty will present itself. For now, focus on what's ahead."

"You have suspicions." Bet laced her moccasin, not taking her eyes off Mandi-lyn.

"Suspicions are akin to guesses," Mandi-lyn said, then stood.

"I think you have more than suspicions. I think—" A low rumble, sounding like an approaching storm, filled the air, stopping her words. Bet got to her feet. "What is that?"

Mandi-lyn didn't answer. Instead, she stared at the sky. Clouds floating in the late afternoon sky sped away, as if pushed by an unseen force. The cerulean sky began to dance in prismatic color, flashing from red to orange to yellow, and then from green to blue to indigo then violet. The colors repeated themselves in reverse order then back again. Then the colors faded from the sky, and the world seemed deathly quiet.

Mandi-lyn looked at Bet, her big eyes growing wider. "The staff has been completed. The barrier from the Din has fallen."

"What do we do?" Bet asked. Her body began to tremble uncontrollably. Her sensing Talent stretched out unwillingly, and she felt the fear of a million beings hit her at once. She clutched her chest, gasping for air.

Mandi-lyn rushed to her side. "What happened?"

Bet shook her head. "I felt the fear."

"Whose fear did you feel?"

"Everyone's." Her eyes pooled with tears. "This is my fault. I have to stop him. I have to make this right."

"No! No, Bet. This isn't your fault. You know as well as I do that the Reacher would have hunted us down, he would have killed us all, and eventually you, to get what he wanted. We must make haste to Moth. There is only one way to stop him. On your feet."

Bet stood, her shaky legs almost giving out beneath her. "I don't know if I can. The fear is crippling."

"Use your fear. Apply it to your strength."

Bet thought of Old Babbers' words of how to use fear to her benefit. Her body clenched. She looked at Mandi-lyn with eyes that seemed to radiate.

"Good." Mandi-lyn secured her bag and pulled her hat down tight against her head.

"We don't even know where Moth is," Bet said, sounding uncertain yet hopeful. "The caves could be anywhere. They could be on the other side of the crater, or in a hole in the ground."

Mandi-lyn took Bet's hand and led her up the slope. "What do you see? Your sight is better than mine." She waved her stubby fingers at the landscape.

Bet peered into the distance and let her senses expand. Free of the Talent-muting fog, she focused on a nearly indistinguishable dark cluster of rock near the center of the caldera that protruded higher than the rest. Something tugged at her instinct—a presence that was both there and not there. "That way." She pointed to the distance.

"Are you certain?" Mandi-lyn asked.

Bet sighed and continued to study the formation. "Not really," she said with a shrug, but a gentle prodding in the back of her mind told her she should be.

Mandi-lyn nodded as she watched Bet. "Good enough. Now run. I will follow."

"You won't be able to. Climb on my back." She gave Mandi-lyn a look of determination so fierce the Flursh nearly recoiled.

"Your leg," Mandi-lyn said.

"It doesn't matter. We get to Moth, and then we find Fealist-Marsh. And we will end this." She stooped low, waiting for the Flursh to climb on.

Mandi-lyn stared at Bet, a wave of sadness seeming to wash over her face. "And so we will." She climbed on the girl's back, and Bet ran.

Thirty-Seven

Bathezine ran to Her-Gad-Ishu after seeing him fall from the sky beneath a canopy of ever-changing color. Old Babbers was by his side in an instant. "Crow! Are ya all right?" she asked, looking the bird over.

"We are fine," Her said after shaking off the fall. All three heads looked to the sky.

Pooch-kin, Errel, and Le'lel rushed up behind the others. "What's happened?" Errel asked, watching the spectacle.

"The barrier from the Din to the Whist has fallen," Gad said.

"Then the staff is complete," Babbers said. She knelt beside Pooch-kin, stroking his ears. "War is upon us once again."

Bathezine clenched his fist. "We're more ill-prepared this time than last. And if'n that Reacher can control every Foul creature he finds, then what chance do we have?"

Errel stepped forward, adjusting his weapons. "We're not as ill-prepared as you think. Andola has the resources to keep King Dalverious at bay. And we have Bet. If we get her to Fealist-Marsh, wherever she may be, then balance can be restored."

"Are you so sure they'll get involved this time? They weren't too eager to help us earlier," Old Babbers said.

Errel looked at Le'lel, then to Babbers. "I have one more card to play."

"What card is that?" the woman asked, eyeing him suspiciously.

"Not so much a card as it's a last resort. But first we have to see Bet through her task."

"Cards or not, if the barrier's down, why don't we just go into the Din and take out the king? You know, lop the head off the beast," Bathezine said, his nervous energy spilling over once again. "We take care of one problem at a time. Then we deal with the Reacher alone instead of two problems. We've got the crew to do it."

"We can't," Her said.

"And why can't we?" Bathezine snapped back.

"Only the Staff of the Din was restored," said Gad.

"The Din can cross into and out of the Whist. We cannot cross into the Din," added Ishu.

"And why not?" Bathezine waved his hands in the in frustration.

"Because we would need the Staff of the Whist to do so," a voice came from somewhere near the oak trees.

Bathezine spun around to find Tiny Nat stepping away from the trunk of the oak tree, changing colors from gray to golden yellow. "Tiny? Where did ya come from? And where in the devil's arse have ya been? And when did ya become a chameleon?"

Tiny Nat buzzed with agitation. "We have been here since Bet's show of power in the caldera. We were drawn to the light. We thought it best to protect you from a safe distance."

"Protect us? Protect us from what?" Bathezine growled. "There ain't been no sign of trouble for days. Least any trouble outside that hole in the ground."

"It's good to see you, Tiny," Babbers said with a smile.

"And us you." He looked at Bathezine. "The Snickers, for one. They didn't appreciate their food being stolen by the Flursh. We convinced them that their pursuit was not in their best interest for the time being."

"Them squirrel-pigs? They ain't no trouble." Bathezine waved the idea of an army of angry furry creatures away. "Well, it's good to have ya back anyway."

Tiny Nat nodded, knowing that was as close to a warm welcome as the Ursian was capable of giving. He went straight to Errel once the Ursian stopped babbling. "We located the source of the contamination of the nectar."

"The nectar? Oh, yeah, yeah," Errel said, having forgotten about it with so much that had happened since then. "What did you find out?"

"The Vapid we encountered in Paskersville told us he met a woman. We discovered she was a contact for the Reacher named Armur Seine. She put the Troojian wasp egg in our food supply while in Illguard, just before our arrival."

Bathezine pulled his attention away from the sky. "Bet gave that wasp a good fight. She didn't say so, but that wasp crawlin' outta the body of your hive mate gave her a fright. Woulda done the same to any of us. Girl's seen so much since comin' here. Your hive mind saved her, Tiny."

Tiny Nat placed his hand on Bathezine's shoulder. "You and us. Your proficiency with the blade saved her as well."

Bathezine shrugged the compliment off. "Least I could do. It killed your friend and near killed Bet." He nudged Errel. "It was a good throw, though. Wasn't it? Took its head off neat as prunin' roses. Remember?"

"How could I forget?" Errel narrowed his gaze at Tiny. "This woman; what does she look like? How did she gain access to our food pantry?"

"She was about Old Babbers' height, and she was a Transmuter, able to take the appearance of any she saw."

Errel crossed his arms and sighed. "So she could have looked like me or Walt, or even Le'lel. Did you find her?"

"Yes. She has been taken to our hive and dismembered," Tiny Nat said, matter of fact.

"That's what I would've done. If I had a hive," Babbers said. She looked over the Vivicon. "You got taller."

"Yes, we have completed the final molt of our lifecycle." Tiny Nat expanded his iridescent wings to their full span of six feet. "In spite of Bathezine's best efforts, we have reached full maturity."

"My best efforts? I didn't tell ya to go get nabbed by that long-toothed beast." He looked at Tiny Nat, fighting back a sadness welling up inside him. From what little he knew about Vivicon physiology, he knew that the final phase of their lifecycle lasted no more than a year or two. "But ya did good out there. Don't know if I told ya that or not. If'n I did, consider it twice the praise."

Tiny Nat tilted his head. He walked to the Ursian. "It is good to see the hardness of your heart chipped away. Keeping the world at an arm's distance only makes your arm grow tired and weak."

Bathezine scratched behind his round ear. "Yeah, ya reach an age where ya either keep on bein' a brick-headed lunk, or try to put the past behind ya. Ain't nothin' I can do to change what's been. And that girl down there, she made me see there's more to livin' than haulin' rocks."

"Your path is clear, Bathezine. Redemption has found you."

"Let's hope so, Tiny." His long mustache raised in a sneer of a smile. "Don't mean I ain't cantankerous no more."

Old Babbers stepped between the two and patted the Ursian's round belly. "I can attest to that."

Bathezine raised his arm like he was going to smack Babbers. "Smilin' while stabbin' me in the back. Ain't that always like a she-devil?" He looked around the camp, content with the friends who surrounded him, but wishing Bet and Mandi-lyn would hurry back so he could feel complete. He looked at the sky. The prismatic display had ended, and the silence which accompanied the end made him shiver. "Since we can't infiltrate the king's palace, what do you suppose we do?"

"It will take several days or longer of travel for the Dalverian forces to reach us. That depends on where the realms rejoined, of course. I suspect they would head to the towns first, to deal with any resistance," Errel said, his voice sounding stoic, yet commanding.

"Unless the Reacher can sense where Bet is. Then they might come after her," Babbers added.

"No, that would put them at a strategic disadvantage. But that doesn't mean the Reacher won't come for her, or the inquisitors. We should be on guard in case that comes to pass." Errel turned his head to the Vivicon. "Are there members of your hive near Illguard?"

"Yes, we have dispersed along the Waste and through the mountains," Tiny said.

"Can you have someone warn Walt and the town of what may be coming their way?"

Tiny Nat looked upward and buzzed quietly for a moment. "It is done. We have learned that the Andolan airships have left Illguard and are headed toward Azural. Why they are going there, we do not know yet."

"I hope it's to organize the resistance. But with my father in command, he might leave the Caldon region to its fate just to spite me. Sharpen your weapons and your eyes. We don't know where the realms will rejoin exactly. It could be a thousand miles away, or ten." He drew his sword and raised it high, looking at the others. "I will fight to protect Bet and defend the Whist until the last drop of my blood has been spilled. What say you?"

Old Babbers raised her hatchet, Bathezine his mace, Le'lel his claws, and Tiny Nat his atlatl. Pooch-kin hopped on the ground, fluttering his wings, while Her-Gad-Ishu raised his beaks. "We say so mote it be," Bathezine said for them all.

"Then, by my authority, I dub thee knights in defense of the Whist." Errel lowered his sword.

Bathezine lowered his weapon. "I ain't never been knighted before. Does this mean I gotta slay dragons and such?"

Errel shook his head with a smile. "After all you have faced, a dragon would be fool to confront you. If dragons were real, that is."

Le'lel watched their exchange and hissed a rebuke. "Dragons are real, if you know where to look."

Errel looked at the Lasoom with a raised brow. "Let's hope that they are. We may need to call on them."

Thirty-Eight

Bet ran tirelessly through the night and into the morning, only stopping to relieve Mandi-lyn of the jostling ride and for sips of water. They traveled lower into the caldera until arriving at a grouping of large basalt rocks thrusting upwards in every direction, towering over them. Porous grooves marked the flow of what had once been molten rock that ran outward, forming bulbous, yet jagged stone.

Mandi-lyn patted Bet on the shoulder. "Let me down. I believe we have arrived."

Free of the Flursh's weight, Bet sat on the cool rock, drawing deep breaths of air into her heaving chest. She let the added strength she had been using ebb away, and felt the dull ache of her injured ankle. She closed her eyes, trying to will away the pain. Unsuccessful, she studied her surroundings, realizing she hadn't actually seen where they had stopped until then. She tried to recall the path they had taken, but it had felt like a blur, like she had been blinded by her intense focus. Bet grabbed her canteen and took a long drink, rinsing her mouth of the trail dust. "Do you think this is the place?" she asked between breaths.

"Maybe," Mandi-lyn said, then pointed to a gap between the rock formations. "But that's the first sign of a cave we've seen."

Bet took an apple from her bag and devoured it, leaving only the stem and a trace of the core. She immediately did the same thing to a pear. "Let's hope so. I think I've exhausted myself. I feel like I should sleep for about a week."

"I tried to warn you last night, but you wouldn't listen." Mandi-lyn dragged her fingers across the rock, studying all she saw. "I'm surprised you're still alive. Messengers in the old era would run for miles and days on end. Some would die at the end of their journey from the toll it took on their hearts."

"We all die at the end of our journeys," Bet said.

Mandi-lyn's bouncing whiskers went still as she looked at Bet. "What made you say that?"

Bet shrugged. "Someone once wrote that no one gets out of this life alive. I was probably ten years old when I read that. It didn't make sense to me back then. But I've grown up a little since that time."

The Flursh's whiskers resumed their twitching, and she looked away. "A poorly phrased philosophy, but no truer words can be said on the subject."

"I guess so," Bet said, standing. She winced at putting pressure on her foot. "Shall we get underway?"

"We need to rest. I need to rest," Mandi-lyn said before Bet could protest. "If Moth is in there, he can wait for an hour."

Bet nodded. "Okay. But no more than an hour. I want to get this over with and get back to the others." She sat back down, closed her eyes, and stretched out her senses. She felt the vague impressions of the Drullids. Free of the Talent suppressing fog, she realized that the creatures didn't feel like anything that was truly alive. It almost felt like they were trapped in a state between life and death. She decided that the Drullids and the undead the legends spoke of were one and the same. She expanded her reach and found something odd, yet disturbingly familiar. The sensation pulled her from the meditative state. Opening her eyes, she saw Mandi-lyn staring at her.

"What did you find?" The Flursh asked while gnawing on a nut.

"I'm certain Moth is somewhere along that path." She pointed to the gap Mandi-lyn had shown her. "My senses were blocked. I'm assuming that's how Moth keeps from being found. But there was another void."

Mandi-lyn's whiskers went still. "This other void; you've felt it before."

Bet picked up a pebble from the dirt, rolling it over in her hand. "I've *seen* it before. In the vision I had after passing out in the woods at Illguard—when I saw the Reacher kill Putrice. I don't know how I know it's the same place, but it is." She flicked the pebble away and listened to it hum through the air.

"Do you believe it's Moth blocking your Talent?"

"No," Bet answered almost before Mandi-lyn finished asking. "It felt different. The blocking in the caves felt fluid—organic, I guess you would say. But the other place... It felt rigid, almost geometric—like it was put there. I don't know if that makes any sense or not."

Mandi-lyn half shrugged. "Maybe. If someone uses a blocking Talent, like Moth's fog, it would feel like you described—fluid, yielding, yet unyielding at the same time. As for the other, the only substance I know of that can block a sensing Talent is lead, but it has to be saturated with silver dust. It would definitely feel rigid. There are stories that prisoners from the Whist were kept in cells made of lead, to prevent them from being found and to stop them from using their Talents to escape. Though, for the life of me, I can't imagine why anyone would build a cell here of all places. Perhaps it is a geological oddity."

"Maybe," Bet said absently while staring at nothing in particular on the ground. Something about it felt wrong. A tickle in the back of her mind told her she might be right. She lifted her gaze and met Mandi-lyn's eyes. "Can someone from the Din cross into the Whist? Someone with no Talents, that is."

"No," Mandi-lyn said without hesitation. "While it may be that the Reacher can cross, and you can as well, in mind only, the Din cannot. That was why the barrier was created." She cocked her head, looking intensely at Bet. "Do you think someone has?"

Bet pursed her lips, wondering what she should say. "No. I thought I felt a presence from the past, but I saw the Reacher destroy her. These visions can make your mind muddled. Sometimes, I don't even know what's real or imagined anymore."

"The imagination is real, so in a sense, everything is real."

Bet put her hands on her hips and raised an eyebrow at the Flursh. "That's no help." She stretched her back and nodded toward the gap in the rocks. "We should go. I don't want to wait any longer. I can carry you if you need to rest."

"Being carried is far from restful, and you should conserve your energy. We don't know what's in store, or even what Moth is." Mandi-lyn threw her half-eaten nut in her bag. She motioned toward the path. "Shall I lead the way, or do you want to?"

Bet looked at the gap. "I will." She adjusted her bags and limped forward.

Mandi-lyn watched her walk. She shook her head and dug into her bag. "Wait." She pulled out a small pouch and fished out a tiny seed, handing it to the girl.

"What is it?" Bet asked, holding out her hand. She rolled the seed against her palm with her finger.

"Falkwith seed. One can ease pain for many days. I was saving it in case one of us suffered a traumatic injury."

Bet raised her eyebrows. "Having your ankle crushed isn't traumatic?"

"While it may be traumatizing, it isn't the same as, say, having a limb torn away or worse."

"We should save it, then. I'm fine," Bet said, handing the seed back.

Mandi-lyn pushed her hand away. "No. I can sense the amount of pain you're in. You may need all of your strength. The seed's properties allow it to seek out the injured areas of your body and deaden the pain. I'm not sure how it knows to do this; perhaps it is a Talent unique to the seed. It won't heal the injury or keep it from being injured further, but it will help until we get back to the camp, where you can rest and heal properly."

"Really, it's okay." Bet tried to give it back once again.

"Take it. I can get more when we get back to civilization."

Bet sighed and reluctantly swallowed the tiny seed. Within moments the Falkwith seed's effects took hold and the pain in her ankle vanished. Her eyes widened in surprise. "Wow, that really works. We should've brought a whole bag with us." She stepped forward, tentatively at first, then with more vigor.

"The seeds are rare and very expensive. In most cases, pain is necessary. It lets us know where an injury has occurred, and shouldn't always be stopped, at least not until a proper diagnosis has been made," Mandi-lyn explained as they walked along. "There are those who say that pain is the essence of life, that it's the pain that lets us know we are alive, for there is no pain after death. Though I believe that is a rather extreme philosophy."

Bet approached the gap in the stones. She rested her hand along the coarse rock looking in. "If that's the case, I definitely know I'm alive," she said absentmindedly, peering through a narrow passage. A chill washed over her. She looked back at Mandi-lyn and motioned for her to follow.

Hours passed as the pair walked, climbed, and sometimes crawled over the rough gray rocks, which scraped and cut bare skin. Both remained silent, as though they expected to see a Drullid or something worse lurking around each twist and turn. The path led them steadily downward, and the farther they descended the darker it became. Bet glanced up, noticing the stone monoliths angled in, leaving only a trace of the blue sky visible above them. The passage narrowed even more, making them shuffle sideways to get through. Rounding another turn, the path widened out once more. Bet came to a stop, spitting a curse she had picked up from Bathezine. She looked back at Mandi-lyn. "Dead end," she said, sounding both angry and disgusted.

Mandi-lyn scurried in front of Bet and looked around, running her hands along the rock. "There were no other ways in that we could see. I was sure of it..." she said, her voice trailing while looking back the way they had come.

"So was I. But then again, this way did look like more of a crevasse, not a cave. That's probably why they don't call it the crevasses of Moth," she said, not noticing that Mandi-lyn's attention was directed elsewhere. She pounded the stone in frustration with the side of her fist, regretting it instantly. "This will put us back a day."

"There has to be a way through. Search the stone face. Find a weak point," Mandi-lyn said, her voice rising to a panic.

"A weak point?" Bet asked without looking at her. "What's got you so upset? We'll head back the way we came." She turned around and saw small streams of water snaking their way along the rocky path. She looked up through the narrow fissure of rock above, noticing the sky was still blue.

"It's not raining." Mandi-lyn looked at Bet. Both heard the roar of rushing water coming their way. "Hurry. I can't swim."

"There's nowhere to swim to anyway." Bet began pounding against the rock face, finding nothing but unyielding stone. She moved from wall to wall in the tight space, repeatedly beating against the rock.

Mandi-lyn joined her, furiously running her whiskers along the rock, trying to sniff out a weak spot. The water came in faster, rising to her waist. "It's no good."

"Try to climb." Bet punched the rock face, using more of her strength. She recoiled, shaking her hand, certain she had broken at least a few bones. The Falkwith seed immediately relieved the pain.

Mandi-lyn clawed at the stone, unable to find purchase for her tiny claws. "I can't," she yelled over the ever increasing roar of water.

Bet moved to help her friend, but a rush of cool air told her it was too late. The sensation reminded her of the strange wave that had hit her when she'd tried to cross into the Whist. She grabbed Mandi-lyn by the shoulders. "Get behind me." Bet turned toward the passage and crossed her arms in front of her, just as the torrent of water hit them.

The powerful blast of water carried her off her feet, and the world became a confusing swirl of white, battering her against the rocks, threatening to steal her consciousness. She felt Mandi-lyn grasp her leg, then slip away, the raging water pulling her back down. The water filled the narrow gap and the rush stopped. Bet spotted Mandi-lyn flailing madly at something to grab hold of. She took the Flursh by the arm and pointed upward, and swam toward the fissure. They reached the crack, but its narrowness wouldn't allow their faces to breach the surface.

Anger began to work its way through Bet as it had when they were attacked by the Drullids. She swam downward, pounding against the stone with ever increasing force, desperately trying to break through. She didn't know why, but she was sure salvation lay on the other side. Her lungs ached from lack of air, and she knew Mandi-lyn was faring much worse. The rage continued to build. A bump beside her drew her eyes away, and she saw Mandi-lyn sink slowly, small pink hands outstretched, reaching for the lifesaving air just out of reach.

The rage grew, and the water began to churn from the fury building inside her. She would break free of the watery tomb one way or another, or die trying. Her hands clenched as the furious energy built, ready to explode outward.

As before, the voice of the Crickshaw echoed in the back of her mind. "Not like this. Remember how you found him on the Waste."

Bet closed her eyes, wanting to ignore the voice; anger was easier than reason. She opened her eyes and let the serenity overcome her, trying to ignore the burning in her lungs. She reached out with her mind, searching for a way through, but found nothing. She tried again, this time letting her thoughts enter the rock, still finding nothing. She grew desperate, but still clung to her serenity.

The memory of how she had found the Reacher flashed back to her, and she let her thoughts touch the elements. She felt the water with her mind, first feeling its coldness, and then delved deeper. She felt the water at its elemental base, the hydrogen and oxygen. A presence in her mind, feeling like the old tree, seemed to nudge her onward. Bet knew what it was telling her. She let herself float downward, taking Mandi-lyn's limp body in her arms. Her vison began to fade from the lack of air. There was no time left. In her final moments of consciousness, her mind tugged at the oxygen in the water and on the surface through the tiny gap. A bubble formed, small at first, and then it grew. It formed over the crown of her head, then expanded, encapsulating her body. Bet clung tightly to Mandi-lyn and sucked in the life-giving air.

The next moment, the water vanished, and Bet and Mandi-lyn landed with a thud on the soft ground. Bet got to her feet at once and looked at the basalt stone surrounding the circular expanse she found herself in. She stooped down and helped get Mandi-lyn to her feet, noticing the Flursh's fur was dry. She looked at her own clothes and felt her hair. Everything was dry, as if nothing had ever happened. The two locked eyes. "Was it even real?" Bet asked.

Mandi-lyn grabbed her hat from the ground. "Or imagined?"

"It doesn't make any sense. We were drowning, and now…"

"This is beyond anything I've read or experienced. If Moth can project this into our minds, it is a Talent that far surpasses what has been written of." She looked around the expansive space, and then back at Bet. "How did you find a way past?"

"Something I recalled from the Crickshaw. I was able to touch the elements. Like when I can touch a mind, but a little different. I don't know how." Bet looked at the beams of sunlight shining down through the small gaps in the stone above.

"If your knowledge comes from the tree, it makes sense. A tree can gather nitrogen from the soil, carbon dioxide from the air, and energy from the sunlight. You must have done something similar with the water." Mandi-lyn studied Bet and nodded as she turned away. "You are discovering new ways to use Talents."

But Bet didn't hear what she said. Instead, she focused on what she saw in the gloom ahead of them. She walked forward, with Mandi-lyn trailing close behind. They approached a flat stone standing on edge, with markings etched in circular paths. "It looks like writing," Bet said, reaching out with her swollen hand, rubbing the inscription.

Mandi-lyn approached the vertical slab. "It is. A primitive dialect from the land of the Hoarsk. Strange to find it here."

"Do you know what it says?" Bet continued to study the etchings.

"The Hoarsk disappeared many millennia ago. But I believe I can translate it." She rubbed her hand along the center of the stone, following the etchings outward in a spiral. "It doesn't make any sense. The letters are jumbled."

"Maybe whoever wrote it didn't know how to write in that language."

"From what I know, the Hoarsk wrote from right to left, not left to write, as we do." She studied it for several minutes, trying to decipher the words. "Wait. That's it."

"What's it?" Bet asked, eager to know what it said.

Mandi-lyn pointed to the top of the circle of letters. "Whoever wrote this, wrote it backward. It's left to right, and the words are backward. See?"

"Not really," Bet said, trying to remain patient. "Can you translate it?"

"Yes. Of course." She rubbed her finger along the words and read aloud:

Center yourself or not,

leave what you left to rot,

try as you may, you might,

choose a path that is right."

"What does that even mean?" Bet asked after repeating the words herself.

"I'm not sure," Mandi-lyn said, then rechecked her work, writing it down in her notebook. "Nor do I know what it pertains to. It could be a forgotten relic with no purpose."

"Why would we get dumped in a cavern after nearly drowning in imaginary water if it doesn't have a purpose? It's a crappy poem, but it has a purpose." Bet shook her head and searched the cavern for a way out.

Sunlight streamed through gaps in the rock ceiling. Mandi-lyn watched the rays travel across the floor with the sun's movement. She stood, transfixed by the sunbeam. One by one, the rays winked out of existence until there was only one. "Bet, come over here."

Bet looked over her shoulder, and felt the rock wall once again, looking for any sign that there was a hidden trigger mechanism which would give them access to another passage. Finding none, she rejoined Mandi-lyn. "Did you find something? Or figure out what the script is trying to tell us?"

"I believe this chamber is like a calendar," Mandi-lyn said.

Bet squinted one eye, looking at the Flursh. "How can a room be a calendar?"

"Think of it like a sundial, except instead of a shadow marking hours, a ray of sunlight marks days. Ancient people would use them to indicate the equinox or solstice, generally for harvest or planting. Some would shine on a particular spot to mark an event."

"Maybe. But if that's true, what's this one for? I don't think anyone ever farmed this lifeless crater." She, too, started watching the remaining sunbeam crawl across the cavern floor.

"Perhaps some peoples lost to history farmed this region. Trees did live here. I have yet to see the light mark anything of interest. But notice the path the beam is taking." Mandi-lyn pointed to the etched stone.

"Maybe it'll show us something we haven't seen," Bet said with a bit more enthusiasm. She sat, stretched out her legs and watched. Mandi-lyn sat beside her and waited to see what would be revealed.

Several minutes passed until the shaft of sunlight reached the base of the etched stone. The light began a slow climb up the stone, and Bet watched in anticipation, while Mandi-lyn scribbled in her book, writing each word and letter the ray highlighted. The beam traveled continuously upward, falling on one last word, and then it disappeared entirely. The two looked around for another hint of light, but no more came.

"Well, that was anticlimactic," Bet said, her shoulders falling in disappointment. "I was kind of expecting it to highlight a secret block or something. You know, so we could press it like a button and open a hidden passage."

"You've read too many stories," Mandi-lyn said, looking over her notes.

"You can never read too many stories." Bet got to her feet and stared at the walls with her arms folded across her stomach. She looked down at the Flursh. "Anything in your notes of any use?"

Mandi-lyn ran her finger along the page, shaking her head. "Depends on whether we can find meaning in them. The beam highlighted not, leave, you, choose. In that order. If it's telling us we can't leave until we choose, it's not much help if we don't know what we're choosing from."

Bet turned the words over in her mind. "Maybe we missed something. Maybe we had to be here on a certain day, and the light would have lit up a different series of words."

Mandi-lyn puzzled over the words, ignoring Bet. "The last word highlighted was *choose*."

"Choose. What am I supposed to choose?" She was about to complain some more, when a low moan came from the far side of the cavern, beyond the stone.

Mandi-lyn jumped to her feet. "That's it. Say it again."

"Say what again?"

"The word…choose." Mandi-lyn threw up her arms in irritation.

Bet gave her a dubious look. "Okay. Choose," she said, putting more emphasis on the word.

The moaning became louder at once, and a rush of cool air came from the back wall, carrying a stale odor. The wind kicked up swirls of dust, causing them to cover their eyes to protect them from the grit. The wind stopped as suddenly as it had begun, and when they opened their eyes, they found three cave entrances along the wall of rock.

"The Caves of Moth," Bet said in wonder.

"Yes, I believe they are." Mandi-lyn scribbled another note, then put her book in the bag.

"Now the crappy poem makes a little more sense. We have to choose between the three." Bet walked toward the caves and stood before them with her hands on her hips. "But how do we know?"

Mandi-lyn peered into the five-foot wide mouths, trying to see inside. "I see well in the dark, but not total blackness. We must decipher the words."

"Right. Read it again," Bet said and sat on the ground. She listened to Mandi-lyn recite the poem and tried to make sense of them.

"If I may say, alluding to what you said earlier, if we had arrived here any other day or at any other time, the sunlight wouldn't have shone on the word. Do you think that a coincidence?"

Bet remembered what she had seen in her dream, and an eerie feeling crawled over her flesh. "No. None of this is. I know it's not a coincidence."

Mandi-lyn studied the girl for a moment. "You say that with certainty."

"I had a dream, or maybe I saw a memory of the tree. In it I saw Fealist-Marsh. She was just a kid. She told the Crickshaw, or maybe it was me, that Moth would tell me how to find a certain place. So yeah, nothing about this place is a coincidence or accidental." Bet grew silent and thought about what was before her, listening to the Flursh take out her book and scribble more notes.

After nearly twenty minutes of brooding over the puzzle, Bet stood. "I think I got it."

"Are you certain? I hate to think of what would happen if we entered the wrong cave," Mandi-lyn said, her whiskers bouncing nervously.

"Thanks for not putting more pressure on me. But yeah, I think so. The first says *center yourself or not*. At first I thought it meant to meditate. You know, center your mind. But that's not it. The next one, *leave what you left to rot*. I was thinking it meant to put the past behind me. But my past is as important as my present and future somehow. The third line is there to create indecisiveness. May and might aren't definite. Lines one and two have negative connotations—not and rot. That brought me to the fourth line, *choose the path that is right*." She looked at the Flursh and smiled. "It's the cave on the right. It even says so."

Mandi-lyn looked at her wide-eyed, whiskers twitching, and not saying a word.

"What?" Bet asked, breaking the stare-down.

"It could be the cave on the right from another perspective. And there are many possibilities within the words themselves."

Bet threw her hands up. "You really make me feel good about my decisions. Is there any other doubt you want to instill in me before I go into the cave on *my* right?"

"No, that should be sufficient." Mandi-lyn adjusted her tricorn and motioned for Bet to go.

Thirty-Nine

The pair entered the mouth of the cave and noticed a faint light, deep within, that hadn't been there before. "See? This is the right path."

"It could be the first glow of magma coming to meet us for choosing wrong," Mandi-lyn said.

"Now who's the pessimist?" Bet asked with a hushed voice. The stone walls did nothing to amplify the sound of her voice. If anything, the porous rock seemed to mute sound.

"Considering all of the possibilities is not pessimism." Mandi-lyn scurried behind Bet, examining everything she saw, even though the tunnel walls were mostly featureless. "You sometimes need to consider the results of your actions before setting forward on a particular venture."

Bet stepped over a large chunk of broken pumice stone. "And sometimes you need to act and consider the possibilities later." She stretched out her senses to get a feel for whatever lay ahead, with no results.

"That is true as well. You must find balance in all things."

"Is that a truism from the Charge of Danthbrook, or a generalization?" Bet asked in idle conversation, trying to mask the eerie feeling the cave was giving her.

"Both," Mandi-lyn said. They followed a sharp bend in the tunnel, and the passage widened out.

The two looked around the ten-yard-wide passage, and continued on. They walked for an hour more before deciding to stop for rest.

"The light seems like it's moving away as we walk. Like a mirage that you can never get closer to," Bet said between sips of water.

Mandi-lyn looked toward the faint light, her whiskers bobbing. "It moves with us, otherwise it would grow dimmer as we sit."

"I noticed." Bet looked back the way they had come. The tunnel was so dark, she wondered if it had even existed at all. A thought crossed her mind. She stood and started walking back toward the narrow tunnel and made it no more than a few yards before hitting solid rock. Fighting back the anxiety rising within, Bet turned to find Mandi-lyn staring at her, and she didn't need her Talents to know the Flursh was fighting the same sense of panic. Running her hand along the stone, the creeping anxiety transformed to a simmering anger.

"Apparently we can only move forward. We should go." Mandi-lyn started to go, but stopped when Bet made no move to follow. "What are you doing? We must keep moving."

"No. I'm done playing these games. People's lives are at stake. The barrier from the Din to the Whist has fallen, and the king's forces will come along with the Reacher. I refuse to solve puzzles and riddles while people die. If all of this is preordained, or whatever you wanna call it, then Moth can come to me."

"You've seen what Moth is capable of. The strength of its Talents is far beyond anything known. It would be unwise to upset something with so much power," Mandi-lyn said, taking Bet's hand to urge her along.

Bet pulled her hand away. "No. Power is…it's an illusion, like these walls and the flood, and the fog. It's a way to control us. I've surrendered to control long enough. The headmistress at the orphanage, Putrice, even the fear of losing my friends—I'm not giving in to it anymore. If this task was appointed to me, for whatever reason, before I was even born, then I'll go forward on my own terms. And if this Ancient One deems me unworthy for not playing these games, then it should kill me now and find someone else to see it through. But I can promise you this—I won't go without a fight." She stood, breathing heavily, searching for a balance between the rage within her and the serenity she knew would protect her.

No sooner had Bet finished speaking her words that they heard the familiar moan of rushing air. The distant light flickered away, leaving them in complete darkness.

"You may have made matters worse," Mandi-lyn said, coming to Bet's side.

Bet breathed deeply, letting the simmering storm of rage dissipate. She did the same for the joyful serenity she carried within, clutching the eternal calm, free of emotion. She stretched out her finger with a flick, and a blue spark of fire floated at her fingertips.

Mandi-lyn saw the confidence in Bet's eyes and her whiskers rose with her smile. "You are quite remarkable. I hope to travel with you to the end of your journey."

The darkness surrounding them disappeared, revealing an expansive chamber with walls of ash-gray stone. Small crystals imbedded in the rock sparkled white and blue, and the stale air became fresh and clean. Bet closed her fist, extinguishing the flame, and stood impassively, waiting for Moth's appearance. A tiny trickle of pebbles at the far end of the cave caught her attention. She watched as a small creature, no more than six inches tall, crawled over the uneven ground on a host of legs.

"Prudence," the tiny creature bellowed in a voice disproportionate to its size. The word echoed off the chamber walls. The creature rose up on its back two legs, shook and doubled in size, taking the form of something similar to a hairless cat with a bushy gold beard.

Mandi-lyn took out her notebook at once and started writing.

"Temperance," the cat-like thing said in a high, shrill voice. It took several steps on its hind legs and shook once more. Once again, it doubled in size and transformed. When the trembling stopped, it had taken a vaguely reptilian form. Narrow slits on its face opened revealing bright blue eyes, which matched the color of the crystals within the rocks.

Bet watched the display, remembering the Pidge messenger's words:

that Moth is everything. She wondered if his transforming ability was a Talent or an exaggerated survival technique similar to Pooch-kin's.

"Fortitude," the creature said next, in an even, tenor's voice. Once more the body shook.

Bet waited to see what type of creature Moth would take the form of next, only this time it didn't transform into a single entity, but a cluster of crystalline butterflies, which scattered and flew around the cave in a brilliant display of color. The butterflies swirled and danced around the visitors, rising high to the cavernous ceiling, then twisted downward, hugging the cave floor. The swarm spun before Bet, flying ever faster, until it resembled a small, yet beautiful tornado. The butterflies rolled into a churning ball, and with a suddenness that stole Bet's breath, exploded into a shower of shimmering dust.

When Bet's eyes adjusted after the dazzling display, she saw a creature that was both beautiful and horrifying. Two sets of eyes sat on small stalks atop a broad, semi-square head. The head rested on a six-foot-tall reptilian body with four feline-like arms, at the end of which deadly looking seven-inch scythe-shaped claws extended outward. Two stout legs, which reminded Bet of the Rhinodon's, supported the husky frame. Two leathery wings, which shimmered in an array of color, extended from Moth's back, waving silently in the cool air.

A wide mouth parted in the center of the noseless face, revealing layers of tiny needle-like teeth. "You have shown these attributes on your journey thus far. Hold true to them, for more trials lay ahead."

"Are you Moth?" Bet asked, unsure of what to make of the creature.

"I am," Moth answered, its opened mouth unmoving.

Bet wondered if there was yet another transformation forthcoming. "Is this your true form?"

"As true as it will be. Many millennia have passed since I came to be, and I have taken the form of many beings, which now reside within me." Moth stepped forward and looked down at Mandi-lyn, who held her book and pen at her side. "Charge of Danthbrook, note what transpires before you. Pass on what you learn to the scribe, and your purpose will be served."

Mandi-lyn hesitated for a moment, seemingly unsure what Moth's words meant. Her whiskers bounced with uncertainty, and she began writing with fervor.

"As I'm sure you know, we've traveled far to see you. I've had a vision telling me to seek you out. But I'm not sure what I'm supposed to ask of you. Will you tell me where Fealist-Marsh is?"

Moth waved its shimmering wings, expelling a cloud of glowing golden dust. The cloud floated in the air above Bet and cascaded over her body. "Breath in."

Bet hesitated briefly, then took a deep breath. The dust felt like the air after a spring rain as it entered her body. The sensation calmed her senses, and she felt warmth fill her entire being. Her eyelids drooped, and Bet swayed on her feet. She stood for nearly a minute, relishing the feeling. A rush of adrenaline coursed through her and, in a moment of clarity, the knowledge the tree had given her flowed through her mind. Bet's eyes snapped open and her body went rigid. All of the memories that had hid in the shadows of her mind since entering the caldera came back to her. Her eyes darted back and forth as she tried to cope with the sudden influx of knowledge and memories. Then her eyes grew still, and she stared unblinking at Moth.

"The knowledge of the Crickshaw was buried within you to protect it from the Null, the one you call the Reacher. If he had found it within you, all would have been lost."

Bet's forehead wrinkled in confusion. "I thought I was destined to come here. Fealist-Marsh told me through the memory of the Crickshaw."

"There is no destiny, Bethany. Preparations were made for this inevitability; however, the uncertainty of chaos may have its way with the best laid plans. None saw that you would give the facet to the Null willingly or otherwise. The drop of a small stone can cause a ripple on placid water. So it is with that which has yet to be. No future is set." Moth stretched out its clawed hand. "Come forward."

Bet walked to Moth without hesitation, and Moth took her hand. "What am I supposed to do?" she asked. "I didn't ask for any of this to happen. I didn't know anything about this realm or even having Talents until a couple of weeks ago."

"You must continue in your quest to find the Omia Temporian. The world will become an ugly place. You must complete your appointed task to restore the beauty."

Bet was getting fed up with vague prophecies and parables. While she understood that certain bits of knowledge had been kept from her to protect her and others, it was time for solid answers. "Where is she? Tell me plainly."

Moth touched Bet's forehead, dragging a single claw in a path from her brow down to her chin. "You have seen where she is kept. The palace of white crystal. It is forever in motion—winking in and out of existence like the stars. I do not know where. There is one who can find it. You must seek her out."

Bet closed her eyes and firmed her jaw. She tried to keep her emotions neutral, but the frustration was overwhelming. "If you don't know, then why did I come here? Is there another purpose to this? Days have been wasted, and now people are going to die."

"Death is inevitable. You chose to save the life of your friends at the expense of many others by giving the facet of the Din to the Null." Moth folded its wings. "But these things must come to pass."

"I thought you said nothing about the future is set." She pulled away from Moth's touch. The thought that she would be responsible for the oncoming war became too much for her to bear.

"As I spoke of the ripples on the water, the flow can change, yet the water will still exist." Moth extended its cat-like arms. "Your emotions serve you well, but they may also prove a hindrance. Stay even and you will prevail."

"Is that it? Will you tell me how I can find this other person?" Bet fought back her rising anger with serenity until once again finding the balance between the two.

"I will. But first, the answer to why you came." Moth clapped its outstretched hands together and a stone chest appeared at Bet's feet. "Open it."

Bet looked at the box, then back at Moth. She kneeled down and stole a glance at Mandi-lyn, who watched her, pen ready to record what treasures lay within. Bet slid the top back. The heavy stone lid fell with a thump at Moth's hooved feet. Seeing a blue silk cloth, Bet reached for it, but hesitated. She looked to Moth, who nodded for her to proceed, so she removed the cloth to find a stalk of quartz, roughly two and a half feet long. She pulled it out and heard Mandi-lyn gasp. Bet looked at the Flursh, then back to Moth. "What is it?"

"A segment to the Staff of the Whist. Continue," Moth said, motioning toward the box.

Holding a piece of the ancient relic filled Bet with a longing she couldn't explain. Knowing what the staff was capable of roused multiple emotions. First came the hope of ending the Reacher's quest for power, followed by the fear of the result if the staff was wielded by him as well. A third feeling emerged—a tinge of greed, which made her recoil, almost causing her to drop the staff.

Bet gripped the length of quartz tightly and pulled away another piece of fabric. Beneath it was another segment of the staff, nearly as long, with a narrowed tip. "Is this another piece?" she asked, to confirm what she already knew.

"It is. The staffs were created here, in this crater, many, many years ago, with the blood of one from the Din and one from the Whist. The Staff of the Din has been reformed by blood. The Staff of the Whist must be, as well."

"I thought both were smashed into a thousand pieces when Fealist-Marsh created the separation. How come it's nearly finished?"

"The fragments were gathered and brought to their place of creation. One piece remains. When you find the Omia Temporian, you will find the joining facet."

Bet shook her head. "Wait a second. If you found these pieces, why didn't you gather the fragments of the other staff and save us the trouble of the Reacher?"

"The fragments were in the Din. Only three can cross the divide. One in body, one in spirit, one in mind." Moth motioned to the box. "Please continue."

Bet looked at the chest. Questions filled her head, but she got the feeling that Moth would only answer what was relevant to his purpose. She pulled aside the next layer of blue fabric and found three gems—a ruby, an emerald, and a sapphire. She waited for Moth to explain.

"You will seek out the Ancient One known to the Charge of Danthbrook as the Wanderer."

Bet held up the sapphire, the size of her palm, admiring it in the light. "What do I do with these?"

"The emerald is to be taken to Mokep the Black in the great city of Azural. Say these words to him—*from pit to peak, the Wanderer I seek.* He will take you to the beacon, and the Ancient Wanderer will come."

She repeated the words and nodded. "Okay. I got it." Bet looked at Mandi-lyn, who motioned to her notebook.

Moth continued. "The sapphire is the memory of the Ancient Wanderer. She has searched the globe for her lost memories since the separation of the realms. She is amorphous. Place the stone within her, and she will be bound to you for a time. She will lead you to the place you have seen in your mind."

Bet perked up at hearing this. They were finally going to find Fealist-Marsh, and all of this trouble would end. Visions of living her life in peace, free from assassins, dangerous creatures, and fighting filled her head, and a smile crossed her face. She held up the ruby. "What about this one?"

Moth's eyes narrowed as it watched Bet. It looked to Mandi-lyn, giving her a warning glare. Fascinated by the ruby, Bet didn't see the exchange.

"The blood-stone is for you," Moth said, pulling Bet out of her fascination. "When the Staff of the Whist is complete, you must seek out the Staff of the Din. The stone will bind the staffs together for all time, and the balance between Din and Whist, between Fair and Foul, will be restored, and the beauty will return. But beware, neither the Omia Temporian nor the Null will give them willingly."

Bet's heart sank at hearing Moth's words. What she had hoped would be a quick and easy end to the mess now seemed like the beginning of a whole new set of troubles. If Fealist-Marsh turned against her, what hope did she have to defeat her *and* the Reacher? She wrapped the items and placed each of them in her bag, trying to make the pieces of the staffs fit before giving up and tying them to the straps instead. She closed her eyes, fighting back a feeling of defeat. Tears welled up, and she closed her eyes tighter, resisting the flow. She looked at Moth with a blank stare, the sadness, anger, and hopelessness numbing her emotions, bringing her to the edge of fatigue. "I understood I had a part to play in this. But why? Am I to be an Omia Temporian, too?"

"You are not an Omia Temporian, Bethany. As to why—it is better to ask why we exist at all. Why do any of us live? It is a question asked since the birth of thought. I have pondered this for over a thousand years. Perhaps we live for life's sake, to perpetuate life. We, the world, the cosmos, are all transient. As our lives are but a blink in time, it may be that these things perpetuate something far beyond our understanding. Free your mind of troubles. Hold to that which you know is good, and you may succeed."

"It doesn't seem to matter much when you put it in those terms," Bet said, looking at the glimmering stones in the rock walls. She imagined them as the stars, winking in and out of existence, with herself a spectator watching them live and die.

"It matters to all who live in this time. And that is what matters most."

Bet took a deep breath. What mattered to her was her new-found family. Above everything, they were the most important thing to her. And as before, she would do all she could to protect them. She looked at Moth, a creature who had lived countless generations, and even it couldn't answer a question as simple as why. "Come with us. Your knowledge and strength would be a great ally to our cause."

"I cannot. As the Crickshaw was bound to the soil, so, too, am I bound to the rock. Go now. Knowledge is yours for good or ill. Remember that and prevail." Moth trembled and transformed to the swarm of crystalline butterflies once more. The sparkling display disappeared into the stone walls. The cave went dark, and the rock melted away, leaving them in the vast wasteland of the caldera as the sun rose in the east.

Bet looked at the landscape and the crater walls in the distance. "Was any of that real?"

Mandi-lyn raised her eyes from her notebook. "As real as our minds determine it to be."

"Seriously?" Bet said, her shoulders drooping as she rolled her head back. "I've had enough contemplation for today. For a lifetime, in fact."

Forty

In the realm of the Din, Anna stood beside the twisted trunk of a bristlecone pine, surveying the rocky landscape below her. Patches of hard snow dotted the mountainsides protected by the shade of granite boulders fractured from once jagged peaks. A palette of orange, yellow, and teal, streaked with crimson, marked the sun's descent into the west, and the icy alpine wind began to moan through ravines and canyons, heralding the coming night.

"Any sign of 'em?" Dalin asked, sitting on a flat rock and adjusting the straps holstering his wooden leg. He stood and shifted his weight back and forth to ensure all was right, then hobbled to his bay, scratching the horse on the neck; the beast seemed to appreciate the gesture. He retrieved a telescope from the pannier and stumbled to Anna. He slapped the matte-black scope against her shoulder. "Here. Try this."

Anna looked at the telescope then at Dalin's face with a doubtful expression.

"Don't worry, the glass don't reflect. Borrowed it from the military." He shrugged. "Since I didn't get a gold watch when I retired."

She took it and scanned the valley below, then toward the path they had taken up the mountainside. "I don't see anything." Anna studied the terrain some more, looking for any sign of movement. "Wait. I see... never mind. It's just a stag. I thought it was a Scow boar."

"Scow boars. Them things can sniff out a duck fart in a deep swamp. I know you're not keen on killing critters, but if they get close enough, I'm puttin' a bullet in their heads," Dalin said, motioning to his long rifle in the saddle holster. "They don't just track you. They'll give you their tusks when they catch you, too."

Anna folded the scope. "Hopefully it won't come to that." She looked to the western sky, watching the sun melt into the horizon. "We need to find shelter from the wind. Spiff is having a hard time with the cold."

Dalin took the scope and walked toward the Saureped, followed by Anna. The reptilian animal sat with his legs folded under his body. Dalin rubbed his chin in thought as he looked at Spiff. "I'd say we could find a cave, but I'd rather not hide out in a place where the entrance is the only exit. We might have to head lower and get in the tree line. At least it'll be a windbreak."

"And it will also put us closer to the inquisitors." Anna looked toward the setting sun once again. "We keep heading west. But you're right; we'll have to go lower. Not just for Spiff, but us, too. It's going to be a clear night, which will make it all the colder."

Dalin nodded and patted the bay. "All right, Phyllis, time to saddle up again." The horse sniffed and her ears drooped. He gave her a brisk rub. "I know, but we gotta keep moving for a bit still."

Anna waved a finger at the Saureped, which told him to prepare for her. He readied his haunches to take her weight. "You're a good friend, Spiff. We'll find a place where you can rest and warm up," she said, climbing on his back. The Saureped stood and snorted, preparing for another arduous trek through the rough terrain.

The siblings rode side by side in silence, with Phyllis' heavy breaths and the clomping of her hooves against the loose rock the only sound beyond the wind. They edged their way closer to the shadowed tree line, keeping a cautious eye and ear for any sign of the Scow boars.

Dalin cleared his throat, breaking the silence just as the last traces of daylight disappeared behind the silhouetted peaks. "What makes you so sure heading west is the right way to go? We can go east toward Suzavale. I know someone there that ain't got no love for the king. I'm sure she can hide us out 'til the heat cools a little."

"And I'm sure the inquisitors know that, as well. No, we have to go west. I'm certain we can cross into the Whist now." She sounded confident, but a hint of doubt floated in her voice.

"What makes you so sure, Sis? That light we saw in the sky?" Dalin kept his head on a pivot, constantly checking behind them and to tree line at their left, feeling reasonably certain he could hear trouble coming from the rocky mountainside at their right.

"Yes. The barrier between the realms has fallen, or at least part of it has."

"And you think Bet had something to do with it? I don't see how that weed of a girl could pull that off."

"Remember I told you that I heard Bet's voice warning us of the inquisitors? No one was supposed to be able to cross the divide. She has Talents I didn't think were possible." Anna leaned her face against Spiff's ear. His movements had begun to get sluggish in the cold. "We're almost there."

"So you think she could do something that nobody has been able to do in the fifteen years since the end of the war? Seems like a stretch. Maybe it was your intuition." Dalin pulled his collar up against the cold wind.

"Her voice was clear, and I could almost feel her presence." Anna pulled back on Spiff's reins, bringing them to a stop. She stared into the trees and made a hooting call. "I don't necessarily think she brought it down. She had an object that made me think of something Mother told me. She told me a story about these staffs that the Omia Temporian could wield, and that they held power over the realms."

"And this Omia person has all the Talents, right?"

"Something like that. After Mom died and before you returned from the war, my friend, Bathezine, said that he had heard that destroying the staffs created the separation. It all seemed like legend until that point. When Bet showed up, I found a piece of crystal in her pocket when I was drying her clothes. There was something about the rock that felt odd, as if there was a power in it. If she or someone else found a way to reconstruct the staffs, or even one of them, that could cause the divide to fall. And the colors in the sky...my gut tells me that's what it was."

"You know, if I can cross over, that means Dalverious can, too," Dalin said. He pushed up on the saddle horn, clicked his tongue, and Phyllis began leading them into to the heavier woods. He pulled his rifle and rested it on his lap, feeling the security of its weight, much as he had during the war. He harbored no delusions of being able to track a target in the twilight, but he would do what he could to protect his little sister.

Anna saw a muted glint of brass on the lever of her brother's repeating rifle in the last hints of light. She shook her head—Dalin playing the part of older brother, even though it was she who'd watched over him these past ten years. She ignored his statement, rode ahead a little way, and once again brought Spiff to a stop. A moment later she raised her arm, and a large gray owl swept through the low branches on silent wings to perch on it. She leaned close to the owl's tufted ear and whispered. The owl spun its head left and right, hooted twice, and then flew away as quietly as it had arrived. "She will act as our eyes and ears in the night."

Dalin ducked, just catching a glimpse of the bird fly overhead. "Some trick. You couldn't do that earlier with the other forest critters?"

"Flit hoppers are much too skittish, and the songbirds and jays are too preoccupied with gathering food and quarreling over territory. Owls are calm and unselfish in their nature. She also told me where we can find shelter from the cold. But you'll have to be on your best behavior."

"Best behavior? I'm always on my best behavior." Dalin spat on the ground in indignation.

Anna gave him a doubtful look he couldn't see. "Sometimes your best behavior is...well, other people's worst behavior. And it isn't people we're going to seek shelter with."

"I was afraid you were gonna say something like that." He let Anna lead the way and slunk low in the saddle, trusting the bay to keep him from any low-hanging limbs that would knock him from her back.

Forty-One

They rode for another hour with no warning from the owls. The wind whispered and hummed through the pines in peaceful forest lullabies, and if not for the biting cold, Anna could have fallen asleep under the sway of Spiff's rhythmic steps. Sleep had become a rare commodity since being on the lam, and the lack of it was starting to wear her thin. However tired she may have been, she knew it was double the burden on her older brother, though he never complained about fatigue. He complained about a great many things—the cold, the king, the king's inquisitors, the cold again—but never the toll the journey was taking on him. Anna smiled at the thought. It seemed Dalin was in his element and happy to feel useful again. She knew he had felt less than whole since losing his leg in the war, and no amount of words or work she had given him had made him feel otherwise. But they were alive because of him, and she knew they wouldn't have made it this far without his pragmatic preparations.

Weeks before, after hearing Bet's warning, and hearing the clank of the inquisitor's iron carriage coming up the muddy road, Anna rushed to one of the three places at the ranch she knew she could find her brother— those being the chair in front of the fire, eating a between-meals snack, the facilities after eating the snack, or the barn, tending to whatever he tended to there. Fortunately for them both, it had been the latter of the three. She threw on a coat and hat and gathered whatever she could carry, which, in her haste, were only a pouch full of coin and a tintype photo of her when she was only three years old with Dalin and their parents. It was the only image she had of her father, taken a week before he died, and the only photograph of the four of them together. She ran to the barn where Dalin was tending to Spiff. "The inquisitors are coming for us," she had said, doing her best to keep her wits.

Dalin didn't hesitate. He cast a concerned but confident look at his sister, grabbed a pitchfork, and hammered its butt end against a loose board on the interior wall. A panel fell open, revealing a hidden storage room Anna hadn't known existed. He quickly grabbed prepacked saddle bags, canteens—filled with fresh water every other day—and a pair of trail packs. He looked at Anna's surprised face, saying, "Been planning for this for some time. Get Phyllis saddled up." He turned to Spiff and adjusted the stirrups. "Sorry 'bout this, boy, but ya gotta do some more running today." The Saureped shook both legs and raised his head confidently as if saying he was ready for more.

Anna's experienced hands saddled the bay with lightning quickness. She mounted Spiff, not waiting for him to stoop. She looked back toward the house, her home since the end of that terrible war, and jerked at hearing the front door splinter under the boot of one of the men coming for them.

Dalin stuffed his rifle into the scabbard, pulled on his gloves and cinched his hat, then, placing the foot of his good leg on the stirrup, hefted himself into the saddle. He squeezed his knees against the horse's side and headed for the back wall of the barn, which bordered their small parcel of land.

"Shouldn't we be going out instead of in?" Anna asked, hooking a thumb at the open barn doors behind them.

Dalin winked at her, then reached for a chain-hook dangling overhead. "Nope," he said with a shake of his head. He pulled the hook with a grunting tug, and a ten-by-ten-foot section of the wooden wall fell outward, exposing the scrubby grassland outside. He set the horse in motion, and the Saureped, carrying Anna, followed.

Anna glanced back one final time, worrying about the animals in her care being left behind. She hoped their owners would come for them once they got word of her exodus. Her last glimpse of home was seeing a large dark figure kick the back door off its hinges and stand watching them from her porch, twirling what looked to be deadly blades. Even from that distance, she could tell he was twice the size of most men, and she dearly hoped he hadn't caught up with Bet, and that it hadn't been the girl's spirit warning her from the afterlife.

Several days passed with them riding east, taking a gradual path to the foot of the Lorde's Mountains, crossing through soggy terrain where days of rainfall had turned the grassland into something more resembling a marsh in places. They took cover where they could, usually beneath sprawling oaks on good nights, sometimes making camp on the open ground, with no good places to make a fire to warm beast or food. When they made their way up the gradual slopes of the lower hills, they caught their first sight of a band of trackers, led by the dreaded Scow boars. At that point, they knew they could no longer make campfires for fear of being spotted during the dark mountain nights, and many cold meals and nights lay ahead.

Along their ride, Dalin suggested several times, sometimes cantankerously insisting, that they should head east, and eventually make their way into the neighboring kingdom of Valdivia, where the king had no love for Dalverious, though he knew that borders would only slow an inquisitor in pursuit of his prey, if even that. But Anna, either through her dim Talent of intuition or by gut instinct alone, refused and, in her own, less gruff, way, insisted they headed west. When she saw the fall of the barrier, she knew it was her Talent that had guided them, and the Whist had called to her.

They had put a day between them and their hunters under the swift legs of horse and Saureped, but the steep mountainsides had slowed their progress. Even though they had lost hours off their lead, she knew the Scow boars and their handlers would fare no better in the rough terrain. Traveling into the high country, where the slow trickle of snowmelt had yet to join other equally small trickles to form streams and rivers, had been a gamble, one that was paying off, as they didn't have to search for crossings. But the ante was paid by Spiff the Saureped, his reptilian metabolism being unable to cope with the high altitude and cold. Anna would do what she could, and pay any price, to protect her friend from the elements and a slow death.

As they traveled farther into the deep woods, they approached a large mound of uprooted saplings, branches, moss, and dirt, barely visible in the pallid moon-glow, and she hoped she could convince the owners of the mound to give aid, and that if help were given, that aid wouldn't be too high a price.

"We're here, Dalin," Anna said, snapping her brother from a half-asleep stupor.

Dalin surveyed the woods. "We're where?" he asked, blinking in the darkness, trying to see what exactly in the old growth of the forest she meant by 'here'.

Anna patted Spiff's long neck, telling him to stop, and slid off the saddle. She looked at Dalin. "Holster your rifle. Keep quiet, and whatever you do, stay calm."

Dalin threw her a doubtful look from the top of his eyes. "You want me to just take a nap here on Phyllis' back?" He scratched at the bay's ear, who leaned her head into his hand for a deeper dig.

"No. It's probably best you dismount. Keep your hands at your sides and don't make any sudden motions," Anna said, her focus on a wide gap in the center of the mound of brush.

The older sibling did as instructed, continuously wiping the condensation growing on his mustache in the cold air and making sure to stand within arm's reach of his rifle in case whoever Anna was expecting to find didn't want company.

Anna took a reaffirming breath, hoping the advice the owl had given her wouldn't lead to her becoming a meal. She straightened her shoulders, and walking with a confidence that was only half true, stepped to the opening. She leaned in and called out in a pleasant, unthreatening voice. "Hello, lords of the wood. I am Anna, friend to you and to all who dwell in these woods." Her words were met by a low, disinterested snort from within, and she stepped back.

Anna glanced over her shoulder at Dalin standing in a beam of moonlight, who quickly unfolded his arms, remembering to put them at his side. He swiped at his nose again and gave her a sheepish grin.

With no further sound coming from within, Anna cleared her throat and tried again. "I pray thee, lords of the wood, we are travelers seeking shelter from the cold and would be indebted to your assistance."

This time the snort was accompanied by another, followed by a loud, moaning yawn. The snap of twigs came from the bowels within the mound as heavy, padded footfalls sluggishly made their way forward.

Anna stole another glance at Dalin, who gave her a half-hearted salute, before wiping his nose once more. She took another step back as the footsteps drew closer, lowered her head and put her hands out, palms up in supplication. The footfalls stopped just short of the breach, and she heard several heavy snorkeling sniffs. She raised her head, putting on her most pleasant face. The steps resumed, followed by more curious sniffing. Anna braced herself.

A large, furry white face emerged from the darkness within the mound, sniffing wildly through a round flat nose. The head came closer, dark round eyes blinked in the bony moonlight, and comically round, fluffy ears twitched, listening for any danger. The nose drew closer, and Anna found herself face to face with the largest Moon Bear she had ever seen. She silently hoped Dalin wouldn't do something impulsive. To her relief, she only heard a muted gasp from behind her. Both Phyllis and Spiff, seeming to know what Anna was up to, remained quiet and still.

"Food?" the Moon Bear inquired in a language only Anna could understand while sniffing at Anna's coat.

Anna hoped the bear meant something other than her. "Yes," she said and produced an apple from her coat pocket. The bear sniffed the apple and took it from her hand, noshing it greedily.

"More food?" the bear asked, sniffing around Anna's waist.

"We do have some. But I ask if you could give shelter from the cold to us weary travelers in exchange. My friend is suffering and is in need of warmth." Anna motioned toward Spiff, who lowered his head, as if exaggerating his fatigue.

The Moon Bear's eyes widened as it smelled the air. "Big lizard," it said, lowering its big round head.

"He is indeed. But the cold wears on him, and he may not survive the night if he doesn't find shelter and warmth. I beseech thee, mighty lord of the wood, to give us aid." Anna held out her hands once again to show she meant no harm.

"Not a lord. Just a bear." It snorted and raised his head toward Dalin standing a few yards behind them, doing his best not to fidget. "Another man? Men hunt us and steal our skin." The bear grumbled and showed its teeth in a silent threat.

Anna nodded and slowly reached out, placing her hands on the Moon Bear's puffy jowls. "He is my brother, and not a hunter. We are not hunters, just peaceful travelers with many miles ahead of us." Her heart ached at the bear's fear. Men had hunted the creatures for many years, using the excuse that they were dangerous predators as their justification for nearly wiping them from the wild, though she had never heard of an actual attack by a Moon Bear unless its cubs were threatened by a hunter. She rubbed the bear's stubby snout. "I promise you we mean no harm. Hunters pursue us as well. We will leave at dawn."

The Moon Bear rocked back and forth, nervous and uncertain. It looked at Dalin, who returned a slight nod with an anxious half-smile. The man raised his hand half way to his face, but thought better of it. "Food? I smell food."

Anna stifled a laugh. "We have more, but we do need to keep some for our journey. May we take shelter in your den?"

The bear shifted its weight, seeming to deliberate between the possible threat and the promise of more sweet apples. When its shifting ended, it looked at Dalin once more for reassurance just in time to see him raise his hand and fall into a fit of violent sneezing. The Moon Bear's eyes widened, and it let out a terrible roar. It charged out of the entry way, barreling Anna aside, toward the offending sneezer.

The bear moved with such suddenness, Dalin had little time to react. He took a step away, reaching for his rifle, and his wooden leg caught a rut, which sent him sprawling backward just as the agitated Moon Bear pounced. The bear landed on top of him, pinning his arms to the ground beneath its wide paws. The bear snarled, showing vicious teeth beneath its goofy, teddy-bear face.

Anna found her feet and raced to her brother's aid. "No! Don't hurt him. It was only a sneeze. He meant no harm."

As if to punctuate Anna's statement, Dalin sneezed in the bear's face. "I think I'm allergic to Moon Bears," he said, grimacing under the bulk.

Anna kneeled beside the bear, looking softly into its eyes and stroking its round ear. "He's not going to hurt you. It was only a sneeze. Surely you know what a sneeze is?"

The Moon Bear bared its teeth more, letting a drip of drool splat against Dalin's face.

"Me hurt him? What about him hurting me?" Dalin tried to wriggle free, but the weight of the bear kept him pinned tight.

"Have you come for our skins?" the bear said, putting its deadly teeth closer to the man's face.

"He doesn't understand you. He doesn't know your language. I assure you, he…*we* mean you no harm, and hate those who do." Anna continued to stroke the bear, pouring soothing words into its ear.

Dalin sneezed once more, wincing afterward as if expecting to have his face bitten off. "He's gonna break my arms if he doesn't eat me first," he said between grunts.

Anna stood, rushed to Phyllis, retrieved an apple from the pack, and hurried back. She held the fruit in front of the bear. "See? We don't want to hurt you."

"Appetizers?" Dalin quipped through a strained breath, looking at Anna.

The Moon Bear sniffed the apple and seemed to come back to its senses. It took the apple in its mouth and chomped noisily, letting the juice fall on Dalin's face. "Food," the bear said, and relieved Dalin of his weight.

"Yes," Anna said. "Food." She helped her brother to his feet. She wiped the slobber and juice from his face and brushed off his clothes.

With the Moon Bear watching, Dalin took a step, and his wood appendage fell from his pant leg. The straps had come loose during the attack. The bear jerked its head in surprise, sniffed the fake leg, took it in its mouth and trotted back inside the den.

"Damn it," Dalin said in a disgusted voice, watching the bear disappear with his mobility, while sitting in a bed of pine needles.

Anna wrapped her arm around her brother, getting him to his remaining foot, and helped him hop to the entrance of the den, grabbing the sack of their remaining apples as they passed the flustered horse. She clicked her cheek and Spiff followed hesitantly.

Dalin squeezed Anna's shoulder when they reached the entrance. He leaned in close. "You sure about this?"

Anna shrugged. "I'm pretty sure they won't eat me. You…not so much." She smiled and returned the squeeze.

Dalin pursed his lips sideways. "Good enough," he said, and the pair entered the warmth of the den, Spiff ducking in behind them.

~ ~ ~

The warmth of the Moon Bear den washed sweet relief over the travel-weary pair, filling their bones with instant warmth. Anna considered Phyllis left outside, but reaching overhead, she knew at once there would be no way to fit the horse inside. She would go outside and blanket the horse after they got Spiff settled. The pungent smell of Moon Bear musk assaulted their nostrils, but it was a small price to pay for the Saureped's wellbeing. Dalin struck a match and spotted his leg beneath the Moon Bear's chin, who had already curled into a ball with its prize. He motioned to Anna, and she traded out the leg for another apple, to which the bear didn't protest.

"Where should Spiff lay?" Anna asked the bear.

The Moon Bear shifted slightly over on its bed of forest litter, indicating a spot close by. Anna motioned for Spiff and pointed to the bedding. The Saureped looked at her with innocent animal eyes. "It's okay. I promise," she said with a smile that Spiff trusted wholeheartedly. Her reptilian-like friend stepped closer, gave her one more look seeking reassurance, and when Anna nodded, he bedded down next to the bear, his body sagging, seeming to relish in the warmth.

Dalin shook the match out, snuffing it between calloused fingers to kill any remaining heat, then put it in his mouth and swished it with saliva to make sure no fire remained. He chewed it a little, then spat it on the ground. Next, he got to the business of reattaching his leg, first rubbing his hand over the appendage to assure himself it hadn't been gnawed through. Finding only a few tooth impressions, he dropped his trousers and reattached the various harnesses, thankful the bear hadn't decided to use it as a chew toy.

Anna took the opportunity to go back outside and blanket Phyllis. When she was certain Dalin'd had enough time to make himself decent again, she came back and sat beside him, patting him on his good leg. "I bet you never thought you'd spend the night inside a Moon Bear's den." She sniffed a laugh at the preposterousness of their situation.

Dalin lay back, wiping his hand across his face, trying to remove the sticky apple juice. "Nawp. But I guess that's what we get for taking in strays."

"Yeah, I guess so," she said, thinking about the girl who had hid in their barn. The girl she thought had something to do with the falling of the divide. Dalin's heavy breathing told her he had already fallen asleep. She listened to the various snores and grunts of at least three other Moon Bears huddled together somewhere in the den, and a soft smile crossed her face. She was never more at peace than in the company of *critters*, as her mother had called them.

The smile faded when her thoughts returned to Bet. She hoped she was safe and that she had found her old friend and fellow conspirator, Bathezine. The girl was no older than she had been when the conflict had abruptly ended. No older than herself when she aided refugees to cross the divide. No older than her when she found that infant in the building and hid her away in the orphanage. Anna's eyes closed, lulled by Dalin's heavy breaths, in sync with the sleeping Moon Bears breath for breath. She fell asleep certain that her path and Bet's would cross again.

Forty-Two

The continuous hoot of an owl outside the den, along with the persistent whinny of Phyllis, pulled Anna from her much-needed slumber. The ground had been hard, but the accommodations, though somewhat heavy with the odor of sleeping bears, were warm and comfortable, and she'd slept hard and sound. Her eyes opened just before Dalin shook her. "I know, I know," she said through a scratchy early morning voice. Anna rolled to her side, trying to shake the sleep out of her head, then stumbled and half-crawled to the breach.

The near-dawn gray light sifting through the tall pines stabbed at her eyes in contrast to the dark interior, making her squint to focus on her owl friend as she blundered out of the den. Finding her feet, Anna stood and met the owl face to face as it perched over the entry. The owl made a series of noises while Anna nodded. When the owl finished its report, she thanked it many times. The owl blinked its big eyes, gave her a final hoot in return, and took flight on hushed wings.

Dalin stepped out in time to see the bird melt into the old growth of pines. He looked at his sister, waiting for the report and buttoning his trail coat. Anna glanced at him from the corner of her eyes, then tilted her head back, sighing at the approaching day. "They were joined by several riders during the night and broke camp about an hour ago. The boars are off their tethers. Get Spiff, will you?" Both knew what untethering the Scow boars meant. They would be able to run at speed once they caught scent, and the riders along with them. And a Scow boar free of its handler could inflict a lot of damage when it caught up with its quarry.

Dalin nodded, took Anna's hand, giving it a soft squeeze, then limped back inside. Anna readied Phyllis, and leaned her head against the horse's cheek. "Today will be a hard run. Take care of the man on your back," she said, scratching her on the neck. Phyllis groaned her readiness somewhat reluctantly, and her ears stood stiff and twitching. Anna patted her. "We'll all have a good rest when we get to where we need to be."

Spiff exited the den looking refreshed and ready, with Dalin trailing behind. The Moon Bear followed them both out, sniffing the air. Anna walked to the bear and pinched its fuzzy round ear between her fingers, massaging the tender lobe. The Moon Bear leaned its head against her, seeming to appreciate the gesture. "Thank you," Anna said, taking Spiff's reins. She reached in the saddle bag and pulled out a brightly colored orange and blue feather fruit, named for the softness of its flesh. She tossed it to the bear and held back a laugh as it bounced off its face. "My last one. Enjoy."

The Moon Bear sniffed the fruit and gobbled it up quickly, then raised its dark round nose to the air once more. "Pigs are coming."

Anna swung in the saddle and stole a glance at Dalin to make sure he had picked up on her urgency. Her brother patted his rifle to show he was ready for whatever may come. She frowned as she took a final look at the Moon Bear. "Mark the ground to cover our scent," she said, hoping the bears wouldn't be troubled by the boars.

The bear snorted with a lack of concern. "Pigs taste good."

~ ~ ~

Anna urged Spiff forward, and followed by Dalin, the two sped through the woods. They rode hard and fast, ducking beneath low-hanging branches for no more than a mile before the constant whip of limbs forced them to slow. An impenetrable copse of tangle-root fir finally brought them to a complete stop.

"We need to get back to high ground," Dalin said, bringing Phyllis alongside Spiff.

Anna spit a frustrated breath while dabbing at one of several scratches on her face with her sleeve. "We'll be exposed up there."

"An untethered boar isn't slowed by thick brush. We can outrun 'em in the clearing." Dalin turned the bay up the slope. "It's our only chance."

Anna watched him for a moment then looked back the way they had come. An uneasy sensation she couldn't place crawled through her, causing a greater sense of dread. She patted Spiff on his neck. "He knows more about this than I do. Let's move."

The pair rode for over an hour before finally reaching the tree line and open ground. Anna dismounted and called out for the owl.

Dalin eased his mount beside her, shaking his head. "We should keep moving. This is where we leave them in our dust."

"We also need to know where they are. If they've figured out we're headed west, they might try to cut us off."

"Five minutes. Then we move," he grumbled, then stole a sip from his water-skin. He sat in the saddle, nervously tapping the horn and checking his pocket watch every few seconds. After several minutes passed, he cleared his throat. "Your bird ain't coming. We gotta go."

"She'll be here. Another minute," Anna said, not masking her impatience.

"We don't have another minute. We go now."

Anna's shoulders slumped and she turned to Spiff when the owl appeared from the trees. She shot Dalin an *I told you so* look and held up her arm for the bird.

Dalin threw up his arms and returned to tapping the saddle horn while watching the conversation.

"Thank you. You've been a great help. Now go home," Anna said, then looked at Dalin.

The look in her eyes told Dalin all he needed to know. "They're gonna try to cut us off."

Anna nodded. "They've split up. A pair of riders are making their way through the trees about a mile back, and the boars are on our scent a little farther back." She climbed back on the Saureped. "We still might be able to get ahead of them. That or we go higher and try to lose them there."

Dalin looked toward the rocky peaks seemingly lost in thought until Anna made a noise. He looked at his sister. "We can't do this forever."

"We won't have to. I know where the barrier is, or was. Once we cross the head of the river, we'll be able to outrun them." Even as she said the words, she knew it was a false hope. She knew that, with the collapse of the barrier, the entire landscape could have changed, and she had no idea what they'd find there. Dalin gave her a sideways look that Anna knew would always be followed by something she didn't want to hear. She shook her head. "No."

"Yes. It's the only way." He looked back up the mountain. "Spiff's a reptile. He doesn't give much of a scent, and the horse does. You keep heading west, and I'll head up and draw them away from you."

"No. We're in this together. I'm not doing this alone. I need you with me. You can't." She tried to sound forceful, but ended up sounding like a pleading little sister. She stared at her brother with worried eyes, returned by an expression that told her his stubborn streak wouldn't be broken.

Dalin handed her an old revolver, holstered, with a strap full of ammunition. "I'll find a good spot and slow 'em down," he said, patting his rifle.

Anna held the pistol. "I don't know how to use it. You're the soldier, not me."

"You've been conscripted, little sister. You're in a war now, and your life might depend on it. We're losing time we don't have." He turned away, looking at the higher peaks. "I'll try to take down the boars, then Phyllis and I will hightail it west. Their horses ain't any fresher than her." Dalin gave her a crooked smile. "Best get going." He jerked the reins and headed up the slope without looking back.

Anna watched him go, sadness and anger battling in her heart for dominance. She guessed Dalin had made his decision the day before, and she knew that once he made up his mind, it was set in stone. She continued to watch his dust cloud disappear farther up the slope for another moment, and her head drooped as sadness won out in her heart. Anna looked westward and clicked her cheek. Spiff took the cue and started running with a jolt.

She rode for no more than twenty minutes before the men who had intended to cut their path off showed themselves at the tree-line below her. A pair of riders broke up the slope at an angle, whooping and hollering wildly. Anna smiled to herself at their stupidity. Had they stayed hidden, they might have had a chance at catching her. She doubled the reins around her fist and leaned in close to the Saureped's ear. "Time to show off your legs," she said, and followed it up with a hollow whistle. She braced herself, and the Saureped, free of restraint, burst into a sprint.

Anna braved a look back and saw the riders disappear with such rapidity it was as if they were heading the opposite direction. The men's calls vanished into nothingness, and all she could hear was the rush of wind and the furious taps of Spiff's feet moving over the ground so quickly she was sure if she spread her arms wide she could take flight. Twisted, windswept Bristlecone pines flew by in a blur as the Saureped kept up its breakneck speed for over an hour, until they reached gullies too wide for Spiff to leap across.

The Saureped slowed to a trot until finally coming to stop at Anna's behest. She slid out of the saddle, bent over to catch her breath, then stretched and shook out her cramped muscles from clinging for life on the wild ride. She had taken Spiff riding on several occasions to 'stretch his legs', as Dalin had called it, but had never had the nerve to let him run at full speed. The escape had at first been exhilarating—the speed and power displayed by the Saureped were incredible—but seeing the rocks whiz by at such speed soon made her exhilaration turn to terror when she realized what would happen if she took a tumble.

But she hadn't fallen, and they had left her pursuers many miles behind them. Anna patted Spiff on the shoulder telling him he had done well. The Saureped lifted his head from gnawing at a sapling poking its tender needles from beneath a patch of snow, snorted at her, then returned his attention to the well-deserved meal. She climbed halfway up a small hill and looked back at the way they had come. The peaks where she had left

Dalin were distant, purple monoliths silhouetted against a graying sky, and as much as she wanted to wait where she was for her brother, her instinct told her they shouldn't linger in one spot for too long. She continued to plod up the slope's loose soil, almost relishing the effort. Using her muscles felt good after so much saddle time.

When she reached the crest, Anna looked to the western horizon and saw something she hadn't seen before. Her jaw fell open with astonishment. From the enormity of what lay before her, she wondered how she could have missed it earlier. As far as she could see, running north and south, a shimmering wall stretched across the landscape, disappearing behind mountains and reaching high into the sky until it hid behind swirling bright white clouds. She pinched the bridge of her nose, blinked several times, and looked again, thinking it was an anomalous mirage. But it wasn't. It was the barrier, or what remained of it, that had once separated the realms of the Din and the Whist. She stood staring, unable to pry her eyes away.

Anna stood in wonderment at the spectacle for several minutes. Coming to her senses, she shook her head clear and called for Spiff. The Saureped plodded beside her, sniffing at her neck, disinterested in the spectacle. "There, Spiff," she said gazing at the scene once again. "That's where we have to go." She forced herself to pull away from the sight, took a swig from a skin, and mounted the Saureped. She didn't know how far they had to travel—it could be a few miles or a hundred; the sheer size of what she saw distorted her perspective—but they were headed toward it, and she would have ample time to stare ahead of her. She gave Spiff a nudge with her boot heels, and he started off at a slow trot toward the Whist.

Forty-Three

Bet sat on a rock eating the last of their provisions as Mandi-lyn hovered beside her, sniffing and chittering over Bet's broken knuckles. The Falkwith seed masked the pain, but the Flursh insisted on healing her injuries. Fortunately the bones were only fractured, not crushed like he ankle, but the healing still took time. "Do you think it's safe for Her-Gad-Ishu to land now? I didn't think about asking Moth."

Mandi-lyn lifted a stubby pink finger for her to wait and continued her work. After a minute, she lifted her head and looked at Bet, whiskers bobbing sluggishly. "That should do it. But do try not to punch anything for the next day or two. Your metacarpophalangeal joint on your middle finger was the most damaged and could take a little more time to heal properly."

Bet scrunched her eyebrows. "My what?"

The Flursh lifted the corner of her hat and looked at Bet with her bulbous black eyes. "Your knuckle."

"Oh," Bet said. She tentatively flexed her fingers, then smiled at her friend. "Thanks. You've been doing a lot of patching people up since you decided to come along."

"I didn't decide to come along. I was sequestered." She kneeled down and ran her nose along Bet's injured ankle. "But you're welcome. And I'm glad I came along." She untied Bet's moccasin and carefully eased it off her foot.

"Do you think it's safe for the others to come?" Bet asked again. "I could really use a ride."

"How would I know?" Mandi-lyn pulled off Bet's sock and ran her whiskers along the black and purple skin. She reared her head back, waving her hand at Bet's foot. "You really need to wash your feet."

Bet waved her hand at their surroundings. "Do you see a bath tub around here?"

Mandi-lyn scooped a handful of dirt and dumped it on Bet's foot. "Rub it between your toes. It will at least mask the smell a little." She worked on the ankle a little more then sat back and handed Bet her sock and shoe. "Surprisingly enough, you didn't cause any more damage, but I doubt it will ever be as it was before. It will ache in the cold and become arthritic if you were to become old."

"Guess I'll worry about that when the time comes," Bet said as she pulled on her moccasin. She looked across the rocky landscape. "Is it good enough to walk on? I have a feeling we shouldn't hang around here."

"Drullids?" Mandi-lyn asked while sniffing the air.

"No. We haven't seen any since that night I did, you know, the thing. Maybe that's all there were."

Mandi-lyn flashed Bet an unconvinced expression. "I doubt it. The caldera is vast and they move slowly. I'm certain there are more on the way. We should do our best to gone before they get here."

Bet ran her hand under hat, and scratched at her unwashed hair. "There's something out there, but I can't quite get a sense of it." Her eyes fixed on a spot in the distance. An eerie feeling crawled over her, and she knew at once that, even though she couldn't see what lay ahead, she had been there during a dream. It was the void she had felt before. As much as she didn't want to go there, a pressure in the back of her mind urged her to go that way. She forced her eyes away to find Mandi-lyn staring at her. "What?" she asked, breaking eye contact.

"Whatever you feel, it may be best we avoid the place you're looking at." Mandi-lyn began busying herself with writing in her journal. "Some things are best left unexplored."

"Yeah," Bet said, sounding distracted, her eyes drawn back to the unseen place in the distance. She flashed Mandi-lyn a half-smile. "But you don't know that until after you explore it."

"Or have the wisdom to listen to someone who does know." The Flursh put her pen and notebook away and cinched her bag closed. "I take it you'll be wanting to disregard my advice and go to the place we should probably avoid?"

"We made it through the dreaded Caves of Moth, didn't we? We escaped the Reacher before that. What could be worse?" Bet said and began walking.

"Many things. Might I remind you that Moth could have killed us with nothing more than illusions, not to mention escaping the Reacher nearly cost two of your friends' lives?"

Bet walked stiffly, looking straight ahead. "Do you want me to trace all of our life lines to see if any of us will die seeing to this task?"

"Seeing another's future alters it. If you saw that one of us were to die and warned whoever it was, it may cause him to die sooner or cost another their life. Altering the future or the past through your Talents can have unseen consequences."

"Then I'd look into the past and I'd prevent—"

"And you'd be stuck in an endless cycle of meditation, forever changing the landscape of what's to come. It's one thing to get a sense of danger and alter your actions, it's another to change what will come." Mandi-lyn adjusted her hat with a jerk. "Your Talents are strong and serve you well, and will help you on this task. But don't let that lull you into a false sense of security. Overconfidence is always the weakness of the strong, and it leads to their downfall. Prudence, fortitude, and temperance are the hallmarks of strength. Remember that."

Bet looked at the Flursh out of the corner of her eye. "You think I'm strong?" She meant it as a joke, but she saw that Mandi-lyn was not in a playful mood.

"Not yet. When you finally learn those three virtues and seriously take them to heart, then maybe. You show traits of all three, but you need to let them guide your actions. When you learn to subdue your impulses and passions, then you'll know strength. Real strength, not the strength of your Talents." They walked a few minutes in silence before Mandi-lyn spoke again, "The three virtues are what truly separate the Fair and the Foul. It's the same for those of the Din as it is for us. It's a universal truth for all creatures of thought."

Bet shuffled along the dusty ground, turning Mandi-lyn's words over in her head. She stumbled when her foot found an unseen rock hiding in the dirt. She grimaced, but refrained from blurting out one of the many new expletives she had learned from Bathezine.

Mandi-lyn looked at her with a bemused expression, seeming to know that Bet had just held back from slandering the rock's mother. "You're learning already."

"Maybe," she said through a laugh. She looked at Mandi-lyn with a suspicious squint. "You're a gambler, and a pretty fair card-cheat, from what I hear, plus you took pecans from those squirrel pigs."

"You speak true," Mandi-lyn said without looking at her.

"Well, doesn't that make you lean toward the Foul?"

"We all have our flaws. I've never claimed to be completely virtuous. Those of us raised in the Whist have that luxury at times." She lowered her head in reflection. "Though perhaps we shouldn't. But there are times in every person's life when you are forced to not be completely honest. When the truth can cause more harm than good at that moment in time."

Bet rolled her shoulders as if working a kink out. "Like how you're holding back from telling me something."

Mandi-lyn took a deep breath. "Bet, there are certain—"

"It's okay. I get it," Bet interrupted, not sounding the least bit upset. "I trust you. And I trust that, when the time comes, you'll tell me what it is. This Talent I have of knowing the truth or at least being able to tell if somebody is not being honest or is hiding something—it's nothing I can turn on and off, like I do the strength, which I can choose to use or not. It's like being an Oragoth, it's active all the time now. I'm not sure if I like it. Sometimes I'd like to go back to being oblivious, like I was in the Din."

"Are you so certain you were oblivious in the Din?"

Bet thought it over. Maybe she hadn't been. She always seemed to know, and if not know then at least had gut feelings when someone was lying. Thinking back on it, her guts got a lot of work during her stay at Malweather farm. Biscuit Head was always saying or doing things that were contrary to what Bet's instinct told her was true. But she usually dismissed it as her general dislike for the woman. "Maybe I wasn't. I just wasn't so in tune with it."

They passed through a group of tall jutting stones, and when they reached a clearing, Bet stopped. She stared ahead, her breath growing shallow, her fist clenched. Mandi-lyn watched Bet instead of what lay before them. "You've seen this before," Mandi-lyn said with a tone of certainty.

Bet only nodded. She licked her lips, desperate for the moisture that had suddenly evaporated. "The dream, or the vision I had," she said in a small voice. She looked at the grove of trees, gray and brittle, dead monuments to the life they once represented, exactly as she had seen it. Beyond that, partially obscured by the tree line, stood the old structure made of crumbling stone and mortar, as dead as the trees. But somehow it felt alive, as if it were calling to her—inviting her to step inside the wooden door she couldn't see but knew was there.

Bet's heart raced. She reached out with her mind to get a sense of what was within the walls. Nothing revealed itself. In fact, she couldn't get a sense of anything within. It was as if there was a great void in the fabric of the world. She had felt it all along while in the crater, like a phantom on the edge of vision, but being in its presence made it real. Sweat trickled down the back of her neck. She wiped at the itch and looked at Mandi-lyn.

Mandi-lyn stared at her with dark, worried eyes. "Perhaps now we should take a different course."

Bet felt herself shaking her head. "No. I'm supposed to go in there."

"Or someone wants you to go in there." Mandi-lyn took Bet's hand, looking at her with pleading eyes.

Bet studied her for a moment, pulled away, and walked toward the ruined building.

Forty-Four

Mandi-lyn hurried behind Bet. "You should really rethink what you're about to do. It could be a trap. If you can't sense what's inside, anything could be in there."

Bet kept walking, jerking at the sound of every dead stick she snapped beneath her feet. "Why can't I feel what's inside? Is it a Talent like a Vapid or some sort of barrier?"

"The only thing that can do that would be lead infused with silver. For whatever reason, nobody has been able to unravel the mystery, and it blocks Talents...all Talents. If you go inside, you'll be helpless, worse than you were in the fog." Mandi-lyn tugged at Bet's tattered sleeve, urging her to turn away.

"Then if something's waiting inside, it won't have Talents either. And I won't be completely helpless." She patted one of her hand picks, pulling away from Mandi-lyn's grip.

"Do you think weapons would do you any good against a pack of rabid Fangors, or an angry Chardragin?"

"What's a Chardragin?" Bet asked, coming to a stop beneath the low branches of a skeletal tree. She stood staring at the door. Its polished brass handle shone in the sunlight, as out of place in reality as it had been in her vision.

"You'd know one if you saw one." Mandi-lyn took Bet's hands in hers, squeezing them softly. "Don't do this. If you go in, I can't go with you, and I can't help you."

Bet kneeled to be eye level with the Flursh. "I don't want you to go in with me. This is something I have to do alone. I don't know why, I only know I have to."

"I fear it's a trap." Mandi-lyn looked at the bleak landscape. Her fur ruffled with a sudden chill.

"I hope you're wrong." Bet stood and squared her shoulders, facing the door not ten yards in front of them. She pointed to a clearing. "Go to that low rise. See if you can spot Her-Gad-Ishu. I think it's safe for them to come now." She looked at Mandi-lyn and gave her an insecure smile.

Mandi-lyn took a step back as Bet walked toward the door. She watched her take slow steps, then looked to the clearing. Glancing at Bet once more, and seeing that the girl wouldn't change her mind, Mandi-lyn turned away and hurried toward the clearing.

Bet approached the old wooden door and stood before it, her hand raised just above the handle. She hesitated and looked at the ancient ruin. Crumbled gray and pale-yellow ashlar blocks littered the ground in heaps along the walls. What remained of the walls stood twenty feet high, with no parapets, towers, or any other adornments to indicate it had been a castle. Why she ever thought of it as such, she didn't know. The word prison flashed in her mind, which caused a shiver to course over her. She shook off the sensation and grabbed the handle.

Her head immediately felt foggy and her legs turned to jelly. She let go of the handle, and put her hands on her knees, trying to rid herself of the feeling. She lifted her torso upright with great effort and stared at the door. *Is this what it's like to not have any Talents?* she wondered. The fog had been different. Her Talents had been muted, but hadn't felt like they were completely gone.

Bet considered Mandi-lyn's words and almost turned away. But the lure was too strong. She had to go inside. Steeling her nerves once again, Bet took hold of the handle and gave it a strong jerk. At first it didn't want to budge, but with a little more effort, the door opened with a protesting moan. A foul, dank breeze rushed through the doorway, assaulting her nose. She turned away from the smell, then peered inside and took a cautious step forward into a vast, darkened room.

Two small openings near the ceiling, like a ship's portholes, allowed shafts of light to enter from either side of the room. The dusty beams of light intersected on the floor ahead of her, highlighting nothing but an empty, rough stone floor. Bet felt relief that they didn't shine on another tablet of archaic script like the one in the cave. Her body felt sluggish and heavy as she walked farther inside. She examined the ceiling and was surprised to find it intact, contrary to the rest of the structure, which had fallen in such disrepair. Surely the ravages of time would have caused the ceiling to collapse by now. Bet reached out, trying to sense any life in the room. A wave of panic swept over her when she couldn't feel anything. She had grown so used to her Talents, it was as if a part of her had been lopped away.

She looked at the interior walls. Through the dim light, she saw that they were dark gray and smooth, not rough like the outer walls. She had seen all she needed or wanted to see. Bet decided that the Flursh's counsel had been right. She had to go. She turned with a jerk back to the door. A stout shadow passed in front of the light. The figure slammed the door shut, and Bet heard a familiar cackle. It was a sadistic laugh, a woman's laugh, a laugh she hoped to never hear again, but one that was, impossibly, in the room with her, more twisted than it had been the last time she had heard it. Bet gripped her pick.

"How did you get here?" Bet asked through a small, shaky voice.

"It's a long story," the woman's voice hissed. "But you're here now. And you've caused me a lot of trouble, girl."

Bet braced herself as Putrice Malweather's corpulent frame rushed toward her.

Forty-Five

Mandi-lyn scrambled up the dusty, gray slope, and began making a loud, chirping noise; a Flursh distress call. It could be heard from miles around by other Flursh, and she hoped a three-headed crow could hear it as well. She scanned the late afternoon sky, hoping for a sign.

"Where is that idiot crow? Circles overhead for hours when I don't need it, but takes a nap when I do."

She looked back to the stone building. Her limited rodent sight made much of the distant landscape a jumble of misshaped blurs, but she was sure she could she the door. And from what she could see, the glint of the brass handle had moved back to the closed position. She hoped Bet had come to her senses and left her adventurous urges behind. She called to her, waited a moment, but no reply came. Mandi-lyn scurried in a circle. Her gut told her Bet was inside, and the door was closed, which meant she was trapped.

Mandi-lyn chirped again and waited. Straining her eyes against the western horizon, she spotted an amorphous dark blob against the yellow-tinted, blue sky. "That had better be Her-Gad-Ishu and not some hungry thorn eagle," she muttered, wondering if their luck had run out.

She rummaged through her pack and found the little knife. The blade felt awkward in her hand. She wasn't much of a fighter, but she'd do her best against a hungry bird of prey. She chirped once more and noticed the shape turn in her direction. Her vantage point gave her an unobstructed view of the vast depression. She scanned the dead landscape and noticed clouds of blurry dust moving toward her from several directions. She knew at once what it meant. The Drullids were coming.

The Flursh's whiskers bounced furiously, her head swiveling between the advancing Drullids, the bird she hoped was the crow, and the stone building. She turned to the ruin, ready to abandon the knoll and rescue Bet, but thought better of it. She needed help, and Her-Gad-Ishu was her only escape if the Drullids fell upon her.

Mandi-lyn fumbled with the knife nervously, preparing herself for an act of violence she was unaccustomed to. Before this journey, her primary method of defense when faced with a threat, usually a sore loser at a card or chips table, was to run and find a nook or hole to hide in until the danger passed. Flursh had an uncanny ability to find the smallest of crevasses to hide in. But she knew that would do her no good here. The Drullids would sniff her out, and they would melt into each other, doubling in size and morphing into any shape they needed to drag her out of whatever hidey-hole she found. Even then, she knew she couldn't leave Bet to her fate.

"Hard-headed girl. Maybe next time she'll listen to me," she grumbled. Mandi-lyn rolled the knife in her hand once more and dropped it. She shook her head, staring at the blade in the dirt. "This isn't going to end well," she said, and pulled out her notebook. She scribbled something down, tore out the page, and folded it behind the cover. Taking a deep breath, Mandi-lyn retrieved her weapon, snapped and tied her bag closed, and waited.

The swirls of dust crept ever closer as Mandi-lyn watched. Fortunately the Drullids didn't move with any rapidity, but she knew they were persistent, untiring beasts that would pursue their quarry relentlessly until it tired or escaped the crater, or in her case, hitched a ride with a crow. She looked to the sky once again and could finally make out the distinct shape of Her-Gad-Ishu and his three heads. She took off her tricorn and waved it frantically in the air, even though she knew the bird's keen eyesight had likely already spotted her, but doing something felt better than standing helplessly idle. She allowed herself a slight sense of relief when the crow swooped low and cawed, acknowledging she had been spotted.

Her-Gad-Ishu swept in and circled just overhead, kicking up clouds of dust with its mighty wings. "Is it safe?" Her asked.

Mandi-lyn threw up her arms in a shrug. "You're not dead, so I'm assuming it is," she called back, shielding her eyes from the maelstrom. Truth was she didn't know if Moth's threat had passed, or if it had been true to begin with, but she'd find out in a moment or, more accurately, Her-Gad-Ishu would.

The crow alighted neatly in front of her. The three heads sagged in relief when they didn't die. "There are creatures coming toward you," Gad said.

"I noticed," Mandi-lyn replied curtly.

"Where is Bet?" Her asked. The three heads swung every direction, cawing and calling for Bet.

"Will you shut up," Mandi-lyn demanded. "She's in that building." She pointed, and when Ishu didn't look, she took his beak and directed him.

"We can't sense her," all three said at once.

"The building is voided. Protected against Users, as those in the Din would say. I'm guessing the interior walls are incased in lead and silver." Mandi-lyn pulled her bags close to her. "You need to take me there."

"You can't walk?" Ishu asked.

The Flursh didn't know if the talking head was concerned that she was injured or being difficult as usual. "I can walk. But the Drullids are coming, and I need to get there quickly, and you need to get the others. Tell them to come immediately and bring a wagon."

Her-Gad-Ishu looked at each other. "Why didn't you stop her?" Her asked.

"I tried. She wouldn't listen." Mandi-lyn turned her back on the crow and braced herself. "Now let's go. You're wasting time." The crow began to cluck. "No. Don't put me to sleep. I won't panic. I need to keep my wits."

Her-Gad-Ishu hopped on the Flursh's waiting shoulders and took flight. Despite her promises, Mandi-lyn felt anxiety rise when her stomach dropped as they skimmed the tree tops and sped toward the ruined structure. They flew for only a minute before the crow released her from its grip, and she tumbled in a graceless landing in front of the door. She dusted herself off and gave the crow a disgusted look, but considered herself lucky that she hadn't sustained any injuries, especially because she was still clutching the knife. She immediately grabbed the door handle and tugged. Touching the door caused a wave of nausea, and her arms felt weak and listless. The door wouldn't budge. She tried again, this time putting a foot against the wall, having the same results. She looked up at the circling crow. "Go get help. The door won't budge."

Her-Gad-Ishu swept down with claws ready to take her. Mandi-lyn sighed. "No. I'll keep trying. Just...just go. Fly like you've never flown before."

In a great swirl of dust, Her-Gad-Ishu flew off faster than Mandi-lyn had seen it fly, save perhaps when they were being chased by the Mastives. She watched her ride fly into the horizon, and as she watched the crow disappear, she hoped she hadn't made a mistake. "You'd better hurry, crow," she muttered and got to work with her knife, trying to disassemble the brass handle.

The minutes passed with Mandi-lyn having no effect on the door handle. There were no screws or seams to pry and it appeared the solid metal handle's locking mechanism was on the other side. She hoped it wasn't a dead-lock, one where once the lock was sprung, it could never be unlocked. She stared at the wood door and stabbed at it near the handle, hoping to splinter it away. The tip of the blade broke with the effort.

Mandi-lyn shook her head with disgust and stumbled away. Free from the Talent-nullifying effect of the building, her head cleared, and she sat with a huff. She looked at her broken knife. "Stonewood. I should've known. This accursed building has my brains in a jumble."

The Flursh walked along the wall, looking for weak points, ears and nose sharp for the Drullids all the while. She hoped they had given up their pursuit when the crow took her in the air, but doubted that was the case. Finding no other ways in, she returned to the door and stood in front of it, trying to come up with a solution. She had read enough about locking mechanisms during her studies to know that dead-locks had at least one iron shaft, about two-foot long, that sprung into place when triggered. Some had four or six that would bar the door in every direction. If someone had gone through the trouble to build this prison in such a desolate place, she figured it was the latter. The stone wall could be chipped away, but that would take the better part of a day if not longer, even if she had the proper tools. She thought about burning the door down, but Stonewood was fire resistant and it would only char at best. Some said that the wood was stronger than stone, which made it notoriously hard to work with. Only those with the greatest strength Talent could shape or cut the wood.

Mandi-lyn threw her hat against the door in frustration. She stood with her hands on her hips, certain there had to be a way in. "But what if there isn't? What if this was designed to imprison someone for life—to let them spend eternity rotting away until they turned to dust?"

Deciding those thoughts would do her no good, she retrieved her hat and returned to her contemplations. Staring at the door, lost in thought, her ear twitched at the sound of a snapping twig near the corner of the building. She spun toward the sound, whiskers bobbing madly, ears stiff, listening. It sounded like something being dragged across the dirt, a steady *swoosh, swoosh, swoosh*. The rhythmic dragging grew louder as it steadily drew nearer.

The same noise came from the other end, and Mandi-lyn stood frozen, trying to see or smell what was coming toward her. She didn't have to guess. The Drullids had found her. She looked back at the door and lowered her head. "I'm sorry, Bet. There's nothing I can do for you now."

Forty-Six

Bet brought her hands up in time to block Putrice's slap. Instead of taking it, as she had so many times before, she lashed out and delivered a solid punch to the woman's chin. Had she been outside, free of the prison where her Talents were blocked, the blow would have shattered the foul woman's jaw. But she wasn't, and all it did was cause her head to jerk back. Putrice came at her again, and Bet punched her square in the nose. This time the woman stumbled back clutching her nose, and fell on her backside.

Putrice sat for a moment, blood streaming from her nose. She rolled to her feet, spat a curse at the girl, and charged forward, head down, ready to tackle her. Bet didn't have her Talents, but she still had Old Babbers' training. She neatly stepped aside, avoiding the woman's bulk and delivered a palm strike to back of her head, sending Biscuit Head sprawling face first on the rough floor. Bet winced, shaking her hand; apparently, the effects of the Falkwith seed were wearing off, or more likely, were nullified by the room.

Bet stared at the woman with contempt. The year spent as her unwilling servant, the insults, the continuous abuse and lashings, flooded back to her. She stepped toward Putrice, right fist clenched, ready to strike again, when a shadow passed over the porthole. Bet looked up just in time to see Her-Gad-Ishu's tail-feathers disappear. She stopped and took a breath. The thought of her friends, her family, brought her back to her senses. As much as she wanted to beat the woman senseless, to pay her back for the atrocities she had laid upon her, she couldn't allow herself to give in to hate.

She remembered Moth telling her to stay balanced in her emotions, and beyond that, she wondered what the others would think of her for beating up an old woman. She stared at Putrice, who was now kneeling in the gloom, head rolled back, spitting the dripping blood from her lips, issuing one vile curse after another toward her, and loosened her fist.

"You're gonna pay for all the trouble you caused me." Putrice tried to stand, but collapsed back to her knees. "Me, an old woman, stuck in this dungeon, wearing nothing but rags, nothing to eat 'cept rats and bugs."

It was then that Bet noticed that Biscuit Head was wearing what appeared to be nothing more than a large burlap sack with holes cut out for arms and head. She would have felt pity for any other person, but she had none for Putrice. She tried to let go of the contempt, but as she looked at her sunken, beady eyes, anger flared again. "You caused your own troubles. Everything that's happened to you was brought on by no one but yourself." She turned away, intent on leaving the woman in the room to rot.

"This is your fault, girl. If you hadn't runned off, I'd still have my farm. And Harrelle, that poor, old, dear man. He'd still be around, seeing to his chores, not locked up in another cell with that demon. Probably dead by now anyways."

Bet spun on her heels. "Harrelle? What demon? What other cell?" Bet looked for another way in or out, wondering what other cell the woman spoke of. She hadn't seen any other doors, but she hadn't bothered to check. And Harrelle, if he was locked up, too, she would do what she could to help and return the favor he had done for her. She had to do something. She flexed her injured left hand, wincing a little, and tucked it under her other arm. She regretted slapping the back of Putrice's head only because it might have reinjured her hand. If the demon Putrice had spoken of was who Bet suspected it was, she would need all of her strength.

Putrice seemed to sense her confusion; her face creased into an oily smile when she saw Bet protect her hand. "The demon, girl. Tell me you haven't had the pleasure yet." She spat out a sickly cackle. "You will. Trust me, you will. Did they blindfold you before they brought you down here? If they caught you, then maybe I'll still get my reward and get out of here. Don't know why they'd bring you here. But the demon did say he wanted you dead."

Bet was puzzled, until she realized Putrice had no idea where she was. As far as the woman knew, she was still in the Din, and in a prison or dungeon. She took a step back as Putrice struggled to her feet. "Whose dungeon are we in?" she asked, keeping an eye on her foe. Bet considered kicking her back to the ground, but the moment had passed. She took a couple more steps back toward the door.

Putrice snorted a derisive laugh. "His lord majesty the king's. Who else's? I'll snap his neck if I ever get out of here. Locking an old woman up. Letting that demon torment me. He'd deserve it." She looked at the walls and ceiling in a panic, as if someone was listening. "But first," she scanned the walls the again. "But first I'll take care of this problem."

"Before you get to doing what you think you're gonna do, answer me a question." Bet took another step back and felt the wall behind her. She stole a quick glance and saw the door to her right. The arched shape was there, but there was no handle, and the wood had been covered by the same lead paneling that covered the rest of the room. She looked back at Putrice, who was wringing her hands as if in anticipation of a long-awaited meal. Bet had to wonder if whatever madness the Reacher had put in the woman's already twisted mind would make her want more than rats for dinner. She watched the woman take one greedy step toward her. Bet put up one finger. "Answer this. If I was a prisoner, like you, do you think they would allow me to carry weapons?" She pointed to the ice picks, the bandolier, and other accessories. Bet was pleased to see Putrice's face contort in confusion as she tried to sort out the riddle.

Putrice stared at Bet, her expression flashing between hatred, confusion, sadness, then to determined violence. Her face curled into something less than human. Bet thought it looked as if all the years of dark thoughts and ugliness the woman had put upon others came together in a single instance of warped, hate-filled focus. She briefly wondered how many 'servants' the woman had purchased from the orphanage before her. She cast the thoughts aside when Putrice began making a guttural growl followed by a sickly cough. The woman spat a wad of phlegm in her direction and clenched both fists. Bet felt for the door once again and gave Putrice a curtly nod. "This is where I leave you," she said and pushed the door. Panic coursed through her when the door didn't budge. She tried again then braced herself when she heard Putrice's gurgled laugh behind her.

Putrice threw her full weight against Bet, pinning her to the door. "You ain't goin' nowhere, sweetie. You're all mine now." She took Bet's injured left hand and twisted it behind her back, and used her other arm to take her in a chokehold. Bet used her free hand to try to pry the woman's arm away from her throat with no effect. She reached for her pick. Seeming to know what she was trying to do, Putrice pulled Bet back and slammed her between the stone wood door and her corpulent frame.

Bet felt her breath leave her from the impact, then felt her feet leave the ground, followed by a brief sensation of weightlessness while Putrice lifted her bodily and slammed her to the stony floor. She tried to shake the stars from her head, pushed herself up, but fell back, rolling to her back just in time see Putrice pounce on top of her. Bet grunted, feeling what little breath she'd regained leave her chest under the woman three times her weight.

"Bigger'n you have tried, little girl. Bigger'n you have tried," Putrice hissed, then slapped Bet across the face with her meaty hand, followed by another. Bet barely had enough time to bring her hand up to diffuse the third blow. Putrice took both of the girl's arms and pinned them to the side. "Others tried to fight back, too. They all ended up the same way you will. Balls of sniveling snot, crying for mercy."

Bet closed her eyes as droplets of blood and spittle rained across her face, and winced at the smell of halitosis stinging her nostrils. She writhed, trying to shift her weight to throw the woman off her and became vaguely aware of the pieces of the Staff of the Whist jabbing into her back. She hadn't come all this way to let this creature destroy all she had worked for. And that's what Putrice was—a creature. Any semblance of humanity, if she ever had any, was gone, destroyed by whatever means the Reacher had taken to bring her to the Whist. Putrice released her arms and delivered a solid punch to her face. Bet felt her eye begin to swell closed almost immediately.

"After I'm done with you, I'm gonna make you my dinner, just like I did your little bird friend." She punched Bet once more and sat on her chest, cackling like a madwoman.

Pooch-kin, Bet thought. Out of all of her friends, the Chook-chook was the one she depended on the most, and she was sure he depended on her just as much. The thought of her friend brought a sense of calm over her, even as she covered her face from another barrage of slaps and punches. The calm let her think clearly, and with it came the familiar sense of serenity she had felt when facing the Reacher. She had thought that feeling was a Talent, but it wasn't. It was something that came regardless of Talents. She could use her Talent to project it on another, as she had with the Mastives, but she realized the peace was internal, a state of mind. She let go of the hate, anger, and fear, as well as the happiness and love, becoming even and still. She opened her eyes as Putrice reared back to hit her again, and with a calm, easy motion, snatched an iron bearing from her bandolier, and slammed it against the woman's mouth, breaking what few teeth she still had.

Putrice reared back in surprise and pain, and Bet shifted her hips beneath her, thrusted upward, and was able to squirm from under the weight. The woman grabbed for her, screaming incoherent profanities. Bet pulled away, took the bearing, and smashed it against her mouth once more, forcing it in the toothless cavity and down her throat. She watched as the woman clutched at her throat, rasping in barely audible whispers, with eyes bulging in horror as certain death came for her.

Bet turned away, took a step toward the door, but stopped, listening to the gurgling Biscuit Head slap her puffy hand against the floor, attempting to beg for help. Bet's shoulders slumped and she went to Putrice, pushed back the woman's shoulders until she was on her knees, then delivered a strong kick to her abdomen. The kick dislodged the ball, which hit the ground with a metallic clunk, stopping at Bet's feet. She kicked it aside and resumed her walk to the door.

"Don't you walk away from me. I'm not through with you yet, girl," Putrice called through heavy breaths in a scratched voice.

Bet turned to her once more, adjusting her bags and belt. She untied a segment of the Staff of the Whist and felt the heft of it in her hands. She thought about what it took to break the staff fifteen years before. She knew she wasn't an Omia Temporian, nor did she have the other staff, and decided it was safe. She walked to Putrice, who was still issuing every vile insult she could, and clubbed her on the head with the crystalline segment. Putrice fell with a whimper. Bet blew out a long breath, spotted her hat and picked it up, then slapped the dust off against her thigh. She grabbed her pick and got to work on trying to open the door.

Forty-Seven

Her-Gad-Ishu hopped to Bathezine upon landing at the camp and the three heads blurted out Mandi-lyn's message simultaneously. The Ursian threw up his hands, urging them to slow down. "Bet's in trouble?" At hearing this, the others hurried to his side.

"Yes," Her said. Gad and Ishu kept their beaks closed, letting the other explain. "She is trapped in a building that blocks her Talents. The Flursh is attempting to free her, but the Drullids are coming for her."

Babbers didn't need to hear more. She rushed to prep the wagons with Le'lel's help.

Bathezine turned and took Errel by his shoulders. "We're goin' for her. I don't care what Moth said, we're going for her. If we die, we die tryin'."

"Of course we are," Errel said. He looked to the crow. "Is there a way down for the wagons?"

"There is a gradual slope several miles away, which should suffice," Gad said.

"And you've seen the building?" Bathezine asked, to which the three heads nodded. "Okay. You'll lead the way." He went to Jangol and helped Tiny Nat harness the wagon.

Errel bounced between the two wagons, assisting where he could. When he could do no more, he went to Bathezine's side. "We'll save her, you know that, right? We'll save them both."

Bathezine nodded, trying to erase the doubt he felt. "I hope so. I ain't gonna lose her. I ain't." He gripped the sideboard, ready to pull himself onto the driver's bench.

"You're not." Errel rested his hand on Bathezine's arm. "She's strong and she's clever, even without her Talents. She's proven herself time and again."

"I know," he replied with a nod and climbed up. Errel took his cue and joined Babbers and Le'lel. Bathezine looked at the others, saw they were ready, then turned his attention to the crow. "Take us there," he said. Her-Gad-Ishu took flight and the others followed, churning up clouds of dust as they rushed to their friends' aid.

Tiny Nat squatted behind Bathezine, buzzing and humming in conversation with other Vivicons somewhere far away. He made an odd click of a noise and immediately stopped his conversation. He sat on the rail board behind Bathezine and tapped him on the shoulder.

Bathezine turned his head away from the road toward the Vivicon. "What?" Tiny Nat hummed for a second and twitched his head, receiving another message. "You have something to tell me?" the Ursian asked impatiently.

"Yes. We have found the joining of the realms."

"Okay. And where is it?" Bathezine grimaced when the wagon rolled over a pothole in the hardpan road. "Watch the ruts, Jangol. You almost tossed me off my seat." The Rhinodon snorted at the exaggeration.

"It borders the Waste at the river and runs north and south as far as one can see. The Twist River is gone, of course. The other side, the realm of the Din, is hidden behind what appears to be a bank of fog."

Bathezine snorted. "Those ain't just storm clouds, then."

"There is more," Tiny Nat said, cutting off further commentary from the Ursian.

"Figured as much," Bathezine said and rolled his hand in the air. "What else ya got?"

"Scouts from the Din have already crossed. As of right now, they have reached Fiverton." Tiny Nat watched Bathezine, waiting for the information to sink in.

He urged Jangol to move faster, then did a double-take at the Vivicon. "If they've reached Fiverton, that means they're no more than a day out from Illguard." He shook his head. "For a sleepy town, that place seems like it's the center of all things. Did ya warn the townsfolk?"

"We have. The remaining Andolan airship has begun evacuating the injured. Fiskers has taken it upon himself to lead a team to confront the scouts. Some of us will join them." Tiny Nat scooted back down and folded his legs beneath him, indicating the conversation was over.

"There's nothing we can do about it now. We've got bigger concerns. I'm sure they have things under control for now," he said to himself, knowing that Tiny had returned to his communications with the hive. He drove on, his mind lost in worry for Bet and for the town that was the closest thing to home he had. Focused on his thoughts, he didn't notice the small girl sitting next to him. He glanced sideways and let out a startled cry.

"You're sure hard to track down, Bear-man," Misty said, her teeth glowing in a bright smile.

"Where'd you come from?" he yelled, followed by a few choice words the girl probably hadn't heard before.

Misty's infectious smile didn't waver beneath his colorful language. "From town. I've been trying to catch up with you for a day now. I found if I look at a place, I can go there—any place, as long as I can see it. You sure made those squirrel pigs mad."

"Snickers. They call 'em Snickers." Bathezine looked at the child and shook his head. "Listen, we're about to do something awfully dangerous, so I need you to go on back home. Ya got me?"

Misty nodded, showing only modest disappointment. "Okay. But I thought you'd wanna know someone came to town looking for you. Both of you. You and Bet."

"I'm sure there's more than a few people lookin' for me. You said he's lookin' for the two of us?"

"Not a he—a she. She's pretty, but looks a little sad. She was riding a big lizard thing and had a fangy dog with her."

"Fangy dog?" He took it to mean a Fangor. "You get a name?"

"She said her name is Anna."

Bathezine sat up at hearing the name. "Anna? You sure she said her name was Anna?"

"Sure as my name is Misty. You know her?" The girl sat proud at bringing the Ursian important news.

"If it's who I think it is, I do." He thought about the last time he had seen Anna. She was no older than Bet back then. He patted the girl on the head. "Ya did good. But ya gotta get back now. And get outta town."

"The men from the Din are coming, huh?" she asked with a trace of sadness. "Ma and Pa are packing, but they wouldn't tell me why. But I knew it."

"I'm sure ya did. If you run into Anna, I want ya to tell her to wait there. No, tell her to leave. Tell her to meet us at Tiny Nat's ferry on the Plece River. And if we're not there within a week, tell her to cross and head for Azural. She'll be safe there. Ya got that?" He looked at her sternly to make sure she understood the importance of the message.

"Right here," she said, tapping her finger against her head. She recited the message to let him know she understood.

Bathezine nodded. "Good. And ya did good, girl. Thank ya. Now ya gotta get lost." He looked ahead, seeing they were approaching the place Her-Gad-Ishu was circling.

Misty flashed her bright smile once more, said 'bye', then disappeared in a blink.

Bathezine sat in thought for a moment until he heard Tiny Nat sit up. He looked back at the Vivicon with a scowl. "You didn't know someone was in Illguard lookin' for me and Bet?"

Tiny Nat cocked his head at the Ursian. "You should know by now that we cannot be everywhere at once."

Bathezine made a low growl and relented. "Yeah, well... I reckon you have a point." He looked at Jangol. "Hurry up. We still got a ways to go before we get to Bet, and the day ain't gettin' any longer."

Forty-Eight

Alternating between running on two legs and all fours, Mandi-lyn had put some distance between her and the Drullids. She had tried unsuccessfully to open the door, working on it until the last possible moment before the Drullids reached her. When she was able to see their horrible, gray, flesh-dripping faces clearly, she decided it was time to go. The creatures, monsters—Mandi-lyn couldn't decide on which, finally settling on aberrations—much like the Floragads, were slow. Not turtle-slow—they could move across the ground in semi-quick bursts—but slow enough for a Flursh who was proficient at much quicker bursts of speed. She stopped and leaned against a tree to catch her breath. Keeping her ears sharp for any approaching enemy, she allowed herself a quick drink of water.

She took off her hat and panted, trying to cool off. The ever present dust quickly coated her pink tongue and she licked her hand to try to remove it, which in turn only added more dirt to her tongue. Foregoing dignity, she did her best to spit. Owing to the fact that rodents aren't the best spitters, she only managed to drool down her front. She gave up and let the dust stay.

Mandi-lyn searched the sky for a sign of the crow. Finding none, she scanned the dead trees for movement. Several minutes passed with no movement heard or spotted. She turned her nose up and sniffed, but the things gave off no discernable scent. Finally, she lowered her face to the ground and her sensitive whiskers picked up the subtle vibrations of slogging feet. She detected three, not more than twenty yards ahead of her, spread out, making slow, deliberate movements. A moment later she picked up the vibrations of a fourth to her right and a fifth to her left. She soon picked up a pattern to their movements. When the two to either side of her moved, the three ahead of her stopped for a time. They would pause, and the process would repeat in reverse order. They were hunting her, and seemed to know her tricks.

Mandi-lyn listened, and heard the subtle scrape of a foot against the dirt to her right. She snapped her head, but only saw the dark shape of the trees. Deciding prudence was the best policy, she turned and began scurrying farther away from the prison. She made it no more than a few yards before the one she hadn't detected, the one that had stood perfectly still, waiting for its prize to be corralled to it, reached out from behind a forked tree and nabbed her by the arm.

Mandi-lyn screeched, squirming wildly, as she tried to break free from the Drullid's powerful grip. The Drullid lifted her in the air until she was eye level with the six-foot-tall beast. She watched the needle-like appendage slide out of its elongated proboscis, twitching in the air, probing its victim. With no other recourse, and with the needling probe drawing closer, she lifted her head and bit into the Drullid's arm, biting clean through with her large rodent incisors. An eruption of viscous fluid flowed into her mouth, coating her tongue with an acrid, rotten taste; it was like biting into carrion. She felt a sharp jab in her neck from the needle just before the hand fell away from the Drullid's arm, still attached to her own.

She slung the severed hand away and stumbled from her attacker while clutching at her neck. She ran for several yards until she saw the Drullid that had been to her right moving toward her with much more speed. Jagging to her left, she sprinted away and didn't stop until she came upon the juts of stone that littered the landscape. Exhausted, injured, and terrified, Mandi-lyn climbed the tallest rock she could find and hoped her pursuers would give up their hunt. She knew with certainty they wouldn't.

Mandi-lyn spent the first several minutes of her reprieve trying to get the rancid taste of the Drullid goo out of her mouth. The purple, almost black gunge coated the fur around her mouth, and its tackiness pinned her whiskers to her face. She looked at her arm, and with the exception of some tenderness, she found she was mostly unharmed. Then she touched the spot on her neck where the Drullid had pricked her. The site was angry and swollen, but surprisingly not very painful. She attempted to heal the wound, and draw out whatever toxin or bacteria she was sure was causing the irritation, but was unsuccessful. With nothing more to do except wait for either the crow or the Drullids to find her, she began writing in her notebook, noting how the Drullids didn't seem to have a skeletal structure, something she'd determined after biting through the arm. She shook in revulsion at the recollection.

From her vantage point, Mandi-lyn could see across the crater, the dead trees surrounding the ruinous looking stone prison and its low arched roof. She estimated she had ran over a mile, and with the Drullids still on the prowl somewhere unseen, she would be hard pressed to make it back with her life intact. Searching the sky for a sign of Her-Gad-Ishu, and on the verge of cursing the bird for not having returned yet, she spotted an oddity that made her question her sense of direction. Large cumulus clouds were rolling in from the east. She looked to the late afternoon sun, making sure it was still on its westward trajectory toward sunset, and it was. Her sense of direction was intact; however, the clouds were headed in the wrong direction. Clouds, without fail, always rolled in from the west, over the Malt Sea and the greater ocean beyond. She concluded that the falling of the barrier from the Din to the Whist had affected weather patterns, and wondered how much more had changed.

Mandi-lyn scribbled a few notes about the weather phenomenon, then scanned the sky once again. Her spirits picked up when she saw the familiar black blob flying toward the prison. She stood and began waving her arms in frantic gestures. The blob that was Her-Gad-Ishu didn't alter its course. Surveying the ground twenty feet below her, Mandi-lyn decided to try her distress chirp once more. A moment later Her-Gad-Ishu changed course, but her relief was short-lived as the sound had also roused the waiting Drullids. "They were trying to wait me out," she mumbled. She hoped they couldn't climb.

Four Drullids closed in on the jut of stone and, when they reached it, Mandi-lyn was puzzled to see that they just stood below, not looking up. The largest of the four reached out and touched the rock, and its arm recoiled on itself, shrinking to half its size. She had her answer to the puzzle of why they didn't climb the rock. Whatever properties were in the stone caused an adverse reaction on the Drullids, and she wrote that in her notes, hypothesizing that Moth had endued the otherwise common basalt stone with some sort of energy, a repellant of a sort. Her ruminations were cut short when two other Drullids began to meld with the first one, tripling its size. The creature's head was now just a few feet below her. Its roiling flesh arm reached over the precipice, avoiding the rock, but still couldn't reach her. She saw that the fourth Drullid was coming to join the other. There was nowhere for her to go but down.

Mandi-lyn considered projecting a render, but it was too late for that. She looked around and spotted a particularly fragile looking spike of rock near the opposite edge. She began tugging on it, hoping she had the strength to break it loose. The fourth Drullid melded in less time than the others took, and Mandi-lyn doubled her efforts, straining with all her strength until a fragment of the stone broke away, causing her to fall back and nearly topple over the side. The broken piece wasn't as big as she'd hoped for, but there was little time to worry over it—the Drullid's elongated arm now stretched over the top, groping the air for its prey. Mandi-lyn barked out in panic and jabbed the rock into the three-fingered hand. The jab had the desired effect, causing the arm to retreat on itself. She did the same to the second arm and looked at the beast, half-amused at seeing the hands wiggle on stumpy little arms.

Not knowing how long it would take for the arms to grow back to their original length, she stepped back to the center of her perch, waiting for the next attack. Standing there, with a small sense of pride in fending off the attack, she heard Her-Gad-Ishu's caw. She had never been so happy to see that idiot crow, and vowed to never be insulting to the bird again.

Her-Gad-Ishu circled the stone tower, examining the Drullid until finally deciding to alight beside the Flursh. "Where's Bet?" Her asked.

"She's still in the building," Mandi-lyn answered.

"Why are you way over here?" asked Gad.

"Those things, the Drullids, were after me." She pointed at the gray-skinned beast whose arms had doubled in length since the last time she'd looked.

"They have little arms," Ishu said.

"Not for long," Mandi-lyn said, swallowing the smart reply forming in her throat. "Where are the others?"

"They are on their way," answered Her.

Mandi-lyn looked to the distance and saw blurry gray fans of dust, which could only mean the wagons were coming as fast as Jangol and Alice could pull them. "Good. Take me to them. We need to warn them of the Drullids." She got in position to be carried and rubbed at the Drullid sting on her neck, noting the swelling had doubled in size.

Mandi-lyn braced herself as Her-Gad-Ishu fluttered above then took hold of her shoulders and carried her away from the Drullid. She watched the jutting stone and trees shrink below her, and clutched the fragment of rock tightly, hoping she wouldn't need it again.

Forty-Nine

Her-Gad-Ishu flew above the wagons and swept in, neatly depositing Mandi-lyn on the fly in the bed behind Bathezine, then flew ahead, leading them toward the stone prison. Bathezine stole a quick glance back. "Where'd you come from?"

Mandi-lyn brushed herself off, then fell to her back in exhaustion. "I was on a rock." She searched the wagon until finding a water skin. She dumped the water on her face, and tried to scrub the dried, purple ooze from her whiskers, saving a few sips for a drink. Tiny Nat hummed beside her and examined the goop. "Hi, Tiny. Glad you can join us," she said, patting him on the arm as he curiously scraped the substance from her face.

"We are glad to be in your company, as well," Tiny said. He studied the swelling on her neck. "You have been stung."

"Something like that." She looked down when Pooch-kin began chirping incessantly. "Don't worry, we'll get Bet. She's clever for a human. I'm sure she'll be fine," she said, though her tone didn't match her words.

"How far 'til we reach the girl?" Bathezine yelled over the rumble of wagon and hooves.

Mandi-lyn squinted ahead. "Not far. But there are things you need to know." She went on the recount the events after leaving Moth, shouting through most of it, and pausing several times to answer questions. She told them all she knew of the Drullids and their apparent immortality.

When she finished her tale, Bathezine urged Jangol onward until they rode alongside Old Babbers. He jerked his thumb to the back of the wagon, and Mandi-lyn gave Babbers and Errel beside her a half-hearted wave. "Tiny, tell them what Mandi told us." Tiny Nat fluttered to them and landed beside Babbers as Errel made room for him.

Her-Gad-Ishu circled back and eased between the two wagons in flight. Both Her and Ishu told them they were nearly there and warned them to mind the trees. Bathezine told Jangol to slow down when they reached the line of dead trees, and checked over the wide array of weapons strapped to him. As they entered the dead copse, he told Mandi-lyn to take the reins, then leapt off the bench. He hit the ground with a stumble, then ran toward the building. To his side, Old Babbers did the same.

Babbers, the quicker of the two, reached the door first, took a single-handed sledge she had tucked in her belt and began beating on the handle. She stumbled back when the Talent-blocking effects made her head swoon. Hearing the howl of Bathezine, she jumped out of the way just before the charging Ursian slammed into the door. He staggered backwards a few steps before falling to his backside.

"That's not gonna work," she said, standing over him, offering him a hand.

Bathezine snorted and accepted her hand. He stood rubbing his shoulder then placed his ear against the door. He clutched his head and stumbled back the same as Old Babbers had. "Reckon the Flursh was right about the lead. Maybe Bet'll just come out when she's done doin' what she's doin' in there."

Babbers raised an eyebrow at him. "You really believe that?"

Bathezine scratched under his beard. "Just talkin'. Lemme see that beater." He took the hammer and examined the door.

"I already tried that. As soon as I got close, the thing felt like it weighed fifty pounds."

"Yeah, well I'm stronger'n you naturally." Instead of beating at the door, he began hammering at the surrounding stone. He hammered at the wall for a minute or two before his arm fell to his side and the hammer slipped from his grip. "Didn't realize how dependent on my Talents I was." He adjusted his tunic and stepped away from the effects of the building. "I don't like her being in there, defenseless."

"She ain't defenseless. She's smart and knows a little about fighting if it comes to that. For all we know, there's nothing in there besides her." Babbers folded her arms and studied the wall.

Bathezine aped her movements but turned away when he heard the wagons arrive. He picked up the sledge and walked toward Errel. "Can you burn through Stone wood?"

"Nothing can burn through Stone wood except acid," Errel said as he climbed down. "I didn't think to pack any acid."

Mandi-lyn peered over the wagon rails and pointed to the hammer Bathezine carried. "That won't work unless you plan on breaking the walls down." She watched Bathezine return to the door. When he had gone, she stood and unslung her pack full of notebooks and various other writings. She held the sack out to Errel. "Moth said I should give these to you."

Errel's blue face crinkled in confusion. "Me? Why would he say that? I'm not a Charge."

"Because not only are you a knight, you're also a scribe. I'm sure you read Flursh shorthand." Mandi-lyn closed her eyes and clutched her neck for a quick moment.

"Yes, I can read most living languages. But you're perfectly capable of transcribing your own notes," Errel said, pushing the bag back toward her.

Mandi-lyn pushed it back, leaned over the rail, and vomited a vile purple fluid. Errel quickly took the bag and tossed it on the driver's bench, and looked at her with concern. Tiny Nat and Le'lel came to her as well. After nearly a minute of retching, she looked up at Errel. Her dark eyes carried a gray pallor. "I think, perhaps, Moth knew something," she said and slid to her side.

Errel leaped in the wagon beside her. He saw the Drullid sting; her fur had fallen out around the swollen flesh, and the skin had turned gray.

"Antidote!" he yelled. "We need an antidote."

"We gave it to Bet when she was stung by the Troojian," Mandi-lyn groaned.

"Tiny, can you do anything for her?" Errel asked, his voice filled with panic.

"We can only counter our own venom." Tiny Nat looked Mandi-lyn over. "But we can see if it will slow the spread." He reached toward her and extended the stinger from his wrist.

Mandi-lyn grasped his hand and shook her head. "No. It might infect you."

Tiny Nat pulled his hand away. "We have gone in search of an antidote." He buzzed quietly for a second. "One has been found, but it will take some time to get here."

"How long is *some time?*" Errel asked.

"No sooner than morning." Tiny Nat looked at Mandi-lyn. His expressionless face somehow seemed to convey sympathy for their friend.

Mandi-lyn sat up and leaned against the rail. "Bet needs our help. Go. Help her. She is what we thought," she said to Errel.

Errel closed his eyes for moment, then set his jaw. "Okay. Tiny, stay with her. You too, Pooch-kin." The Chook-chook chirped his affirmative. "C'mon, Le'lel."

Before he left, Mandi-lyn clutched his arm. She looked at him with pleading, earnest eyes. "Don't let me turn into to one of those things."

His shoulders fell. "I'm not going to kill you. You can't ask that of me," he said, shaking his head adamantly.

"I'm asking you on your honor as a Knight of Andola. Do what you must before I change." Mandi-lyn's whiskers bobbed a little, then she closed her eyes.

His eyes met the others, and his chin fell against his chest. He sighed and shook his head almost imperceptibly. "Watch over her," he said and ran to assist Bathezine and Old Babbers.

~~~

Bathezine stole a glance at Errel when he and Le'lel arrived. "What took ya?" His brow furrowed when he didn't see the others. "Where's Tiny and the Flursh?"

Errel kept his focus on the door. "Mandi-lyn is sick. Tiny is taking care of her."

Babbers and Bathezine exchanged a glance. "That Drullid sting?" Bathezine asked. Errel made the tiniest of nods. "Is she gonna make it?"

Errel filled his chest with a deep breath. "I don't think so." He flicked his wrist, igniting a ball of fire in his hand. "One problem at a time. I doubt this will be hot enough, but it might be able to soften the metal." He took a step closer and thrust his hand against the brass handle. He spat something indecipherable when the flame died before making contact. "Any other ideas?"

Bathezine stroked his beard, trying to keep his mind on Bet and not Mandi-lyn. He heard Old Babbers mention something about using a ram. There were plenty of dead trees to use, but he doubted it would do much good. He spotted Her-Gad-Ishu circling overhead, watching for the Drullids, and called for him. "Any sign of those creatures nearby?" the Ursian asked when the crow landed.

"Just one," Her answered.

"It is still by the rock we took the Flursh from," Gad added.

"Is there any way in through the roof of this place?" Bathezine asked. He rocked on his feet in frustration.

"There are two small openings. But they are too small for Bet to fit through," Her said.

"We've flown over them, but can't see Bet," Gad added.

"Okay, okay. You're gonna have to land on the roof and tell her to get as far away from the door as she can."

"We speak your language because of our Talents," Her said.

"And Bet won't be able to understand crow without hers," Ishu followed up.

Bathezine nodded. "Right. Okay, so fly over the hole in the roof and call her name. I'll give you a note. Drop it inside." He turned to Errel. "Get something to write a note on." Errel nodded and ran back to the wagon.

"What do you want me to do?" Babbers asked. She gave Bathezine a look that said she already had an idea of what he had in mind.

"It's right up your alley." His mustache twitched with a smile. "Better move the wagons back a little ways."

"We're gonna blow a hole in this thing?" she asked. Bathezine replied with a nod. A smile crossed her face, but quickly faded. "What if she's lying near the door unconscious or something? What if the whole damn place falls down on her?"

Bathezine looked at the deep orange creeping in the west and the thunderheads rolling in from the east. "We're losing daylight, and there's a storm coming. I don't see as how we have a choice. There's two feet of dust in every direction on the floor of this crater, and if we don't move soon, we'll never make it out of the mud. And I doubt those Drullids will stay dormant all night. We gotta do something, and if'n you don't have any better ideas…"

Babbers wiped the sweat from beneath her hat, hesitated, then threw up her hands. "I don't. How many bombs you want?"

Bathezine studied the stone walls. He tried to come up with another idea to get the job done expediently. Not being able to, he looked at Babbers. "A bunch."

Babbers studied the wall, hands on her hips, bobbing her head in agreement. "Yep. A bunch ought a do it."

Fifty

Bet chipped away at the interior wall, making little progress and dulling her pick in the process. She stopped for breath and glanced at Putrice sprawled out, still unconscious, on the floor. It crossed her mind that she may have hit the woman too hard, but realized she didn't really care. The woman was going to kill her if she hadn't done what she had. Putrice groaned softly, and Bet grunted with frustration in reply. If she woke up now, she'd have another fight on her hands. She rummaged through her bags and found a length of twine. She prodded the woman with her foot. Satisfied she wasn't feigning unconsciousness, Bet rolled Putrice to her stomach and tied her arms behind her back. She tugged Putrice's sack of a dress lower, as much to save the woman's modesty as sparing herself the sight.

Just as she started to get back to her work, she heard Her-Gad-Ishu call her name. She snapped her head up in time to see the crow's fleeting form pass over the porthole. "I'm here," she cried, waving her hands and running beneath the opening. She waited, craning her neck to see if the bird would return. A moment later the crow called again, and something fell through the hole. She heard it clunk against the stone floor, and dashed to whatever Her-Gad-Ishu had dropped. She fell to her knees and snatched the small rock wrapped in paper. Squinting in the faint light, she skimmed over the note, smiling at the rough image of a smiley face at the bottom drawn by Old Babbers beneath Errel's exquisite handwriting. The swelling over her left eye made it difficult to read, and she blinked her right eye several times to clear the scratchy dust. After reading the note, her good eye went wide open.

Bet ran to the far side of the room and hunkered down against the wall. As she knelt, she saw Putrice begin to stir. The woman was no more than ten feet from the door. The message didn't say when they were going to blast the wall. Bet stood, hesitated a second, then ran to Putrice. She spat a few choice words for being too kind to leave the woman there—she had tried to kill her, after all—but she couldn't let her get crushed or blasted in good conscience. She gave the woman a few light slaps, trying to wake her. She ran her hand across her own cheek, remembering all the slaps she suffered from Putrice's hand. Bet reared back, hand raised, ready to give the woman what she had given her for so long. Instead, she clenched her fist and let her arm drop to her side. It wasn't forgiveness, neither was it forgetting and letting bygones be bygones; she was fighting revenge.

When Putrice didn't respond to her attempts to wake her, Bet stood and tugged at the heavy woman, trying to drag her by the collar of her dress. She managed to move her a few feet before she fell back exhausted by the effort. Bet got up and leaned over her, and tried to hook her arms under the woman's shoulders. Putrice's eyes flashed open, and she head-butted Bet square in the nose, sending her to her knees. "Where ya taking me, girl? Gonna feed me to that demon again?" She stumbled to her feet, twisting her body, trying to free her hands.

"No," Bet yelled, her injured hand cupped over her nose, trying to slow the flow of blood. "The door's gonna blow any moment now." She raised her hand limply, indicating the door. Putrice paid her no mind and tottered toward her in a clumsy rush. Bet tried to get up and run, but Putrice slammed against her, knocking her back down. She found herself in the same position she had been in earlier, with Putrice's large frame sitting on her stomach, stealing the air from her lungs. "Will you listen to me? They're going to blow—"

The door exploded inward in an ear-splitting blast, sending chunks of stone and lead flying at the pair, trailed by a rolling ball of fire. The force of the blast sent Putrice sprawling on top of Bet, shielding her from most of the debris. The explosion was mercifully brief, and through the ringing in her ears Bet could hear the creak of the ceiling's wooden support beams and the steady patter of crumbling rock. Through the echoes in her head, she heard someone call her name. She coughed a laugh. It was Bathezine. Of course he would be the first one in. She blinked open her eyes, only seeing dust illuminated by a shaft of sunlight, and raised her hand. "Here," she called weakly through a cough.

Heavy footfalls came crunching through ruins, and a large shadow appeared over her. Bet peered from beneath Putrice's shoulder and gave Bathezine a half-smile. "Hey, bear man. Did you use enough explosives?"

Bathezine snorted at her comment. "Some appreciation." He flipped Putrice off Bet. "Who's the..." he paused, examining Putrice. "Who's the woman?" He scooped up Bet in both arms.

"That would be Putrice," Bet said, looking her over. Her sack of a dress was singed black, and most of her sparse hair had been scorched away.

"Putrice? The Biscuit Head?" he asked, prodding her with his foot.

"Yeah. And don't ask, because I don't know. Is she alive?"

Bathezine nudged her with his foot again, and noticed the woman's chest rise a little. "Sorta. Let's get you outta here before this whole place falls on our heads."

Old Babbers met them on the way out. "You're alive," she said, wiping the dust from Bet's face. She scowled at Bathezine. "Told ya we didn't need ten. Five woulda worked just fine."

"Nag me later, woman. This whole thing is 'bout to collapse." They stumbled over the broken ashlars and through twisted sheets of lead paneling on either side of the breach. Free of the building, Bathezine gently laid Bet on the ground. "Rest easy. We gotcha now." He looked back at the hole and bent steel rods that had locked the door in place. "You want me to get the woman?"

Bet stared at the breach for a moment or two. Putrice really wasn't worth the effort, but again, she couldn't just let her die if the roof caved in. And if she did somehow survive, she didn't put it past her to cause trouble later. "Yeah. If you think it's safe."

Bathezine followed Bet's dazed stare inside. "Reckon it is. Come on, Errel. There's a biggen in there."

Errel stopped beside Bet. "I'm glad you're safe," he said, but his face didn't express much joy.

Bet's Talents came flooding back to her. The effect was dizzying at first, but it soon felt like the comfort of a returning friend. She heard an excited Chook-chook chirp, and she sat up in time to catch Pooch-kin in her arms. She hugged her friend tightly, pressing her cheek against his feathered body. She held him, relishing in the comfort of her little friend. A tear traced a line along her dirty cheek.

Pooch-kin purred and rubbed his beak on her nose. "I was really scared this time. We didn't know if you were alive or dead. And I thought for sure that bear had blown you to pieces with that blast. Don't ever do that again."

"I can't make any promises, but I'll do my best," she said with a self-conscious grin.

Tiny Nat walked up and looked down at Bet. "We are pleased you are alive."

"Thanks, Tiny. So am I. Glad you could make it." She wiped the muddy blood from her lips.

"The Ursian expressed similar sentiments." Tiny Nat hummed something, which Bet took as a version of a Vivicon laugh.

They turned their heads toward the crumbled wall as Bathezine and Errel reappeared with Putrice in their arms. With their opinions of the woman already firmly established, they dropped her with a lack of gentility.

Putrice moaned and struggled to sit upright. With intense effort she managed to get her knees under her. She blinked her eyes beneath the harsh late day sun and spotted Bet. Snarling like a wild beast, she made a motion toward the girl. Bathezine, Errel, and Tiny Nat stepped between them, Bathezine clutching the sledge, Tiny Nat a pair of throwing knives, and Errel flicking both his wrists and holding balls of fire. Putrice looked at their large frames and seemed to reconsider her actions. She looked at Old Babbers squatting beside Bet twirling a hatchet and carrying a closed-lipped smile that invited violence and quickly averted her eyes. Her gaze fell on Pooch-kin on Bet's lap. She snorted. "I thought I ate all of you." Her voice was coarse and devoid of any traces of humanity.

Pooch-kin looked at Bet. "How did she get here?" His feathers turned a shade of red that Bet hadn't seen before. It didn't take her Talents to sense the anger rising from the little bird.

"The Reacher did it. I don't know how." Bet stroked his feathers to try to calm him. She looked at Bathezine. "Give her a drink then gag her. I've had enough of her talking." Bathezine did as instructed, then double-checked the knot binding the woman's wrists. Bet got to her feet with the aid of Babbers' arm. "Where's Mandi-lyn? I could use a quick heal of my nose and a few other places."

Old Babbers squeezed Bet's arm, her eyes telling her that Mandi-lyn wouldn't be healing any one. Bet caught her breath. "Where is she?" she asked, her words catching in her throat. Babbers pointed to the wagon. Bet's knees went weak, and she braced herself on Babbers. She glared at Putrice then looked at Tiny Nat. "Watch her. If she tries to move, sting her." She ran to Mandi-lyn.

Fifty-One

Jangol lifted his head and sniffed at Bet as she approached. Trees stretched long dead limbs through the dusty haze like the arm of a reaper pointing toward the wagon. Bet ran her hand along Jangol's back, letting it linger for a scratch on his hip. She saw the corner of Mandi-lyn's tricorn hat lift and half-closed eyes squint against the hanging dust from the explosion. Bet hesitated then climbed over the sideboard and took a seat in front of the Flursh. She sat in silence for a moment or two as they stared at one another. Her eyes fell on the gray skin, now stretching from the side of her neck along her arm to the notebook in her lap. She swallowed then looked up. "Does it hurt?"

Mandi-lyn shifted, sitting up a little. "Not much."

"The Drullids?" Bet asked, even though she already knew. Pangs of guilt churned in her chest, and she struggled to keep them from bursting into a fit of tears. Mandi-lyn nodded. "I'm sorry," she said, her voice just above a whisper.

Mandi-lyn shook her head. "Don't be. No one is to blame."

"You can't heal it?" Mandi-lyn shook her head. Bet fought back the tears threatening to spill over. "I should have listened. You were right, of course. I gained nothing and lost a lot."

Mandi-lyn stared at her, seeming to read her thoughts. "What did you find?"

Bet lifted her head and looked at Le'lel leaning against the other wagon, keeping a watchful eye on the trees, tongue flickering, tasting the air for danger. "Nothing good. Putrice, the mistress from the farm. The Reacher brought her here somehow. It was a trap."

"You found more than a trap," Mandi-lyn said. She reached out with her good arm and touched Bet's knee. "You found balance outside of your Talents. It will serve you well in the days to come, if you heed its lessons."

"Balance?" Bet balked at the statement. "It feels more like indifference... apathy."

"It is more than that. You learned to not let emotion guide your actions—to do what is necessary regardless of the consequences. You found serenity in your decisions. Your choice to not kill the woman, not giving in to the passion of retribution, saved you, whether you know it or not. Had you given in, you would have been lost, and all those around you, and those yet to come would be, as well. You were given knowledge from the Crickshaw and from Moth, but having knowledge doesn't mean you know it. Sometimes you have to learn it. You gained much."

Bet started to say something, but stopped. Instead, she gave Mandi-lyn a trace of a smile beneath the first tear trekking along her battered face. "You read my mind, huh? You've always been able to." Mandi-lyn shrugged at her secret being revealed. Bet took a deep shaky breath. "I'm sure there are easier ways to learn something than...than this." She motioned toward the ruined structure then at Mandi-lyn, then wiped her face with the back of her hand.

"Perhaps, or perhaps not. How we learn a lesson can be as important as what we learn. Take it from the Charge of Danthbrook—I've learned many things the hard way, and there wasn't always an easy way to learn them." Mandi-lyn wrapped a band around her notebook and handed it to Bet. "Give this to Errel."

Bet took the book and stared at it, rubbed her fingers along the smooth leather cover, over the fire-stamped words written in Flursh, words she couldn't read. "What do we do now?"

"Now you see to your task. And now you go get Errel. He's has his own task to perform." She reached for a pouch on the skinny strip of rope she used as a belt. "But first, take these."

Bet took the pouch, pulled the drawstring, and dumped the contents in her hand. She sniffed a laugh, raising her eyebrows at the Flursh. "Pecans?" She had thought the contents would be something more meaningful, some profound knowledge or artifact to aid her on her journey. Even if they weren't, they were important—a gift from a dying friend. "I'll cherish them," she said only half sarcastically.

"Don't. And they're not for eating. The Snickers, squirrel pigs you called them, will stop at nothing to retrieve their stolen nuts. Use them wisely. They may come in handy. Now go." She raised her gray arm; the flesh had begun to take on the familiar look of the Drullids. "And Bet, remember that balance doesn't mean foregoing love and compassion, and at times, fear and anger. Encompassing all emotions will be required when the time comes."

Bet reached for her hand and Mandi-lyn offered it, not pulling away as she had when they'd first met. She wasn't sure what she meant by encompassing all emotions; she had been sure balance meant the opposite. She tried to find words that wouldn't come. "Thank you," she said. It was all she could say, though the words seemed small and insignificant.

Mandi-lyn closed her eyes and nodded. "Go. My work is done, and time is running short."

Bet forced her legs to move, stood, and hopped down. She stole a final glance back at Mandi-lyn, the Charge of Danthbrook, her friend, and ran to Errel.

Fifty-Two

Errel Handover's body sagged when he caught sight of Bet. His eyes fixed on the ground, reluctance showed in every step he took in her direction. He paused for a moment when she arrived, and looked at her. "Time?" he asked. The tears on Bet's face told him the answer. Bet swallowed dryly and nodded. Errel looked back at Bathezine, Babbers, and Tiny Nat, and they fell in line behind him.

Bet watched them go with Pooch-kin at her feet. She sucked in a deep breath, trying to calm the overwhelming pain in her heart. Her body became too heavy for her legs to support, and she sank against the dusty ground and stroked Pooch-kin's ears. The Chook-chook cuddled beside her, silent in his sympathy, doing his best to ease Bet's troubled heart. She turned away when she saw her friends, her family, take one of their own from the wagon and carry her away.

She sat staring at Putrice, not really seeing her, lost in thoughts of what her actions had cost not only her, but Mandi-lyn, and all of them. A grunt from Putrice pulled Bet from her thoughts. The woman was shaking with muffled laughter, eyes sadistically happy at Bet's pain. She fought back a flare of anger; not just anger, but a deep rage, yearning for her to take an iron ball a send it flying through the woman's fat skull and silence her once and for all. She clenched her fist and shut her eyes until the urge passed. When she reopened them, she looked at the joyless crease of smiling eyes still trained on her, as if Bet's pain was her greatest accomplishment. Bet wondered what could make a person so cruel. Putrice had been cruel before—mean, nasty, an all-around horrible person—but now, free of the restraints of society and responsibility for her actions, Putrice had become something less than human, twisted into something worse than the demon who had sent her here.

The thought of how Putrice got to this place, in the middle of nowhere, in a crater in a different realm, in a building designed solely to trap, in Putrice's words, *Users*, itched in her mind. It was time to scratch the itch. She would find out exactly what happened and how. Bet shifted on her knees and stared deeply into the horrible woman's eyes, stretching her senses to touch Putrice's mind. She felt Putrice recoil when she realized Bet had entered her mind. Bet didn't care. Let her squirm, let her be afraid; it was the least she could do in return for the trouble she had caused.

She delved deeper into Putrice's thoughts and memories; the woman was powerless to stop her. Bet could have masked her presence—she had done it when she determined the Vapid had been lying—but she didn't, she wanted Putrice to know what she was doing, that none of her thoughts, none of her secrets were safe.

She went into Putrice's past. She saw her evil deeds. She saw what happened to those who had come to the farm before her, and saw their unhappy ends. A boy, fifteen, ill will choke pox, left to die when the woman had refused to buy a simple, inexpensive cure; a girl of the same age drowned in Silt Creek for dropping a dozen eggs, then buried in the woods. She saw the beatings, cruelty, and the pleasure Putrice had taken in delivering the punishment. Bet felt—a subtle knowing and understanding—the orphanage's indifference toward the woman buying a new child every other year. They knew, and they didn't care; it was money in their pockets and nothing else mattered.

A few youths had escaped, ran away, and Bet could vaguely trace their fates. Some became smoke addicts, living, homeless, in the slums of various cities, some became soldiers in the King's service, and some met more tragic ends. It had gone on for over forty years. Bet felt sorrow for their suffering.

She pulled away from those memories and lineages, lest her anger boil over and rip apart the woman's mind from the inside. She focused on her time at Malweather Farm. Seeing the events unfold through Putrice's eyes, she saw the night she had taken ill, saw herself sleeping, unconscious with fever. She watched herself grow closer as Putrice crept forward. She saw a pillow in one hand and a mallet in the other, and felt Putrice's intent to murder her in her sleep. Then a flash of greed came, and the thought of a reward. The thought hadn't originated in Putrice's mind; it had come from somewhere else...somebody else. Putrice turned away, tossed the pillow in her own bedroom and went outside, barefoot. The mud squished between her toes, cold and sticky. She still held the mallet, and through Putrice's eyes, she saw the Chook-chook coop. Bet recoiled at Putrice's memories.

Next came the struggle and being pushed to the floor by Bet from Putrice's point of view, and then seeing Harrelle take his time to go in search of her. She saw Putrice's hand pick up the destroyed door knob from the mud, and felt a trace of fear at knowing what could have happened had she provoked Bet further. The old man returned, and he and Putrice had argued for an hour, as Putrice was convinced he had helped. The woman may have been insane, but she was intuitive. The inquisitors arrived the next morning, and Putrice rambled repeatedly about her reward and how Harrelle had helped the girl escape. Bet saw the inquisitors leave and witnessed another one-sided screaming match as Putrice berated the old man. The next day came, and with it came the inquisitors once again. She felt her fear, anger, and sense of betrayal when the large, black-bearded man with the red ribbons ordered them shackled and taken to the dungeons.

She sat in the back of the iron carriage, shackled to the hard bench. She saw one of the inquisitors tend to another who was missing his lower jaw. She saw the bloodied bandages and heard the man's moans. Putrice offered a few venomous words, and she saw the caretaker pull a long needle from a bag, and felt the jab of a needle in her neck. Then blackness.

Her eyes fluttered open, and she saw the irons around her arms and legs and the stone walls of a prison cell, faintly lit by a sconce high above. She could taste the leather strap in her mouth, tied around her head much tighter than necessary. She saw Harrelle curled in the corner on the stone floor, chained as well. Days passed as Bet fast-forwarded through the various feedings and insults at those bringing the food. A man in uniform entered, and Bet listened to the questions asked and the answers Putrice gave, painting herself as the victim to Bet's spells and torment. She watched the man do the same with Harrelle, only the old man sat stone-faced and silent. Then a blindfold.

Time passed again; Bet didn't know how long. And then she heard the door open, the blindfold was removed, and she saw King Dalverious. The Reacher by his side, floating like a dark, vaporous cloud, hovered close. She saw and listened to the exchange through Putrice, and then she felt the Reacher enter Putrice's body, and the pain of being torn apart, then a brief sensation of nonexistence.

Bet tried to pull away from the connection but was unable to; she was trapped in Putrice's mind. She saw the interior of the stone building and felt her own nakedness, and saw the sack dress laid out for her. Her mind disconnected from Putrice, but she was still inside the prison. All turned black, and a voice came.

"Bethany," said the voice. It was the familiar voice of the Reacher, the Null. "Since you are hearing this, you must have somehow escaped my prison, likely by the aid of your friends, and this worthless sack of a woman failed to carry out what I had hoped she would do. And because you are here, I assume you have come to see Moth, and it will undoubtedly give, or has given you fragments of the Staff of the Whist. The choice, of course, is yours. But if you continue on your quest to find Fealist-Marsh and reconstruct the staff, I will have no choice but to kill you. And I will kill your friends. Anna and her brother, Dalin, that little Chook-chook you care so deeply for, so much so that you stole his time of dying, the woman, the Vivicon, the Flursh, the Prince of Andola, and the Ursian, they will all die long and painful deaths. I will kill all who have aided you, befriended you, or came in contact with you knowingly or not. Or…you can cast aside what you feel is your duty, your destiny, so to speak, and I will not harm you or your friends. I can't speak for the inquisitors; they seem to be carrying a grudge for what you did to their comrade.

"If you complete the Staff of the Whist and free Omia Temporian, I will die. I'm sure this gives you great pleasure. But know that I only want to live. Life is all I truly desire. The same can be said for Fealist-Marsh. She knows the consequences of your actions, as well, and she will not give in so willingly. And of course, by now you know what will happen if you join the staffs, if you happen to take them from us. You will die along with us. The Null, the Omia Temporian, and you, the Medius Proles, will cease to live.

Return the fragments to Moth. I cannot take them—I have no power over the Ancient Ones—and there they will stay for all time. Again, the choice is yours, but I know you desire life over death. It is what we all want—to live."

The Reacher's voice faded away, and Bet fell back, her head spinning. She crawled to her hands and knees, and saw Pooch-kin's anxious eyes looking up at her. She feigned a smile and patted his back. "I'm okay. I'm okay."

She twisted and sat, her breath coming in rasps. She looked at Putrice. The woman sat swaying as if some unheard song was playing in her head. Her eyes open but unseeing, glazed and unblinking.

Bet turned away and saw a flash of blue light in the copse of dead trees. She reached out and felt Mandi-lyn's essence—her life—fade away. Bet fell, clutching her head, and wept.

Fifty-Three

Bet blinked open her eyes at Babbers' soft touch against her cheek. "Hey there, little sister. Let's get you up." She hooked her arm around Bet's back, guiding her to sit.

"I'm okay," Bet said. She looked at Putrice, who was on her knees. Putrice glanced up at Bet, any mirth, psychotic or otherwise, gone from her eyes. Recalling what she'd learned from Putrice's memories, Bet glared at the woman. She reached for the climber's pick at her belt, but her hand found nothing. She must have lost it in the building. Putrice reared back, shaking her head, eyes wide and terrified. Bet let calm wash over her. She stood without Babbers' assistance and surveyed her surroundings. "Where's everybody?"

"They'll be here in a few." Old Babbers squinted at Bet suspiciously. "What happened?"

Bet shook her head. "I...I just got a little overwhelmed."

Babbers raised an eyebrow. "You wanna try again? That ain't it. Not all of it, anyway."

Bet looked at Pooch-kin for a moment, then let her gaze fall on Putrice. She nodded toward the woman. "I probed her memories. I wanted to find out how she got here. She was here before the barrier fell."

"What'd ya find?"

"I found a lot." She continued to stare at Putrice. "The Null...the

Reacher, brought her here, or sent her here. He wanted her to kill me." Bet felt revulsion rise as she looked at Biscuit Head. "As bad as that is, it's not the worst of it. There were others before me at the farm. She's a murderer. Worse, a serial killer, in a way. So many kids died or were killed by her outright at that farm."

Old Babbers glowered at Putrice, the potential of violence showing on her face. "What else? I know there's more."

Bet looked at Pooch-kin again. "You were lucky to escape."

"She killed every one of them. Every Chook-chook died. Not for a meal. Just for the pleasure of it," Pooch-kin said. He turned his fiery eyes toward Putrice.

"I know. I saw. She was going to kill me when I was sick, while I slept." Bet turned away and watched Bathezine in the distance, readying the wagons. "I should kill her." She turned back toward Putrice. "But I can't. It's not the way a…" Her words caught in her throat and she closed her eyes, wondering if what the Reacher had said was true. Was she the Medius Proles? If so, who else knew? Had Mandi-lyn known? She was certain Moth knew but hadn't told her.

"Well, if you can't do it, I don't have a problem with it," Old Babbers said and withdrew her hatchets, taking a step toward Putrice.

"No," Bet said, grabbing Babbers' shoulder. "Don't. It's not worth the stain it will leave on you." A thunderclap exploded in the distance, and Bet smelled the promise of rainfall. She raised her head toward the sky, then back at Putrice. "We'll leave her for the Drullids."

"Are you one to judge the deeds of another?" a voice said from behind them.

Bet and Old Babbers spun around to find Moth, in its chimeric form, standing behind them. Babbers gasped and raised a hatchet. "Moth," Bet said, putting her arm in front of Babbers, steadying her.

Moth's leathery wings shimmered with color and spread wide as it glided closer. "The judgement of others is not a task appointed to you. Your task is ahead of you."

"As the Medius Proles, you mean?" Bet's voice carried an accusation that she didn't care to hide.

Moth's bulbous eyes narrowed, and two of its four cat-like arms crossed while the others steepled in front of its chest, claws tapping together. "The Null told you?"

Bet was surprised to find that Moth hadn't known. The pressure in her head told her it only knew by probing her mind. "Yes. I looked into her memories," she hooked her thumb at Putrice, "and when I finished his voice came to me. Like a preplanned message. He told me everything."

"Not everything," Moth said.

"He said enough," Bet countered. "Why didn't you tell me? Is what he said true?"

"You weren't ready. The Wanderer would have told you when the time had come." Moth laced its fingers. "All that he said is true, or will be true if you choose to continue."

"That's a tired excuse...*you weren't ready*. Was it really you, Fealist-Marsh, or whoever is trying to protect me? Or was it that you were afraid I wouldn't see this to the end if I found out the truth? That I'm gonna die if I join the staffs? The Reacher is a terrible person, I have no doubt. But the one thing he hasn't done was lie to me or keep me in the dark about what's really at stake. I'm sure he thought the same thing—*that I'm not ready to hear the truth*. And that's why he told me. But I've had my life on the line nearly every day since I came here. And it's going to be that way until the end. I know that now." Bet stopped and looked at her friends, who had gathered around. "I'll see this through. And you know what? I don't know if I'll be able to do it when the time comes. That's upfront honesty. Maybe I'll find another way. Who knows? But if I get that far... I'll know then."

Bathezine gave Moth a wide berth and walked to Bet's side, putting his big arm around her. Babbers did the same, and Pooch-kin stood at her feet. Moth stood silent for nearly a minute, until its toothy maw seemed to almost smile. "You are strong, Bethany. I have no doubt you will do what needs to be done. I have no more to teach you. The Wanderer will impart further knowledge on you."

Bet slid from beneath Bathezine's arm and took a step closer to Moth. "Then this is where we part ways. Thank you for the lessons," she said. She did little to mask her bitterness. Whether it was the hurt of losing Mandilyn, or the sense of betrayal at not being told all she should have known, her encounter with the Reacher's psychic message, and Putrice, she didn't know, and didn't really care. Maybe it was all of it or none of it. Over the course of a few weeks her world had drastically changed so many times it appeared as if change would be the one constant forevermore. She squeezed her eyes shut, fighting the rush of emotions swirling through her. Fear, doubt, anger, and sadness battled with courage, confidence, love, and joy, all swimming in a pool of anticipation of what lay ahead. She grimaced at her acceptance of whatever may come, looked at Bathezine and waved her hand at Putrice. "Make sure she's bound. She's coming with us."

At this, Moth raised its arms. "Those who enter my realm are bound to my judgement. Putrice Malweather must face hers."

Bet looked at Biscuit Head. The woman's face showed her fear, and she looked at Bet with her beady eyes begging for mercy. Bet thought of all the horrible things she had seen in Putrice's memories and walked to her. She touched the woman's head, who recoiled at her touch. Bet focused and looked for Putrice's possible futures. There were none. A thin smile crossed her face, and she let her hand drop away. "You will live in the memory of my contempt." Bet walked away and scooped up Pooch-kin.

Moth stopped Bet as she walked by and extended a closed fist. "Take this." Bet gave Moth a suspicious look and held out her hand. Moth deposited a long, smooth, green nut resembling a large acorn.

"What is this?" Bet asked. She felt the weight of it in her hand. It was surprisingly heavy, even for its large size.

"It is part of the future, should you choose to let it grow."

Bet stared at the acorn. A part of her seemed to know what it was—the part of her that was the old tree's memory—and that pleased her.

"Prudence, fortitude, temperance," Moth said. "Remember and keep them well, Bethany."

Bet tore off a piece of fabric from her ragged sleeve, wrapped the acorn, and put it in her satchel. "I will," she said, then gave Moth a crooked smile. "And my name is Bet."

Fifty-Four

Bathezine and Old Babbers walked side-by-side with Bet to the wagons, with Errel walking in silence ahead of them. Tiny Nat had already flown ahead and began batting down the supplies in anticipation of a fast and hard ride out of the caldera. Bet spotted Le'lel walk toward the wagons from the opposite direction, carrying a medium-sized crate. Bet immediately felt the anguish within Le'lel and didn't need to ask what was in the box. Some said that Lasoom didn't have emotions, owing to their expressionless reptilian faces, but Bet knew better. She watched him put the makeshift casket in the back of the covered wagon, and felt relief that it wasn't riding with her. The pain and the guilt may have been too much for her to handle.

Old Babbers patted Alice the Fleet Ox on the rump and checked over the hitches. Bet heard her spit out a swear-laden exclamation and turned to see what the commotion was. Babbers pointed, and they all watched as Moth transformed into a massive swarm of gold and glittering butterflies. The sight was awe-inspiringly beautiful. The swarm twisted and circled, flying high above the trees in a silent display of magnificence none except Bet had seen before. They watched, mesmerized, as the crystalline wings reflected the dwindling sunlight into a thousand twinkling bursts. The swarm reached its zenith then descended like a tornado reaching from the sky. The spectators let out a simultaneous gasp when the cloud cascaded on Putrice and swarmed over her like a hive of angry bees. Moments later the swarm scattered and disappeared, leaving the skeletal remains of Putrice Malweather lying in the dust.

Nobody said anything for a moment until Bathezine cleared his throat and nudged Old Babbers. "We should get going before Moth comes back and passes judgement on us."

Old Babbers licked her dry lips. "I hear ya. I gotta lot to be judged."

They loaded up and made haste with Her-Gad-Ishu flying above them silhouetted against the falling sun. Riding hard and with the crow's guidance, they made the edge of the crater just before sunset and began the slow trek up. Thunderclaps of the approaching storm chased them up and out of the caldera like an angry god warning them never to return. None of them had the desire to do so.

The muted yellow glow of a single lamp beneath the bonnet of Old Babbers' wagon scarcely illuminated the road. Tiny Nat's vision led the way as he sat on the bench beside Bathezine. When they approached the old oak trees where they had previously camped, the Ursian called a halt. Bet sat up and looked around. "Why're we stopping?" she asked. Bathezine didn't answer. Instead, he hopped down, grumbled something about his knees, and walked to the dead fire pit.

He stood staring out beyond the trees. Lightning flashed, brightening the landscape as the cold air of the Din battled with the warm air of the Whist for dominance. He didn't speak, he just stood with his hands clutched in front of him hanging below his waist.

Several minutes passed until Bet decided to go to him. She eased herself down, making sure she didn't land hard on her injured foot. The Falkwith seed had worn off, and the ache let her know her ankle wasn't fully healed. "Stay here," she said to Pooch-kin, and walked over to Bathezine. "Hey, there. Whatcha doing?"

Bathezine stared away for a few more moments then looked down at the girl. "This is as good a place as any," he said and walked to the back of the wagon, leaving Bet alone.

She watched him rummage beneath the tarp in the wane light and come back carrying a hand spade. He knelt and began digging without saying a word. Her-Gad-Ishu landed near Bet, and Old Babbers, Errel, Tiny Nat, Le'lel, and Pooch-kin stood and watched as the big Ursian dug with intense purpose, working through the pain of Mandi-lyn's death.

When Bathezine finished his work, he tossed aside the spade and came to Bet's side, wrapping his burly arm around her. Bet leaned against his chest, breathing in his musky scent mixed with the smell of fresh earth. The smell brought her to a safe place. It was the smell of the father she would never know and never could know, and it was the smell of home. She wrapped her arms around him and hugged him tightly. Bathezine gave her shoulder a soft squeeze.

Errel stepped away and came back carrying the pine box. He dropped to his knees and placed the box in the hole. He stood, removed his hat, and pulled a brass coin from his coat pocket. "Your debt is payed, and you are released from your duties, Charge of Danthbrook," he said softly, and dropped the coin in the grave. He stepped back and stole a glance at Bet. His shoulders drooped and went to her.

Bet lifted her head and took his hand. He tried to pull his hand back, but she held it firm. With a squeeze, a blue flame ignited in her palm. Errel's eyes widened, then narrowed with a smile, and his yellow flame joined hers. They raised their hands and a small ball of green fire floated above them, hanging in the dark for several heartbeats before disappearing.

Bathezine patted Bet then retrieved the spade and began filling in the grave. With Pooch-kin at her side, Bet watched the work. She closed her eyes and felt a tug in the back of her mind. It was a familiar presence, and she could almost hear its voice calling her *Little Monkey*. A soft smile crossed her face and her eyes welled. She opened her satchel and pulled out the acorn. She carefully removed it from the torn fabric and held it up, examining it in the gloom. She looked at Babbers and Errel, who both gave her questioning looks, then walked to the nearly filled gave and kneeled before it.

"Whatcha got there?" Bathezine asked.

Bet didn't answer. She held it out then looked at her friends. Her-Gad-Ishu's three heads looked at her curiously while Errel and Babbers stood either side of her, and Pooch-kin scooted close to her knee. She placed the acorn in the soft soil and spoke softly, "Take care of this, my friend." She scooped the remaining soil over the nut and patted it down.

Bathezine stood scratching at his beard. "What is it?"

Bet met her friends' eyes one at a time, then looked at Tiny Nat and Le'lel standing a little farther back. She inhaled deeply then smiled. "It's the future." She picked up Pooch Kin and walked to the wagon, taking a seat on the bench. The others stared at the fresh grave for a minute longer then turned away as the first droplets of rain began to fall.

About the Author

Steven Hammond is a Sci-fi/fantasy author, artist and photographer. He has written six books in the *Rise of the Penguins Saga* including *Rise of the Penguins, The Warlord, The Warrior, The War, Crosscurrents, Whispers of Shadows, The Royal Creed,* and *Order of Kings.* He also penned *The Talents of Bet,* the predecessor to *The Journey of Bet.* He is currently working on two new titles in the *Rise of the Penguins* series, and the follow-up to *The Journey of Bet.*

Steven lives in California's Central Valley, his home since birth, where enjoys spending time with his family. When not slapping at his keyboard like an enraged Siamang, while his Buster Dog curiously looks on, he can be found working on any number of art projects, or enjoying a good movie.

To learn more about Steven and his talents, visit his Web site at http://www.stevenhammondbooks.com/.

More from Rockhopper Books

The Staffs of Omia Series

The Talents of Bet

Rise of the Penguins Saga

Rise of the Penguins
Book 1

The Warlord, The
Warrior, The War
Book 2

Crosscurrents
Book 3

Whispers of Shadows
Book 4

The Royal Creed
Book 5

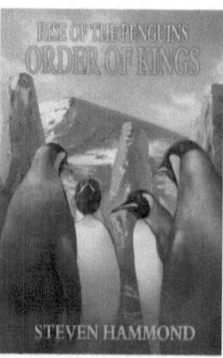

Order of Kings
Book 6

The Great Auk War
Book 7
(coming soon)

www.ingramcontent.com/pod-product-compliance
Lightning Source LLC
Chambersburg PA
CBHW031219120726
47905CB00002B/394